CLOVER

THE ITALIAN CARTEL #9

SHANDI BOYES

Edited by NICKI @ SWISH DESIGN & EDITING

Photography by 612 PHOTOGRAPHY BY ERIC MCKINNEY

Illustrated by SSB COVERS & DESIGN

ALSO BY SHANDI BOYES

Denotes Standalone Books

Perception Series

Saving Noah *

Fighting Jacob *

Taming Nick *

Redeeming Slater *

Saving Emily

Wrapped Up with Rise Up

Protecting Nicole *

Enigma

Enigma

Unraveling an Enigma

Enigma The Mystery Unmasked

Enigma: The Final Chapter

Beneath The Secrets

Beneath The Sheets

Spy Thy Neighbor *

The Opposite Effect *

I Married a Mob Boss *

Second Shot *

The Way We Are

The Way We Were

Sugar and Spice *

Lady In Waiting

Man in Queue

Couple on Hold

Enigma: The Wedding

Silent Vigilante

Hushed Guardian

Quiet Protector

Enigma: An Isaac Retelling

Twisted Lies *

Bound Series

Chains

Links

Bound

Restrain

The Misfits *

Nanny Dispute *

Russian Mob Chronicles

Nikolai: A Mafia Prince Romance

Nikolai: Taking Back What's Mine

Nikolai: What's Left of Me

Nikolai: Mine to Protect

Asher: My Russian Revenge *

<u>**One Night Only Series**</u>

Hotshot Boss *

Hotshot Neighbor *

<u>**The Bobrov Bratva Series**</u>

Wicked Intentions *

Sinful Intentions *

Devious Intentions *

Deadly Intentions *

COPYRIGHT

Copyright © 2021 by Shandi Boyes

All rights reserved.

No part of this book may be reproduced in any form or by any electronic or mechanical means, including information storage and retrieval systems, without written permission from the author, except for the use of brief quotations in a book review.

 Created with Vellum

WANT TO STAY IN TOUCH?

Facebook: facebook.com/authorshandi

Instagram: instagram.com/authorshandi

Email: authorshandi@gmail.com

Reader's Group: bit.ly/ShandiBookBabes

Website: authorshandi.com

Newsletter: https://www.subscribepage.com/AuthorShandi

DEDICATION

To Tammy,

Thank you so much for all your help. Your twisted heart weaves so well with mine, without fail, you make my books better.

Love
Shandi xx

#FamousCousin

1

ESTELLE

When the droning buzz of an ancient doorbell shrills through my tiny apartment, I curse a poor education and unwealthy parents. I can't really blame my parents for my unstable amble into adulthood. If I had paid more attention at school, I could have been awarded a scholarship like my best friend, Roxanne.

Alas, I thought I'd flirt my way into a trust fund baby's heart, and he'd be so smitten, he would demand his parents rip up the prenup they had drafted before he was born before we sailed off into our twenties in wedded bliss.

What? My dreams aren't a stretch from reality. Almost every book I read has a similar plot. And what kind of life would a romance novel lover have if she didn't occasionally dream that she was a fictional character being swept off her feet by a tormented soul hiding under a black cape.

I'm not ashamed to admit I find the beast more attractive when he's precisely that—a beast.

"I'm coming," I shout at my caller, annoyed by their second

buzz.

Can they not hear how monotonous the ringing is? It's enough to drag a girl out of ecstasy mid-climax. I don't know about you, but that would be the equivalent of waking up a dragon with a sore head. It would end disastrously.

My thought process quickens my steps. Brayden said he'd pop by sometime today. Although his contact has been rather sporadic the past couple of weeks, I'm willing to forgive just about anything for the right amount of groveling.

Brayden is my on-and-off-again boyfriend. We're on anytime he's away from the prying eyes of his parents. Off pretty much anytime we're in public.

His family knows of me, I was formally introduced the weekend before Roxanne secured a job paying thirty-five big ones an hour, but they don't believe their son should 'settle' until he's at least thirty. Since that's over six years away, it leaves me a little perplexed on how to title our relationship.

The stigma their values cloud our relationship with is almost enough for me to call it quits, but what can I say? Not only does he treat me like a princess when we're alone, he's also exceptionally skilled in the bedroom.

So much so, my voice tremors as much as my thighs when I swing open the door and purr out, "I told you there's no giving up daytime sex."

With things tight and money needed elsewhere up until Roxanne landed the ideal job, I only allowed Brayden to visit during the day. It was the only way I could hide the fact that they had cut the electricity due to an overdue bill—many of them. We only changed things up a couple of weeks back when the water, electricity, *and* cable switched back on like Roxanne's new position is more about polishing Mr. Petretti's knob instead of wiping his wrinkly backside.

"Daytime sex is almost as good as public escapades."

My unsubtle smirk sags a little when my eyes lock with what I believed would be Brayden's face. Instead of piercing blue eyes, dirty blond locks, and the cutest dimple-blemished cheeks, I'm confronted with a broad chest, massive tattooed biceps, and a sneer that has me convinced I'll once again be cheering for the villain in the next book I read.

Fuck dark and dangerous, this man is devastatingly savage.

Plump lips, perfectly trimmed black hair, and a cut jawline my tongue is begging to trace. His face is exquisite even with his aura screaming anguish and suffering. I can't recall a single time I've met a man I want to climb like a jungle gym and nurture at the same time. Not even Brayden has evoked those responses out of me, and his childhood, although wealthy, was as awry as mine.

"Hi," I squeak out, both shocked about how far I have to extend my neck to lock eyes with the stranger and the depth and darkness of his narrowed gaze. Usually, you see pupils when you stare into someone's eyes. All I'm seeing are deep pits of blackness. They're so mesmerizing, not even the four-leaf clover tattooed below his right eye can detract from their allure. "Do you have the right apartment?"

I swear I've seen him before, but for the life of me, I can't place exactly where. It isn't like he has a face that's easily forgettable. I'm basing my theory more on his aura than us having a face-to-face meeting. He seems like the type of guy who'd watch from afar.

When I attempt to scoot past him, jealous as hell one of my neighbors have lost their tall, dark, and tempting bedmate, the stranger folds his arms in front of his chest, blocking my path. The girth of his shoulders alone hogs the doorway, much less the thrusting of his chest when he drinks in my body as hungrily as I did his. I'm wearing booty shorts that leave *nothing* to the imagination and a ribbed tank top without a bra.

Don't judge. Youth is in my favor, so I work it for all it's worth.

I'm also in the comfort of my home. If I can't be myself here, where can I be?

I startle as if the brooding stranger told me he's here to kill me when my cell phone unexpectedly vibrates on the coffee table. My apartment is so small, even with me being in the foyer of my home, the living room is only two strides away.

When the stranger grunts out, "You should answer that," I fling my eyes back to him. His accented voice is thick and dangerous, a perfect match for his surly attitude.

"It's fine," I reply, waving off his offer like it was a suggestion instead of a command. "It's probably just my boyfriend checking in."

I don't know why I bring Brayden up. I could blame the unease filtering in the air, but that would be the cheat's way out. I am as interested in the stranger's response to my confession I have a boyfriend as I am to discover who's calling me. Excluding Mr. Monroe reaching out to roster me on for extra shifts, my phone rarely rings.

I arch a brow when the devastatingly handsome man replies, "It isn't your boyfriend."

"How do you know that? He calls me all hours of the day *and* night."

His accent is thicker than first perceived when he murmurs, "Popping over for a booty call and calling to see how you are aren't close to the same thing." My thighs shudder when he steps closer to me. I'm unsure if it's in fear or excitement, so take your pick. "It's the curse of the golden pussy. It may taste as sweet as honey and hug a cock like it's never been touched, but rarely will it see you granted a dinner invitation." He drags his eyes away from the buds of my erect nipples before asking, "That's what you want, isn't it? Approval from the rich schmuck's parents."

"No," I deny, even with his comment being more truthful than dishonest. "But I do think it's time for you to leave."

As I grip the rusted doorknob for dear life, my cell phone commences hollering again. It curdles my stomach with worry even more than a stranger spotting a truth Brayden hasn't once attempted to acknowledge. I don't want his parents' approval, but it would be nice not to be treated like a lecher anytime we're in public.

I shake my head when the mysterious man asks, "Aren't you the least bit interested in discovering who it is?"

"If it's important, they'll leave a message."

He smirks about my stubbornness before he wholly removes any trace of it from my face. "I wonder how Roxanne will feel when she learns she isn't important enough to take up a moment of your precious time to gather a package for her."

I'm torn on how to respond. Roxanne is my best friend. We've been through so much, but I'm also angry about how distant she's been the past couple of weeks. Don't get me wrong. I'm grateful she organized for the electricity and water to be reconnected before she left, but this is the longest we've been out of contact since we were thirteen. I'd rather have cold showers and be left in the dark than act as if our friendship is worthless.

"Roxanne will—"

"Stop blowing up your phone when you get her what she needs." He says his comment like I should be grateful to see the back end of my best friend. "So answer her fucking call."

"Excuse me!" I tolerate rudeness to keep my job. I even occasionally give it as good as I get it, but there's no way in hell I'm going to let a stranger disrespect me in my own home. I don't care how handsome he is. "Leave before I call the police."

He laughs a murderous chuckle before he shakes his head, straight-up denying my request. "I was sent here by Dimitri to collect a package..." He stares straight into my eyes as he digs a business card out of his suit jacket to hand it to me. It isn't his credentials. It is for a Dimitri Petretti. "So I ain't leaving until he either orders me to or you give me what I want."

His reply stumps me for a couple of seconds. Dimitri is the name Roxanne mentioned when she went for her job interview, but Brayden said I should keep that detail on the down-low, so only he and I know who she works for. Furthermore, my lust-fueled head heard his demand as more amorous than threatening.

Against my better judgment, and after several long seconds of deliberation, I request for the dark-haired man to wait in the doorway while I check to see who's calling me.

Proof he's telling the truth confronts me when I glance down at the screen of my cell phone. Roxanne's name and picture are flashing up on the screen.

When I shoot my eyes back to the stranger, he smirks a smug grin. He loves being right just as much as he appreciates the slightest snippet of my backside poking out the bottom of my booty shorts. He's quick to drag his eyes away but not quite quick enough.

I give him the stink eye before sliding my index finger across my phone's screen. Confusion bombards me when my phone's speaker shrieks like I'm calling Roxanne instead of the other way around. It rings on repeat until my call is eventually sent to voice-mail. It did the same thing a couple of days ago.

"She hung up," I say in shock, more to myself than to the mysterious stranger.

"She'll call back." My living room shrinks in size when the man steps far enough into the foyer, my front door shuts behind him. He's so tall, he had to bob his head to stop it from colliding with the doorjamb. "Until then, we wait."

"Ah. No." I splay my hand across his broad chest, wordlessly advising him to stay where he is before I dial Roxanne's number. "I have places to be and—"

"A friend so uneager to see you, she sent me in her place."

As anger bubbles in my stomach, I wordlessly demand the stranger to stay in the foyer, squash my cell phone to my ear, then pace toward Roxanne's bedroom. Our apartment only has one bedroom, and although Roxanne has been gone a little over two weeks, I've stayed out of her realm. Everything is where she left it, waiting for her, including the pencils and drawing pad she was rarely without before her ex-boyfriend tried to kill her.

If I know Roxanne as well as I do, that's what she's seeking. The knowledge that her love of drawing has returned doesn't make the stranger's comments any less frustrating, though. If Roxanne wants her art supplies, she could have come and got them. She didn't need to send a brute over to knock my ego down a peg or two. I've been dying for her to revamp the skills she let slide when she was hit with back-to-back losses. I would have cheered her on, not criticized her.

My brows stitch together when my scan of Roxanne's room has me failing to locate her sketchpad and nubs of charcoal. I could have sworn they were on her bedside table. They were next to the picture of her nanna she took when she packed. Her beloved dressing gown and photo frame were the only things removed from her room when she left, which is the sole reason I didn't call the police to report her missing.

I love Roxanne dearly, but not even the homeless man on the corner would steal her dressing gown. Its lack of appeal is why Roxanne cherishes it so much. She doesn't have to worry about anyone stealing it. Her dressing gown, Nanna, and I were always there for her.

Now it appears as if I've been shoved down on the list.

I'm not exactly sure what I did wrong. Yes, Brayden and I were in a hot and heavy make-out session the last time she saw me, but her spirits were so high about a possible job placement, she didn't once glare at me when she unearthed Brayden was hiding his hands under the flare of my dress. She encouraged Brayden to grill me about working a double shift at the establishment owned by a man with as many shady business dealings as Brayden's uncle before she skipped out the door like she had the world at her feet.

I was happy for her.

'Was' being the prominent part of my comment.

Anger isn't a go-to emotion of mine. I lean more toward berating than screaming, but I can see my patience being stretched thin today, especially when Roxanne doesn't bother greeting me when she finally answers my call.

All I get is silence.

"Roxie? Are you there?" I breathe out slowly to subdue my nerves. It does little to douse the fire igniting in my stomach. "If you ignore my call one more time, I'm going to scream." I feel it bubble in my chest when the stranger dares to chuckle about my warning. I am glad he's entertained. I'm far from it. "What's the go with you lately? Are you too good for your friends now?"

My mood worsens like a storm rolling in on a dedicated beach day when the stranger grunts, "Less talk. More looking. I haven't got all day."

I snap my eyes to his, my teeth bared in warning. "Don't push your luck, mister. After the way she left me high and dry the past few days, she should be grateful I took her call. I'm pissed, and it's that time of the month, so you better watch yourself." My comment doesn't come out as snappy as intended, but I'm hopeful it will remind Roxanne that our friendship is not to be messed with. Nothing comes between us. Not money. Not a man. Nothing.

"Estelle—"

"Oh, so you do remember my name. How kind of you." I bite

on the inside of my cheek, needing pain to override the anguish in my tone. "Now tell me what I'm searching for so I can get on with my day." My bitchiness takes a backstep when Roxanne sucks in a sharp breath. She only ever does that when she's confused.

After locking my eyes with the brute taking up every inch of space in my foyer, I disclose, "Mr. Cranky Pants said he was ordered here to collect a package, and that he isn't leaving until he gets it. Considering he handed me your boss's business card, I'm assuming the mysterious package has something to do with you."

My throat feels suddenly parched when Roxanne's silence allows me to hear her steadily rising pulse. She sounds seconds from collapse as she begs, "Don't do this. She has nothing to do with this."

"Nothing to do with what?" I query, confused and somewhat frightened. Roxanne was run over by a car—twice. She has experienced pain and loss like no one else, yet she sounds more scared now than she ever has.

On instinct, I back away from the man glowering at me like not the slightest bit of panic slicks my skin when Roxanne stammers out, "I've done as you asked. I followed your rules."

I barely make it to the other side of the living room when the brute with dark, gleaming eyes bridges the gap between us. His strides are slow and steady, vastly contrasting to the words shooting out of my mouth. "Excuse me, I asked you to wait in the foyer."

With a smile as sexy as it is evil, he digs leather gloves out of his pocket while he continues stalking my way. Instinct should have me bolting for the door, but the self-defense classes the gym teacher at Erkinsvale PCYC forced me to endure when I was thirteen are long forgotten as I back myself into a corner I'll have no chance of escaping without carnage.

As I shake my head at the stranger, silently begging for him to alter the murderous glint in his eyes to amicable, Roxanne sobs. "Please, Dimitri. She's all I have. I won't cope without her."

Her begging makes me realize how wrong I have everything. She didn't withdraw contact to hurt me.

She did it to protect me.

When the back of my knee scrapes against the bathtub, I shift my focus to my only lifeline. "Roxie..." My one word is so breathless, not even I recognize my voice. "What's going on? I thought you were working for some old geezer who can't wipe his ass."

"I am. I'm just—"

The stranger stops just inside the bathroom door when a thick Italian voice drowns out the frantic throbs of Roxanne's pulse. "Not following the terms she agreed upon." It's obvious he can hear what I'm hearing, I am just lost as to how. I didn't activate the speaker function on my phone, and he isn't close enough to hear anything over the raging beats of my heart echoing around my dingy bathroom. "And since she's too stubborn for her own good, I had to get inventive."

"So you sent a member of your staff to collect her belongings?"

I sound dim, but it can't be helped. I am truly lost as to what the hell is happening. The man doesn't sound like he wants to hurt Roxanne. His voice is brimming with way too much protectiveness for that to be the case, so that can only mean one thing— he wants me to help him end Roxanne's determination.

I'd find his endeavors amusing if I weren't being crowded into the bathroom by a giant with murderous eyes.

With the odds stacked against me, I revert to a commonly used mechanism when I'm feeling snowed under.

Humor.

"If you want Roxie to fall into line, you should have threatened her family."

My snappy attitude sails out the window when the brute standing across from me winks, smirks, then murmurs, "Bingo."

"Oh, shit."

The stranger bats away the ceramic toothbrush holder I peg at his head. The direction of his push sends it hurling into the vanity mirror. Its crack sprinkles the tiled floor with shards of jagged glass.

I don't consider how hacked up my feet will be before commencing my endeavor to flee. After tossing towels, a free-standing rack, and rolls of toilet paper at him like they're life-maiming weapons, I sprint the three steps between us, barge him with everything I have, sidestep him, then race for the door.

"Please!" Roxanne screams just as the stranger catches up with me in the living room. "I'll do anything you want."

When he bands his arm around my waist to fling me away from the door, my cell phone slips from my hand. It clatters across the living room floor, landing a mere inch from the wall he crowds me against with his imposing frame. He doesn't respond to my violent outburst with the same feverish rage I'm exerting. He merely deflects the jabs of my fists as if they're as painless as butterfly wings fluttering across his chest before he stills the jerking thrusts of my legs with his chunky thighs.

"You're a sick fucking prick," I spit out when it dawns on me that he is hard. His cock is extended well past my belly button, and its girth and hardness are too perverse to excuse him as being a shower instead of a grower.

The dangerous stranger doesn't deny my claim. He steps closer to me, his eyes twinkling with amusement as he anchors my arms above my head with one hand while the other moves toward my neck.

When he curls his hand around my throat, I try to pull away from him, to push him back with my body, but the more I fight him, the firmer he clutches me. I don't get the chance to plead, scream, or beg for mercy before he steals the air from my lungs with a brutal clutch on my throat. I wouldn't even if I could, though. If your day is done, it's done. No amount of wishful thinking will alter that fact.

Being choked to death isn't as scary as I thought it would be. With the stranger's hold on my throat firm enough to lift my feet from the floor, and his erect penis aiding with the hoist, my body confuses his aggression as pleasure. It can't feel the screams of my lungs because they're being denied oxygen nor the panic hazing my mind of rational thoughts. It feels the throbs of pleasure I've been too scared to explore and hears the manic whisperings of the nymph who resides inside my heart.

The disturbing thoughts assuring me I deserve everything that's happening to me deepen when the stranger loosens his grip enough, small portions of air sneak down my throat.

When you're squashed against a wall by a man who exudes danger, victory is the last emotion you should feel, but there's no denying it. It rains down on me like a torrential downpour when the loosening of his grip is quickly chased by him scrubbing his thumb across my bare lips.

He drags the worn leather material on his glove over my mouth and down my jaw before he uses it to shove my head to the side. The tiny breaths subduing the panicked squeals of my lungs come out in a hurry when he braces the tip of his nose against the throb in my throat, and he inhales deeply. I feel his growl more than I hear it. It rumbles between our conjoined bodies, strengthening my belief that I've lost the plot.

After what feels like minutes but is barely seconds, he whispers in my ear, "You owe me." He drops his hands to his sides, steps back, then locks his eyes with mine. "And I'm not a man who doesn't collect what's owed."

He waits for me to see the decisiveness in his murky black gaze before he nudges his head to my cell phone. "Hurry, Estelle," he murmurs, shocking me that he knows my name. "Before I change my mind."

Confused but very much assured that I need my head examined, I dip my chin before bobbing down to snatch my now cracked cell phone from the floor.

"Go," Roxanne begs when I squash it to my ear.

"Where?" I reply.

I have nowhere to go. Not even my place of employment is open this early in the day.

"Anywhere. I'll find you. I promise."

The grogginess of her voice breaks my heart. "Roxie—"

"I'm fine. I promise you I'm okay. I just need you to go."

"Okay," I reply, willing to say and do anything to lessen her heartache. "I love you."

As she returns my declaration of love, I gather my purse and car keys off the entryway table before hot-footing it into the corridor. Roxanne sighs in relief when the creak of the safety gate on the elevator announces I'm in the clear.

We don't speak during the seven-floor descent to the lobby of our apartment building or the twenty-step trek to my car. I'm too busy replaying the words the unnamed man whispered in my ear to have cognitive thoughts.

Roxanne's silence exposes she's facing a similar battle of her conscience. Except she doesn't run away from the monster instigating her subliminal thoughts. She faces him head-on by declaring war as only she knows how—with straight-up anarchy.

"Send one of your goons to deal with me now. I dare you."

2

CLOVER

I kill for the money.

The thrill.

The condemnation.

I plan to go to hell, so why not have some fun during the prolonged detour?

But today... today I made an exception.

I've murdered gangsters and political diplomats and killed an entire family who thought I'd be too blinded by a set of big tits and an untouched cunt to let justice prevail. Estelle Armstead was an easy mark. I could have ended her life the instant she opened her front door, refunded Dimitri the one hundred thousand dollars he paid to cause a ruckus, then went on my merry way.

What stopped me? The simple answer is entertainment. One person's death can be easily replaced by another, but true entertainment for a man as fucked as me is scarce.

Most men flounder when they see me, and almost all of them don't have balls big enough to approach me, much less put me in my place, yet Estelle took my surly attitude in stride like it's a nasty side dish she can make more pleasant with a sprinkling of seasoning.

I don't have the heart to tell her that won't be the case. I was born evil, bred evil, and I will die evil. But just like everyday strait-laced men, murderers have needs too.

Needs I can see Estelle's tight cunt, firm ass, and rocking body fulfilling.

I've just got to take care of one matter first.

The three-hundred-thousand-dollar bounty on her head not even Dimitri is aware of.

3
———

ESTELLE

When the accented voice booming out of the security box at the front gate of the Katz mansion tells me Brayden will be down in a minute, I sag into the driver's seat of my beat-up Honda. His voice isn't as foreign as the man who tried to strangle me. It's Spanish and mature, whereas the stranger's voice was deep, rugged, and still ringing in my ears even with my escape occurring over thirty minutes ago.

I can't stop thinking about his threat.

You owe me, and I'm not a man who doesn't collect what's owed.

I have nothing, not a single thing I own is of any value, so I'm lost as to what he thinks I owe him and how he thinks he will recoup my so-called debt. He must have me mistaken for someone else. I can't be the only Estelle in this area of Florida. But how does that excuse his impeccable timing?

It doesn't, which can only mean one thing—my name is at the top of his hit-list, and it was placed there by the man Roxanne is working for.

"Come on, Roxie," I beg when I drop my eyes to the screen of

my phone. My messages have been delivered, but not a single one
has been read.

12:13 PM

Estelle: *I'm out.*

Delivered

12:16 PM

Estelle: *Call me when you can.*

Delivered

12:22 PM

Estelle: *Are you okay?*

Delivered

12:32 PM

Estelle: *Pls message me back.*
I'm worried about you.

Delivered

12:42 PM

Estelle: *Roxie...*

Delivered

Desperate, I type out a final message.

12:53 PM

Estelle: *I'm calling the police.*

.   .   .

I don't breathe when three little dots ripple across the cracked glass. My threat was frivolous. I don't trust the police in my hometown any more than the mobsters who run the towns bordering it, but I'm desperate enough to pretend.

12:54 PM

Roxie: *I wouldn't do that if I were you.*

I'm partway through typing out a response to the person who clearly isn't Roxanne—she would have called out my bluff—when another message pops up.

I don't know whether to be pleased or concerned when I read his response.

12:55 PM

Roxie: *For one, I'm in control of your cell phone and the 2016 HP Spectre you watch Netflix on every night with the neighbor's account you unearthed when their bill was placed into the wrong mail slot at your apartment building, so any calls you attempt to make will come to me. And two, contacting the authorities would impede Roxanne's safety, not improve it.*

I stare at my phone for a couple of seconds, contemplating what to do. I want to call out the stranger's bluff, but I'm worried I've used all my good luck today. I escaped the grim reaper with a bruised neck and nicked feet. The murderous gleam his eyes held when he choked me exposes it should have been much worse.

Confident not all law enforcement officers are as corrupt as my employee has made them out to be, I breathe out slowly, dial 9-1-1, then activate the phone's speaker.

I gorge on fresh oxygen like its candy when I'm connected with a dispatch officer a couple of rings later. "Emergency services. Fire, police, or ambulance?"

"Police, please." I stop deliberating the uniqueness of the operator's voice when my location dawns on me. "But not Ravenshoe PD. I need someone outside of this region."

"Why is that?" the operator asks while tapping away on a keyboard.

"Umm..." I'm not on the ball when it comes to thinking. At the very least, I need a couple of seconds to come up with the goods. While tucking a strand of platinum blonde hair behind my ear, I mutter, "Because Ravenshoe PD—"

"Is full of corrupt cops who accept bribes from gangsters?" It's the fight of my life not to toss my phone into the air when the call connect screen is replaced with a face of a man with dark hair and an immorally corrupt smirk. "Because if that's your reasoning, your assumptions are correct." A thousand articles about corruption, misconduct of officers, and the cases associated with them flood my phone. "Despite the millions of dollars invested in the Ravenshoe area, Ravenshoe PD has yet to remove the riffraff from their department." The man's face returns to the screen. "I should know. I am responsible for depositing their bribes each month." He smiles at the shocked flare darting through my eyes before asking sincerely, "Is there anything else I can help you with, Ms. Armstead?"

The smugness on his face clears away when I mutter, "Your hacking skills are impressive, but they can't stop me from walking into a police station and reporting Roxanne's disappearance in person."

"That's true," he counters with a bob of his head. "But then you'd need to explain this..." He inundates my cell phone with images of me at work slipping ecstasy pills to clients. I don't sell them to make money. It's part of my undocumented job description. "And this..." The dollar bills Mr. Monroe pays me with make his next lot of pictures appear more sinister than they are. "And if that isn't enough, I can always become more inventive."

"What the hell?" I mutter before I can stop myself. I haven't done any of the horrifying things this man bombards my phone with, but my face is in every single image.

Once he's confident he has me worried enough to listen, he removes the disturbing gallery from my phone before saying, "It will be more convenient for all involved if you simply forget what happened this morning."

I shake my head. "Roxanne is my friend. My *best* friend. I don't care what you do to me, but I won't stand by and watch her be hurt. *She's been hurt enough.*" My last sentence is a whisper since Roxanne's story isn't mine to share.

Debilitating silence occupies the next couple of seconds before a man with green eyes joins our conversation. He doesn't speak to me. He whispers something into the dark-haired man's ear, instantly softening the agitation on his face.

My head has to remind my heart to beat when a montage of photographs plays on my phone. They show Roxanne doing a range of activities. In one image, she's sketching portraits on a large bed in an elaborate room. In another, she's grinning at a tattooed man whose backside is sprawled on fancy-looking marble tile, but it's the last image I pay the most attention to. It's zoomed in, and since her tiny body is being engulfed by a man with broad shoulders, only a portion of her face can be seen, but there's no denying the expression on her face.

She's in love.

"If she loves him, why is he hurting her?"

I'm not granted a verbal reply but thrust back into a nightmare that's only forty minutes old. I'm given access to the event that unfolded in my apartment from Roxanne's perspective. The ten-minute video leaves no stone unturned, so when it progresses toward a ransom worth over seven million dollars, I'm left speechless.

It's for the best. If I hadn't been rendered silent, I might have missed what the bearded man says a nanosecond before Brayden knocks on my driver's side window, scaring the living daylights out of me. "Dimitri won't hurt Roxie, Estelle. He's trying to stop her from being hurt. You've just got to trust the word of a stranger." As Brayden opens my door, the green-eyed man stares straight at me while saying, "If you're anything like Roxie, I'm sure you can do that. She has blind faith in everyone." He winks, smirks, then the screen goes black.

I dart my eyes between my phone's screen and Brayden when the messages the man sent when I threatened to call the police disappear from the chat window. He covers his tracks so well that even the 'read' notifications at the bottom of my messages revert to 'delivered.'

"Hey. What are you doing here?" Brayden asks after coercing my eyes to his, seemingly unconcerned that I'm shoeless and my feet are bleeding. "I didn't think you knew where I lived."

I sound more confused than panicked when I reply, "I looked up your address in the directory." A new emotion takes hold of my senses when air whizzes out of his nose. "That's okay, isn't it?"

An immediate 'yes' is what I'm seeking, but Brayden doesn't give me anything close to that. "Not really." He twists me so I face away from his family's mega-mansion. "My parents are home. Now isn't a good time—"

"Not a good time! I was just attacked... *in my home*... but now isn't convenient for you." I pull away from him, aware I'm taking my anger out on the wrong person, but also furious two months of dating hasn't granted me the right to do a pop-in visit. "Well, excuse me, I guess I should go and check with my intruder on a more suitable time for all involved."

"Hold on, wait." He grabs my arms and forcefully yanks me back out of my car. As his eyes scan my face, he asks. "You were assaulted?"

"Yes!" *Why is that so hard for him to believe?* "We got into an altercation in the bathroom, then he tried to choke me in the living room."

The movie rolling through my head pauses when Brayden asks, "How did he get inside your apartment, much less your bathroom?"

"I don't know... he knocked. I answered." I'm torn between laughing at my stupidity and defending myself when memories of my confrontation with the stranger roll through my head. Although it was surreal, it doesn't make it any less scary. "Does it really matter how he got in? He tried to kill me."

"It will matter to the police." I assume he's taking my side until he adds, "They won't take your case seriously if you tell them you invited him inside your home."

"I invited him into the foyer. I didn't ask him to kill me!"

"Okay. Okay. Calm down." He opens the door he shut with his hip after forcefully evicting me from my car, then guides me into the driver's seat. "Let me grab a couple of things, then I'll be right out." He jogs two steps away before he spins back around to face me. "I told you Roxanne was messing with the wrong crowd."

No sympathies for my injuries.

No pledge to hurt the person responsible for hurting me.

Just judgment I don't need and a surly attitude.

"Don't worry about getting your things. I'm fine."

I slam my car door shut, drowning out Brayden's request for me not to be so dramatic before cranking on the ignition. It takes three attempts and several curse words for the motor to kick over, but when it does, I reverse out of the Katz driveway like they won't order one of their many butlers to scrub away my tire marks with their one and only toothbrush.

"Elle..." Brayden calls out as he follows me down the street. "You're being unreasonable."

After winding down the window, I flip him the bird. It won't give me a place to stay while I unmuddle the confusion in my head, but it sure feels good responding how I want instead of what is expected.

4

ESTELLE

I stray my eyes over the empty alleyway before peeling open the door of The Commission, a club I've worked at for the past six months. It's owned by Mr. Monroe, a wannabee gangster who waited until his fifties before aspiring to reach mobster status.

The Commission is registered as a dance club, but anyone in this part of Erkinsvale knows it's more a strip club than a nightclub. Mercifully, the waitresses don't work topless as per Mr. Monroe's wish, but our uniforms leave nothing to the imagination. They're even more revealing than the booty shorts-midriff top combination I'm wearing now.

I'm grateful my dash out of my apartment two hours ago was done without shoes. It makes my steps across the polished floors of The Commission soundless. I don't know why I'm so panicked. I'd rather face a breaking-and-entering charge than be incriminated for selling molly to patrons.

I don't profit a dime from the multiple illegal transactions this company makes each night. I only do it to ensure I'm given shifts the following week. We've lost over half a dozen waitresses the past month, and none of the losses were because of the skimpy uniform.

I freeze outside the door leading to The Commission's staffroom when an unusual smell streams into my nose. The scent of whiskey and cigars is nothing out of the ordinary, but blood is rarely on the agenda, and the only time men sweat here is when their wives track their cell phones. We're not open for another three hours, so it's too early to consider a disgruntled wife. And Tommy, the lead bouncer of The Commission, only ever gets his knuckles bloody when the clients are too handsy with the staff.

"It's just the cuts in your feet," I murmur to myself while summoning the courage to continue my tiptoe walk.

"Or not," replies a thickly accented voice that hasn't stopped playing on repeat in my ear the past two hours. "Your scent is pure and clean. His was not."

My heart thuds in my chest when a shadow moves away from the booths surrounding the main stage. The dark and gloomy stranger doesn't charge for me like he did when I sprinted for the front door of my apartment. He takes his time. His steps slow and noiseless.

"Why are you here?" I ask just as his bruised and bloody hands come into view. They weren't damaged like that when he stole the air from my lungs. They didn't have a mark on them. "You shouldn't be here. I called the police."

"You did," he replies with a chuckle, somewhat amused. "And you also sat outside the station for almost an hour." My chest thrusts up and down when he emerges from the dark enough that half of his face unshadows. "But you never went inside."

I dart my eyes from his smirk to his dress shirt when I notice it's dotted with blood. I've barely had a cognitive thought since my near-death, but I'm reasonably sure the blood isn't from him. The direction of the spray is wrong, and tiny snippets of tissue that doesn't appear to be skin is mottled throughout it.

My throat burns through a brutal swallow when it dawns on me what the matter could be. I hated biology at school, and a dissection of a sheep's brain during my sophomore year was the cause of that.

"What did you do?"

My hands seek something to grip when he answers, "I killed a man."

I'm too far from the bar to reach it, and I'd have to bypass the man confessing to a murder to slump into the safety of a high-backed booth, so I stay put instead.

"W-Why did you that?"

I drench my dry throat with spit before shaking my head when he commands, "Sit before you fall."

My legs are shuddering a million miles an hour, and my head is woozy, but I've got a grip on reality—just. "Answer the question. Why did you kill a man so soon after leaving my apartment?"

My heart launches into my throat when he exerts his authority with a chest shuddering roar, "*Sit* before you fall!"

When I shake my head for the second time, determined to work out if the pardoning of my life is responsible for the loss of another person, he charges the three steps between us, grips my throat like he did earlier, then thrusts me back until my ass lands on one of the leather-topped stools dotted around the bar.

After bringing his lips to my ear, his breaths uneven, he snarls, "If you don't start doing as you're told, the goods will be damaged before I've had the chance to sample them."

Goods?

I almost slip off my chair when my scrambled mind unjumbles his riddle.

I have nothing to offer him—*except me.*

"I have a boyfriend," I blurt out, panicked.

He drops his hand from my neck to my collarbone, his touch so soft it barely registers. "Who let you leave injured and upset." My knees pull inward when his nostrils flare from leaning in close. He seems as intoxicated by my scent as he is my lips. After exhaling the big breath he sucked in through his nose, he locks his deadly black eyes with mine. "He doesn't deserve you."

"And neither do you," I snap out, confident in my assumption of what he's chasing.

Spit pools in the corner of my mouth when he replaces his snarl for a smirk. "I know. That's what will make this so much fun."

I begin to wonder how much time has passed since our last exchange when he removes an official-looking contract out of the breast pocket in his suit jacket. It's pristine and uncreased like it was recently printed, but it's already been endorsed by Nadir 'Clover' Hadi and a witness.

Air traps in my throat when my eyes scan the document. I'm not solely shocked Nadir is thirteen years older than my almost twenty years, I'm also gasping over the debt I supposedly owe him. "How can I be indebted to you for four hundred thousand dollars? I don't even know you."

Nadir flips over the pages of the contract until he arrives at the itemized billing section. Even with English not being his first language, his contract spells everything out in a way a foreigner could understand. Murder is a globally recognized word.

Confident I've seen the term as hoped, Nadir states, "My rate is five hundred thousand for a non-dignitary. After deducting the one hundred thousand dollars Dimitri paid to..."

"Scare Roxanne," I fill in when words elude him.

He also scared me, but I refuse to let him know that. The flare that shoots through his eyes anytime I give him lip assures me my sassy attitude is the only reason I'm still breathing. If he thinks I'm more scared than excited, our conversation could end before I understand all his terms.

After lifting his chin in agreement, he states matter-of-factly, "So you are left with a four hundred thousand deficient."

"I can see that," I reply, somehow capable of forming sentences. "But why would I pay you five hundred thousand dollars? I didn't order your services."

I'm glad I am seated when he places a Polaroid on top of our 'contract.' The particles on his shirt now make sense. It's brain matter, as suspected. It came from a man who's no longer identifiable since half of his face is missing. His back is propped against a long counter, and although he's wearing a black button-up shirt, the bruises on his neck and torso are the darkest parts of the photograph.

"You killed a man... *for me*?" I breathe out slowly as the dots slowly join together. When he nods again, I blubber out. "Why? I didn't ask you to do that."

The heaving of my chest doubles when he mutters, "I killed him so you wouldn't be killed." He wipes at a bead of sweat pooling near my temples, sucks the droplet into his mouth, then drifts his eyes between mine. "Did I make a mistake?"

"Yes! You shouldn't have killed him for *any* reason, much less for me."

"Why not?" He doesn't wait for me to answer. "If I hadn't killed him, I would have had to kill you."

The struggles of my lungs are heard in my reply. "Why? Why can't you just not kill anyone?"

He laughs. It isn't a butterfly-producing chuckle, but it does cause a tingle to an area below my stomach. "You had a contract on your head. A bounty I had intended to cash before I realized your death would give me ten minutes of pleasure." He lowers his eyes to my lips. "But your mouth could give me so much more."

For some stupid reason, his murmured comment excites me more than it scares me, but not enough for me to completely lose my mind. "I'm not signing that contract. I didn't ask you to kill anyone for me, so it isn't my debt to pay. Furthermore, why should I believe there was a bounty on my head? I don't know you, so there's no way in hell I'll just take your word on something so absurd."

Wooziness bombards me when I slip off the barstool. I want to blame low blood sugar for my dizzy state, but that would be a lie. It's from what Nadir says next, "You killed his daughter, so he wanted you dead. Since he couldn't stomach the idea of doing it himself, he sought outside help."

He waits for me to spin and face him before he places down a second Polaroid. It's of a girl I'd guess to be in her early twenties. She has a bright smile, black hair, and a ton of innocence in her eyes. She looks starkly different from the girl I performed CPR on in an alleyway for thirty minutes while waiting for paramedics to arrive last month.

"Mary overdosed. Her death wasn't my fault."

Tears threatened to roll down my face when he sets down a third photograph. This one isn't a polaroid. It's blurry since it was taken from the surveillance device hanging above the main bar at The Commission. "You supplied her the drug that killed her, so her father blames you for her death."

"E doesn't cause the symptoms she had. She must have taken something else before she arrived."

Salty blobs slide down my cheek when Nadir discloses, "The coroner found traces of N-methoxybenzyl in her system. It's more toxic than standard MDMA and often causes heart attacks, strokes, and renal failure." He stands, shrinking the room with his impressive size. "You'd know that if you were more than an unpaid distributor." A reason for the increased smell of alcohol is unearthed when he leans across the bar to snatch up an open bottle of whiskey. "When I explained that to Mr. Van Den Brink and promised to take down the true culprit, he agreed to remove the bounty from your head."

Nadir fills two glasses to the brim before sliding one to my side. I'm not much of a drinker, and it's early in the afternoon, but I raise the glass to my face, confused as to why the club emblem isn't the standard one the patrons use.

I take a staggering step back when I realize the glass is sprinkled with blood and is engraved with the initials AM.

Aaron Monroe.

Youngest son of Mr. Rule Monroe.

Excluding the glass he leaves on the counter to be washed each afternoon, the regular staff never sees him. He arrives outside of trading hours to do the books and prepare the banking. I only see him during business hours when he's dropping off the latest shipment of ecstasy he wants to be sold to his father's customers.

After dumping Aaron's glass onto the counter, spilling a generous portion of the contents inside, I drift my eyes to the mirrored wall at the back of the bar, suddenly mindful of the backdrop of the photograph Nadir showed me. Liquor from around the world is spanned across the glass shelves mounted to the mirror, but they don't hinder the image of a man without a face propped against the bartenders' side of the bar.

A blood-curdling squeal erupts from my lips as I stumble away from the bar. I barely get in two steps when my wish to flee is thwarted by Nadir's big, imposing frame. He stands behind me, his raging pulse unmissable since my ear is closer to his heart than his face.

He is also hard, either turned on by my fretful scream, or

worse, his earlier comment about getting pleasure from murder works for both male and female victims.

My breaths come out in a quiver when he drags his index finger down my wet cheek before he stops it at the throb in my throat. "I'll give you twenty-four hours to come up with a response. If you agree to my terms, none of this will be your fault."

"If I don't?" I have no clue how I am negotiating. I'm shocked I haven't passed out from a lack of oxygen.

My knees knock when Nadir spins me around to face him. He doesn't step back to place much-needed space between our bodies. He remains super close. Even our breaths are shared. "The video footage of you sneaking into The Commission before opening hours will be returned to the surveillance hard drive. Add that to your fingerprints on Aaron's glass, and Ravenshoe PD will have a slam-dunk case. I've seen them put away people with less evidence." He acts as if I'm not already scared by tacking on another threat. "And I could always convince Mr. Van Den Brink that my assumptions were wrong. Then I'll only be out of pocket one hundred thousand dollars. A small price to pay for ten minutes of fun."

In silence, he drinks in the fear slicking my skin with sweat for several long seconds before he takes a step back, dangles a set of keys in front of my face, then places them into my shaky hand. "You'll be safe here until you make your decision." He brings his plump lips to within an inch of mine before whispering, "From everyone *but* me."

Before I can blink, he disappears into the shadows.

My getaway is just as quick, but only once I've wiped my fingerprints off Aaron's blood-splattered whiskey glass.

5

ESTELLE

"*R*oxie..."

The hope fueling my high tone slips away when her voicemail finalizes her greeting, "Can't take your call right now. You know what to do." *Beep.*

"Roxanne, it's Estelle," I blurt out like her childhood phone number isn't displayed on the screen of her cell phone. "I really *really* need to talk to you. Something has happened, and I don't know what to think about it..."

I pause for the second time when an unfamiliar click sounds through my ear. It's like the clank of a landline call being disconnected even with the receiver still being in my hand.

"Hello..."

I push down on the hook switch of an outdated house phone three times when I fail to get neither a dial tone nor a response. With the calls from my cell phone going straight to voicemail, I checked to see if the landline was still in operation. They're a lot harder to hack.

Well, so I thought.

When an additional three pushes on the hook doesn't award me a dial tone, I slam the receiver down, then pace to the window spanning one half of the living room. It took me longer than I care to admit recognizing the key Nadir placed in my hand.

Neither Roxanne nor I have been to her grandparents' ranch in over a year, and even before the death of her beloved Nanna, my visits were sporadic. I don't like being reminded about how poor I am. The apartment I share with Roxanne isn't close to flashy, but it's a step up from the residence I was raised in.

Erkinsvale is infamous for the tough kids it reared. It's that notoriety that has us forgetting how far away we are from the one-percenters who rule this country.

Unease makes itself known with my stomach when something in the far corner of the rugged landscape catches my eye. It's reflective and shiny like the holes spread across the sandy plains were from treasure hunters seeking buried loot.

Forever curious, I pace closer to the shimmery object like the sun didn't set over an hour ago. I make it across five acres of flat yet overgrown terrain when my heart leaves my chest for the third time today. Even with my cell phone being in my pocket, it has no trouble getting reception.

After gathering my heart from the ground, I dig my phone out of my pocket, hopeful my caller is Roxanne. I'm left disappointed when I discover who's calling. Mr. Monroe hates when his staff calls in sick for a shift, and his annoyance is even more stubborn when they do it via text message.

My cowardice can't be helped. I know what happened to his son. Cheerful, non-disclosure conversations aren't my forte right now.

I'm not sure they will ever be.

Another contact request pops up within a second of me denying Mr. Monroe's call. It isn't a standard call. Brayden is trying to FaceTime me. I'm tempted to deny his request as well, but the hundreds of apologies he bombarded my phone with this afternoon have me doing the opposite.

Perhaps I was being unreasonable.

A change in personality is expected after a traumatic experience.

"Estelle, baby, thank god. I've been panicked out of my mind," Brayden mutters down the line a second after our chat connects. "I shouldn't have let you leave the way you did. I was just so shocked by what you said, I wasn't thinking straight..." He pauses, glances past me like he's never seen untouched land before, then shifts his eyes back to me. "Where are you?"

The silence the past couple of hours has been good for me. It allowed me to think on the spot, a trait I didn't have access to previously. "I've gone away for a couple of days to think."

"About?" he queries while giving me his best puppy dog eyes. "It's about me, isn't it? You're angry about how I responded."

I shake my head. I'm too confused to be angry. "I didn't want to go back to my apartment, so here seemed like the next logical choice." I twist until Roxanne's grandparents' ranch fills the screen behind me. We've only been dating a little over two months, but Brayden is aware of its sentimental value to Roxanne enough to recognize it.

A new type of anxiousness twists my stomach when Brayden asks, "Can I come?"

"I don't think that's a good idea, Brayden. I'm not in the right headspace."

He drops his bottom lip. "Because I'm not there with you. You know I make everything better." He ramps up his wooing by adding the slightest pop of dimples to the mix. "I've got flowers to deliver..." The two dozen red roses he thrusts into the screen aren't exactly a girl's first pick when it comes to groveling flowers, but it's meant to be the thought that counts, isn't it? "And your favorite chocolates."

I mentally heave when he shows me a large box of dark chocolates. Only three groups of people eat dark chocolate—men, women on diets, and anyone over the age of sixty.

Although he missed the mark with his first two gifts, he goes from being near the line to over it when he murmurs, "And I collected a takeaway menu from *all* your favorite restaurants so you can splurge on anything you want for dinner tonight." A giggle rumbles up my chest when he holds up a handwritten menu for my favorite hole-in-the-wall Mexican restaurant five miles out of town. "They didn't have any menus, so I made my own." He takes a moment to relish my grin before asking again, "So, can I come?"

He jumps into the air like a child when I dip my chin before he sprints to his sports car. He tosses the roses into the passenger seat like they're worthless before dumping the box of chocolates on top of them. I realize he's only just purchased his groveling-approved products seconds before calling me when the lights of Erkinsvale's main street reflect through the rearview window of his ride.

That means he needed over six hours to realize he made a mistake when he let me leave this afternoon. That's five hours and fifty-nine minutes longer than what's acceptable.

The anger keeping my veins warm subsides a little when Brayden arrives one hour and forty-five minutes later. The trip usually takes three minutes, but my annoyance subdues somewhat when I discover the reason for his delay. He's grasping a picnic basket and blanket in one hand, and the other is overloaded with grocery bags.

He winks at my doe-eyed expression before quadrupling it. "You said you wanted to get away for a couple of days, so I brought you some home comforts to make your stay more pleasant." He hands me the blanket and picnic basket before nudging his head to the living room. "Set this up in there while I put the perishables away."

I swoon like crazy when he places milk, cheese, ham, and butter into the recently switched-on refrigerator before he dumps a selection of fruit into a bowl on the two-seater dinette. "Have you thought about what you'd like to eat?"

I spread the velvet blanket across the bottom half of a two-seater sofa before fanning the leftover parts over the carpet. "Not yet. Do you have a preference?"

Brayden twists his lips. "I'm down for anything as long as it isn't too heavy. I don't usually eat before hitting the club scene." When my brows furrow in confusion, he attempts to smooth them. "My uncle is opening the Blue Dragon tonight. I got us a set of tickets for the VIP section. I thought it would be nice for us to go out in public together. Announce our relationship, so to speak."

The excited butterflies his comment instigates almost have me forgetting I nearly died today. If it weren't for the tinge of pain in my neck, I might have agreed with his suggestion. "Although I've been waiting for this day for weeks, I really don't want to go out tonight. I'm super tired." Brayden looks like I told him I'm moving interstate when I say, "Perhaps we could watch a movie instead?"

"Do they even have cable?" When I shrug, he paces further into the room, snatches up the outdated remote, then switches on the square television. "They don't even have standard channels," he murmurs a couple of seconds later, his tone way too privileged for my liking. "So that leaves us only one option. We have to go out. What a shame."

"Or..." I wet my lips before raking my teeth over the lower one. "We could stay in and make our own entertainment." I've never felt dirty using sex as a means to get what I want. I guess times change when the entire basis of a half-million-dollar contract is sexual contact.

"That could also work," Brayden replies with a grin, his brows waggling.

He gets to within an inch of me before I stop his panther-like strides by splaying my hand across his chest. It's ludicrous for me to say I'm disappointed we stand at almost the same height, so I won't mention it. "But first, we should order food. I was born and raised in Erkinsvale, but that doesn't mean I'm willing to eat their cuisine."

"What is it?" I ask when Brayden returns to the living room, looking as white as a ghost.

Although we've fooled around the past hour, our PDA didn't step over a PG rating. I used the excuse I didn't want the delivery driver stumbling onto me in a half-dressed state as the reason for my lack of interest, but in all honesty, that's a copout.

I didn't want Brayden touching me.

I'm still angry about his response earlier today, and the fact he hasn't once brought up the injuries to my feet or neck amplifies my annoyance.

I can only hope the greening of his gills is because our heavy petting session has him realizing how close he came to losing me today, or I'm about ready to blow my top.

Brayden's head lifts from his cell phone before he mutters, "Aaron Monroe was found dead this evening. Foul play is suspected."

I scoff. "Of course, there's foul play. You can't lose half your face and not suspect criminal activity."

I curse my hotheadedness when Brayden asks, "How'd you know he lost half his face?"

"Umm..." I stare at the black screen of my cell phone before shifting my eyes to the even blacker scenery outside. "Mr. Monroe called me earlier. He was devastated."

I'm the worst liar, but up until today, I didn't realize Brayden's inbuilt lie detector was broken. "I can imagine. Although his grief can't be that bad. He kept The Commission open."

"He kept it open?"

I accept the cell phone he's holding out before peering down at the screen. A reporter is broadcasting a live stream in front of The Commission. It appears as if all hands are on deck.

"I guess we all grieve in our own way," I mumble, truly unsure.

I'm about to ask Brayden if he would have grieved me for longer than an afternoon if Nadir had been successful in his bid today, but before I can, a knock sounds at the door.

"Finally," Brayden grunts out on a moan. "I'm starving."

My throat becomes scratchy when I stray my eyes in the direction he's pacing. Our delivery driver isn't the standard fresh-faced teen you anticipate around these parts. He's tall, steaming mad, and the murderous gleam in his eyes is exactly what you'd expect from a hired hitman.

I don't breathe when Brayden sketchily slaps a ten-dollar bill into Nadir's hand, shakes it, then attempts to snatch the takeout bag he's clutching in his left hand. Nadir is already pissed, so disregarding his forty-minute trip with a stingy tip won't make things any better.

"It's unpaid," Nadir bites out, his tone low as he drifts his deadly black eyes to Brayden. "There was an issue with your credit card."

"Really?" Brayden queries, as suspicious as me.

His family comes from old money.

They never have payment issues.

When Nadir lifts his chin, his movements tight, Brayden shrugs. "All right. Let me grab my wallet."

He's barely left the room when Nadir's aura overwhelms his ten to one. After dragging his eyes across the untouched picnic basket and blanket sprawled on the living room floor, he raises them to my kiss swollen lips. He doesn't speak. Words aren't needed to relay his annoyance. His jaw is so firm, it appears seconds from cracking. And don't get me started on his fists. Even balled, they leave no doubt to the damage they could do to Brayden's face if given the opportunity.

"I gave you time to make a decision, not fuck around. Get him out of here. *Now*." The growling of Nadir's last word sees my head bobbing up and down before my brain has the chance to object.

My fast agreement pacifies the agitation on his face by a smidge, but not enough for Brayden not to bounce his eyes between us when he returns to the living room. He doesn't get jealous, but it's obvious he isn't a fan of the tension sizzling between Nadir and me.

"Here you go?" He steps in front of Nadir like his five-foot-eleven height will interrupt our stare-down before he thrusts a fifty-dollar bill into his chest. "This should cover it."

"It's on me." Nadir's reply is for Brayden, but his eyes remain on me. The height difference between Brayden and him means he can continue staring at me even without slanting his head.

After hitting me with a final warning glare, he drops the takeout bag onto the floor with a thump, spins on his heels, then walks away. Even scared, I can admit his walk is arousing. It's full of arrogance but with a touch of grace that exposes he knows how to move his body both in and out of the bedroom.

I stop staring in the direction Nadir went when Brayden mutters, "Fucking rude." He shoves his wallet into the back pocket of his pants, bobs down to pick up the now mushed sushi, then spins around to face me. "I knew he'd be a prick. That's why I went light with his tip."

My eyes roll about his deplorable excuse for his regular stinginess a mere second before a brilliant idea pops into my head. "You should go to your uncle's opening. Show your support." I only glance outside for half a second when I add to my suggestion, "Give me a second to get dressed, and I'll come with you."

Nadir's instructions were to kick Brayden out. He didn't mention anything about me going with him. Roxanne's grandparents' ranch is practically in the middle of town, but since the landscape is dotted with ancient trees and scrubs, it has an eerie feeling associated with it. I don't feel safe here, and surely the chances of being murdered in public would have to be lower than in a cabin in the woods.

I send silent thanks to Roxanne when my entrance into her childhood bedroom has me stumbling onto a partially full closet. We've been the same size since our senior year, and mercifully, her goth stage included plenty of LBDs.

Faster than Brayden can scoff down three sushi rolls, I saunter out of Roxanne's room in a body-hugging black dress with a flirty hemline. Brayden almost chokes when he spots how high the hemline sits. Roxanne and I are similar body types, but I'm several inches taller than her.

"Is it okay? It isn't too risqué, is it?" I'm not asking for Brayden's benefit nor mine. I want to make sure I don't give Nadir another excuse to intervene in my life. For some reason, I feel a daring outfit selection would do that.

My ego gets a boost when Brayden mutters through a mouth full of rice and seaweed, "You look fucking hot!"

My back molars grind together when he dumps the sushi I had planned to eat during our commute onto the floor like Roxanne's nanna's house is a trash site. I loathe wastage almost as much as I hate his lack of respect. This place isn't the Ritz, but it deserves better.

As do I.

"Let's head out before traffic gets too heavy." With no regard for the cuts on my feet, Brayden snatches my shoes out of my hands, bands his arm around my waist, tugs me into his side, then races us to his car. "There are Band-Aids in the first-aid kit in the glove compartment. You can fix your feet on the way."

So he knows I'm injured, he just doesn't care enough about me to ask if I'm okay.

Jerk.

6

ESTELLE

I shift my eyes from the side window of Brayden's sports car to him when he mutters, "What do you think that's about?"

He nudges his head to two police cruisers coming up on our right. Their lights are flashing, and a dark sedan is parked two places up from it.

"Probably some teens drag racing. We get a lot of street racers in Erkinsvale since the roads are so flat…" I swallow the remainder of my reply when Brayden's slow cruise past the police crackdown has me spotting the driver of the sedan. He's wearing an Uber Eats shirt, and although it isn't tucked into the front of dark pants, the length of its hem does little to hide the wet patch spilling from the crotch of his uniform to his running shoes.

As recollection dawns that he was most likely our assigned delivery driver, I return my eyes to the side mirror of Brayden's swanky ride. Within seconds, I spot a single headlight tailing in the distance. It's the same size and shape as the one that's been following us the past seventeen miles.

When I originally spotted the shadow, I brushed it off as the security detail Brayden's parents forced on him months ago. I can't do that this time around. My intuition won't allow it, let alone the tingles in the lower half of my stomach.

Certain I'm a hair's breadth away from being sentenced to hell, I stack evidence to the overflowing pile I've amassed so far today. "How fast can this thing go?" When Brayden's eyes drift to mine, eager to assess if the purr of my words matches the intensity in my eyes, I nudge my head to the flashing lights disappearing on the horizon. "Erkinsvale PD is a two-officer unit. If they're occupied..."

Brayden clicks on to my suggestion remarkably quick. "We can let off some steam."

After giving his engine a rev for good measure, he flattens the gas pedal to the floor. I'm thrust into my seat, the brightness of the taillights we whizz past adding to the adrenaline thickening my veins.

With a grin showing he's in his element, Brayden weaves his sports car through the traffic that grows thicker the closer we approach Hopeton. It's got nothing on the number of vehicles that hammer the streets of Ravenshoe every night, but there are plenty for concealment.

"Wow," I mutter a couple of minutes later when Brayden lowers his speed so he can pull down the street his uncle's new dance club is on. "If I hadn't blown out my hair this morning, the wind would have taken care of it this evening."

His chuckles drown out the gurgle of my stomach when my eyes lock onto a fat-wheeled motorbike parked next to the entrance of an overflowing parking lot. It isn't the aesthetically pleasing glossy black and shiny chrome combination I'm paying attention to. It's the man staring at me as he pulls an all-black helmet off his head.

Nadir has once again found me, but he didn't follow Brayden's dangerous weave through traffic.

He helmed it.

I shouldn't be excited by the knowledge, but I am.

What girl doesn't want to be chased?

One who doesn't want to end up dead in a ditch, that's who!

I don't get a chance to reprimand my inner monologue as Brayden has jogged around his idling car to help me out. "Come on. It's time to shine, baby."

I was so caught up drinking in Nadir's smug smirk, I didn't notice Brayden pulled to the curb at the front of the club so the valet could park his car. I've watched him attend events like this on local blog pages, but they only showed him once he reached the red carpet. I didn't consider how he got there.

The hiss of pain I release when I slip my left foot into my stiletto is gobbled up by the clicks of the paparazzi's cameras when they snap my awkward maneuver out of Brayden's low ride. I almost sprain my ankle to ensure my lady bits aren't exposed, but Brayden seems none the wiser. He grins at the men racing our way with flashing cameras before he tugs me into his side to ensure the focus remains on him and not my risqué hemline.

After correcting my footing and tugging down the skirt of my dress, I peer past the bright lights blinding me. Brayden's uncle has gone all out for the opening of his club. The number of guests on the red carpet is in the hundreds, and a handful of them are well-known celebrities.

I don't know if the glitziness of the guestlist is responsible for Brayden dropping my hand like a hot potato the instant we walk through the front door of the Blue Dragon or annoyance that the paparazzi's questions were focused on me instead of him.

He hates when anyone steals the limelight, and his annoyance is undeniable when he spends the next twenty minutes ignoring me instead of introducing me to his uncle's guests.

Usually, I'd bite back just as hard. Tonight, I don't. I use his ignorance to investigate the cause of my quickening pulse. Nadir is here. I can sense his presence, but I can't see him even with his black gaze burning up every inch of my skin.

My eyes float of the crowd pauses when Brayden stops at my side. He's still pissed, but it's cooled somewhat since a small-screen starlet stroked his ego by greeting him by name. He thinks she knows who he is. In reality, her PA whispered his name in her ear when he approached her. "Let's grab a drink before we hit the dance floor."

I lift my chin before shadowing his walk to the bar. A trip that shouldn't take longer than a minute extends to fifteen when Brayden stops to greet numerous skimpily dressed women, men in tailored suits, and a handful of staff. He even greets the bartender with a sloppy cheek peck before she can take our order.

I'm about to request a martini, but Brayden orders me a daiquiri before I can. It doubles my annoyance. I prefer tequila over rum. He should know that by now.

When the busty bartender sets down my drink, I chug it down as if it's water. Not only am I thirsty, my throat dries like a desert when I finally spot Nadir across the room. He's seated in the roped-off VIP section. Just like Brayden, his striking features attract him a lot of attention. Women are practically tripping over themselves to get close to him, and it appears as if every man in the room knows who he is.

"Do you know who that is?" I ask Brayden when a man in a buttoned-up black shirt and dark trousers approaches Nadir. Although Nadir is flanked by men and women of all ages and sizes, the gentleman with a colorful array of tattoos is the only one game enough to get within touching distance of him.

My interests pique even more when the unnamed man slants his head enough, he exposes his face. I'm reasonably sure he's the man who convinced me earlier today that Roxanne is safe and protected. A horrifying brain injury couldn't have me forgetting his handsome face and roguish green eyes.

Although my curiosity is at a pinnacle, I don't miss the generous tip Brayden gives the bartender. Not even the high-end nightclubs in Ravenshoe charge one hundred dollars for two cocktails. He's just being flashy since we're in public.

After swallowing a generous serving of his drink, Brayden discloses, "That's Rocco Shay. He got out of lockup a couple of months back. I'm not sure what he was incarcerated for."

I bet I can guess.

"He isn't someone you should be associating with, Elle." He gives me a stern look, places my empty glass onto the sticky counter next to his, then curls his hand around mine, thankfully blind to the fact he's seen Nadir previously. "Roxanne's placement already puts you on the Petrettis' radar. You don't need to associate with them more than that."

For the first time ever, there's a hint of jealousy in his tone. It's about time. I could rile him twenty-four-seven and never get a peep out of him. This time, he gave up the goods without a single bit of provoking.

Good.

It doesn't make up for him being a jerk, but it is a step in the right direction.

After thanking the bartender for our drinks with a wink, Brayden guides our walk to the dance floor. It isn't a long trip, and it also is not done without scrutiny. I feel Nadir's eyes on me even with every inch of the thumping space being filled with sexy, sweat-slicked bodies. The only time he removes them from me is when Rocco farewells him with a slap on the back, and that lasts for barely a second, then they're back on me, as heated as ever.

Within a handful of songs, I've lost Brayden to the thrumming crowd and have progressed from the middle of the dance floor to the roped-off area Nadir is seated behind. I'm not solely endeavoring to remove the massive groove Brayden's grinding of my backside our first two minutes on the dance floor etched between his dark brows, I'm endeavoring to unearth how deeply engrained in the Petretti entity he is. Brayden disclosed that Rocco is part of the Petretti crew. He seemed close with Nadir, so I'm interested in discovering how far their friendship extends, and I'm willing to use any means necessary to find out.

My heart beats louder than the *doof-doof* music banging out of the speakers when Nadir's eyes rake my body. His tongue doesn't roll out of his mouth like Brayden's did when he takes in the short hemline of my dress. His gaze turns murderous.

After ensuring I've felt the fiery burn blistering out of his narrowed gaze, he signals for the bouncer to let me into the roped section. I don't miss the numerous hisses of disdain from women both in and out of the elusive bubble, but I act ignorant to ensure not a sprinkling of indifference is heard in my voice when I greet Nadir like he didn't try to end my life earlier today. "Hey... do you come here often?"

Don't start. I already feel like an idiot. I don't need your judgment.

When my greeting is answered with a prolonged bout of silence, I raise a shaky hand to Nadir's face. It's obvious he's showered since our last altercation, his hair is wet and slicked off his face, and not a droplet of blood can be seen on his hands or neck. However, he still smells like murder and mayhem. It could be classified as an enticing scent if I didn't know how factual it is.

A squeak pops from my lips when Nadir snatches my wrist before my hand gets close to the bristles on his cut jawline. I assume he's swatting me away, so you can picture my shock when he uses his hold to drag me out of the VIP section and through the club of sweaty dance patrons.

When a hiss of pain seeps through my lips from his brutal pace, he scoops me into his arms like a groom carrying a bride over the threshold before he continues his military-swift walk.

Panic makes itself known with my stomach when he walks us into Brayden's uncle's office like he owns the place. We've met before, so I'm convinced he will recognize me.

I have no reason to fret.

Although Marc peers straight at me, recognition fails to dawn on his face. He scurries out of his office without Nadir speaking a word, his lack of balls convincing me that approaching Nadir was the right decision to make.

Only Petretti crew members are given free rein in this town.

When Nadir sets me onto my feet, I tug on the hem of my borrowed dress until it sits at a respectable level, then raise my eyes to his face.

It's a lengthy trek since he's so tall.

I call bullshit.

When Nadir mistakes my screwed-up nose as disapproval of my gawk instead of annoyance about my accurate inner monologue, he angles his head to the side and arches a brow. His glare alone should assure him I wasn't mocking him. If my knees pull any closer together, my thigh gap may never return.

The sticky situation between my legs goes from embarrassing to downright horrifying when he barks out, "Ask what you want to know, angel, before I use the delay to part your thighs with my tongue."

Don't kill me for my tardiness. You couldn't see the twinkle his eyes got when he growled out his words. He seems more interested in making me come than killing me. It's a step up from the way he treated me this morning.

Although I'm equally scared, confused, and aroused, I keep my focus on the task at hand. "Roxan—"

There isn't an ounce of dishonesty in his tone when he interrupts, "Is tucked up in bed, asleep, like you should be."

I fold my arms under my chest to hide the trembling of my hands. "I need proof."

He cuts me off with a headshake this time around instead of words.

"Why not?"

I sound as annoyed as I feel, but my emotions are pushed aside for intrigue when Nadir steps closer to me. "Because Dimitri has her security locked up so tightly, not even I can get in."

A tinge of pain rockets up my leg when I take a step back, but I suck it up. If I don't put some distance between us, my brain will turn to slop. That's how hot the energy teeming between us is. "Are you trying to get to Roxanne?"

Do you want Roxanne? is the question I want to ask, but this will do. I can't be envious of the attention my friend forever gets *and* be worried about her safety. It isn't possible.

I gulp down a relieved breath when he shakes his head. "I don't *want* anyone." He hovers in close until I'm wedged between his imposing frame and a large wooden desk. "Why *want* when I can *take*?"

My brain screams at me to run, to knee him in the groin, and bolt like more than my virtue is on the line, but no matter how loud it screams, I don't hear anything but Nadir's panted breaths when he drags the tip of his nose across my jawline and down my neck.

He drinks in my scent for what feels like hours but is only seconds before he presses his lips to the shell of my ear. "Why do you keep whimpering?"

He peers down at me for a moment when I whisper, "Because you're big... and scary."

A flare detonates in his eyes as he inches back with a grin that would have you convinced I told him I want to ride his face. "I asked why you're whimpering, not why are you cowering." He cocks a brow, his grin mocking. "There's a difference."

He snickers about my 'duh' expression before he lifts me to sit on the desk. I watch him in confusion, unmoving and unspeaking when he glides his massive hand down my leg.

Brayden's only ever travel one way.

It dawns on me what is happening when he slips off my left shoe. It's the one causing me the most pain. I washed out the cuts as well as I could in the shower after leaving The Commission, but it's still throbbing hours later.

After inspecting the cuts in my feet like he actually gives a shit about me, Nadir drops my foot, then nudges his head behind me. "Scoot back."

While I do as requested, ruining a stack of freshly printed paperwork on the way, he removes a rectangular box from his suit jacket. "If you scream, I'll be forced to gag you with my cock."

I'm completely lost as to why my body responds positively to his threat instead of panicked but lose the chance to deliberate when my eyes lock on the instruments in Nadir's travel kit. There are multiple scalpels, tweezers, and pliers.

"Please don't tell me you carry that with you everywhere you go?"

Some of the fret on my face fades when he plucks a set of

tweezers from his portable torture kit. After raising my foot an inch from his face, he drops his eyes to the immodest shadow the hem of my dress casts over my barely covered pussy.

It's the fight of my life not to cover my vagina when he mutters, "Although circumcision is not mentioned in the Quran, at the school I attended, it was a legal obligation under Islamic law. Uncircumcised men cannot go to pilgrimage." His lips tuck at one side when he confesses, "So I grant them a final chance to Salah for clear passage before I…" He doesn't need to finish his comment. The murderous gleam in his eyes tells me everything I need to know. My stomach gurgles when he mutters. "The tweezers come in handy more times than you'd think."

Although I am confident he uses his medical travel kit more to maim than help, the furl of his lips at the end of his sentence exposes he's being playful. Many assumptions are made about certain ethnicities, but very rarely are they true. Nadir is playing off the notion I am unaware of that.

A spasm of pain jolts up my leg when Nadir digs his tweezers into a cut in my foot. "Ouch."

When I attempt to yank my foot out of his clutch, he firms his grip before tugging me even closer. "Don't whine. I'm barely touching you." My stupid insides clench when he murmurs, "*Yet.*"

After a handful of silent seconds, he removes a shard of glass from a cut in the middle of my foot. Although it's tiny, its extraction offers an immense amount of comfort. My foot instantly stops throbbing, and the spasms I've been handling all afternoon subdue to a faint buzz.

My brows become lost in my hair when he holds his tweezers in front of me while asking, "Would you like to keep it as a memento?"

"Of the time you tried to kill me?" I don't give him the chance to respond. "No. I'm good. I doubt the memory will leave me anytime soon."

He sighs while dumping the shard into the bin next to the desk, then he returns his tweezers and portable torture box to his pocket. I assume his tidy-up is the commencement to the end of our exchange but am proven otherwise when he flattens his palms onto the desk on each side of my thighs. "How much do I get?"

"For?" I ask, truly confused.

When he slants his head, the clover tattoo on his cheek glistens in the light above his head. "For fixing your foot. Torture comes at a price, so shouldn't repairs as well?" A tingle of excitement skates over my skin when his deep, raspy voice murmurs, "I won't even make you pay with cash."

Without notice, he grips my butt cheeks and skids me across the desk until my lace-covered ass dangles off the edge of the sturdy material. My brain's screams for me to run ramp up when he slings off his jacket and tosses it over the polished wood, but the image of the bulging veins in his arms as he rolls up the sleeves of his dress shirt has me acting ignorantly. Even knowing he's a killer doesn't alter the facts. He is ridiculously good-looking, and his cut body is as divine as his handsome face.

"You better reach a figure, angel, before I calculate my own." He licks his lips before cracking them into a murderous smirk. "I'm almost certain my tally will be much higher than yours."

When his hands move from his sleeves to the buttons hiding his pecs from my rapacious gaze, I ask, "What's with the nickname? No one calls me angel."

My clit pulses when he growls out, "Because your face is as close to heaven as I'll ever get since I have a one-way ticket to hell."

A squeak vibrates my lips when he plucks me off the desk, then spins me around to face it. I asked a question instead of answering his, so to him, that means he's now in charge.

I'd be panicked at the thought if I weren't so lightheaded from his closeness.

His erection is the only thing keeping a gap between us. It's pressed against my back, causing me to swallow thickly about the arousal flooding my nether regions.

My lungs take stock of my oxygen levels when Nadir raises the hem of my dress until it sits above the waistband of my lacy thong. His growl this time around is more dangerous than his scowl. It scuttles excitement through me at a million miles a minute and has me confused on the difference between a captor and a savior.

"Why wear it if it leaves nothing to the imagination?" Nadir asks as his finger softly glides beneath the skimpy material to peel it off my heated skin.

I don't get the chance to respond. I'm too busy moaning through the sensation of him snapping my thong off my body with only the slightest grunt to form words.

After sliding the damp material into the pocket of his pants, he pinches some of the excitement keeping my clit firm with a threat. "Now I know what to look for when I hunt the men who couldn't respect you enough not to photograph you while your panties were showing."

"Y-You don't have to kill them," I stammer out. "I was covered."

I don't know whether to swoon or fret some more when he replies, "Yes, I do. Because just the thought of them wanting to photograph your panties has me wanting to rip their hearts out of their chests. They clearly have no use for them, so why should they keep them?"

My lungs struggle to secure air when he drops to his knees.

"Still," he grunts at me when I turn to face him.

He twists me back around before he kneads the bouncing globes of flesh in front of him. It isn't a gentle grope that exposes he appreciates the number of squats I do per day, it's a mauling with the intent to mark. A good hurt, but a hurt, nonetheless.

When his teeth unexpectedly sink into my right butt cheek, I bite on the inside of my cheek to stifle an unexpected howl. My shoulders roll forward in fear as tears prick my eyes.

"Break through the pain to find the pleasure behind it," Nadir suggests between the frantic breaths whizzing out of my nose. "You can endure more pain than you realize when you stop considering how much it hurts."

I brace my hands onto the desk when he bites my left butt cheek with the same amount of cruelness he did to the right. Although he gnaws down on me hard enough, I'm convinced the scent of blood mingling in the air is coming from me, the sensation is different this time around. I'm not howling in pain. I am moaning about the unusual throb lighting up my insides. The sensation isn't anything I've experienced before, and although I'm not sure I'd sign up for it again anytime in the future, there's no doubt it's an experience in itself.

The reasoning behind his savagery comes to light when Nadir murmurs, "Let's see how eager he is to grind against you when he sees my marks."

After soothing the burn of his bites with spit from his tongue, he stands, bends me over the desk until my ass is high in the air, then cups my pussy.

I don't understand the word that rips from his throat when he feels how wet I am, but I am reasonably sure it is an Arabic curse word.

His breathy pants batter my ear as the tip of his middle finger locates my clit without the hunt most men endure. "This is your last chance, angel. State your terms."

"I... I... I..."

Can't seriously be contemplating this?

He's a stranger.

A murderer.

The man who tried to kill me.

But my god, the way he looms over me with his big, brooding personality on display is a massive turn-on. I've never felt more craved, and it has me acting the most reckless I've ever been. "Isn't the provider in charge of invoicing?"

Nadir's exploring hands still before the heat of his grin warms the back of my head. "You're right. How silly of me."

Our location, my morals, and the fact I have a boyfriend leave my mind when the strokes of his finger awaken something inside of me I ignore more than I encourage. I rock against his hand when he slips his fingers between the drenched folds of my pussy, then my moans fill the silent void in the office when he murmurs, "You're so fucking wet. You've wanted this all along, haven't you?"

"No," I push out with a shudder, certain I'm seconds from climaxing just from the deep richness of his accent.

Heat rushes through me when his palm slaps an area of my ass still on fire from his teeth. "Lie to me again and I'll remove your clit with my teeth."

Jesus Christ.

I'm too scared to move but also so turned on at the thought of his mouth on my pussy, he faces not an ounce of resistance when he slides a single finger inside of me.

When the tip of his index finger finds the sweet spot in my warm center, I grind into the desk, then double the rocks of my hips.

"Good girl," Nadir praises. "See how good it can feel when you stop resisting."

Minutes pass in a hazy void. The sensation is amazing. I'm so taken aback by the tingles firing in my core, I don't care who hears how brilliant our exchange is.

"Please. More. Oh," I beg a short time later when the thought of Nadir replacing his finger with his cock filters into my head. With how long and thick his fingers are, I'm certain his cock will be just as impressive.

My lips part to suck in desperate breaths when he pushes a second finger into my hot, wet pussy. I arch my back and call out, overwhelmed by the attention he pays to my clit and G-spot at the same time.

When I bite my lips to lessen my moans, Nadir pumps into me faster. Harder. He finger-fucks me like he owns my body, his command undeniable. I'm virtually screaming, and my climax is so close, I'm not ashamed to beg for it.

My pleas for him to make me come fade to a whisper when a familiar shout of my name overtakes my grunted words. Brayden is searching for me, and if the loudness of his shouts is anything to go by, he's seconds from bursting in on me bent over a desk, being defiled by the man who wanted me dead.

"No!" Nadir growls before he pins my head to the desk with his big hand, then doubles the strokes of his thumb over my clit. "Finish first."

"I-I can't," I blubber out, suddenly riddled with guilt. "He's right there. Right outside that door... *ooohh*."

Guilt has nothing on lust. It roars to life when Nadir uses the wetness coating his fingers to stimulate my clit. It convinces my lust-muddled head that he's once again fallen to his knees, but instead of biting my ass, his mouth is on my pussy.

I'm blindsided by an orgasm so fierce my screams cause Brayden to bang his fists on his uncle's office door. As I shudder through an earth-moving climax, he begs for me to open it.

"Estelle!" The polished wood warps under his poundings, but it has nothing on the intense throb pulsating through me. It's strong, blistering, and so fucking wrong, I feel like crying when I come down from my high instead of reveling in it.

I'm a horrible, horrendous person, and the knowledge has me slipping out of Nadir's grip, ruefully tugging on the hem of my dress until it covers my dripping pussy, then racing for the closest exit.

I feel Brayden's bangs more than I hear them when Nadir beats me to the door. He slaps it closed like he doesn't need an industrial lock to keep Brayden out, then pins me to the gleaming wood with his brooding frame. As his heaving-with-anger body stills mine, he brings his lips to the shell of my ear. His stiffened shaft bracing against the globes of my ass prompts me to the marks he left, so he doesn't need to issue the threat he does to have me falling into line. "If he touches you, I'll drain every drop of blood from his body *before* I kill him." He grips my throat, then angles my head back to face him. "Do you understand, angel?"

It's virtually impossible for me to nod with how hard he's gripping me, but I manage—somewhat.

When he accepts my unvoiced confirmation, I suck down my first full breath in what feels like minutes. I'm not grateful he can read my responses without a syllable slipping from my lips. I'm gasping in shock about him pulling a gun out of the back of his trousers and directing it at the door Brayden is endeavoring to knock down.

"That isn't necessary."

Nadir doesn't look at me while replying, "I'll be the judge of that." He cocks back the hammer of a gun that looks capable of shredding a man's face off before locking his eyes with mine. "Seventeen hours, angel, and not a second more."

Aware I either nod or force Brayden's family to organize a funeral, I bob my chin before pushing down on the doorhandle Brayden hasn't realized I unlocked before Nadir slammed it shut.

When Brayden trips over his feet from my abrupt opening, his head stops at the exact area Nadir's gun is facing. Not thinking, I push him off me, then take a giant step back.

It switches the panic on Brayden's face to fury. "What the fuck, Elle? I thought someone was murdering you. Why were you screaming like that if you're not walking toward death?"

While ignoring Nadir's snicker that triples my raging pulse, I rack my brain for an excuse.

I'm stumped of a reply until Nadir pops his glistening fingers into his mouth. Remembering that my orgasm was payment for his help sees me blurting out, "I had a shard of glass in my foot. I had to dig it out. It really hurt."

"Clearly." I silently relish Brayden's lack of care when he asks, "Are you good now?" He's too pissed to check for himself, and it is that stubbornness that saves his life.

"Yep!" I rush out in a hurry before spinning to collect my stiletto dumped onto the desk next to Nadir's suit jacket.

Gratitude fills me that Brayden's focus rarely stays with me when we're in public when he fails to notice that the jacket on his uncle's desk is much larger than his uncle's below-average frame. He barely glances my way when I slip my foot into my shoe, then hightails it into the hallway with only the briefest glance Nadir's way.

His murderous eyes aren't floating between inanimate objects. They're locked on my flushed cheeks and dilated gaze, and they are as evil as ever.

7

ESTELLE

"Are you sure you don't want me to tuck you in? I brought supplies." As Brayden drags his teeth over his lower lip, he wiggles his brows.

I unlatch my seat belt, then shake my head. "I'm not feeling well. It's lucky I only had one sushi roll. My stomach might not have handled more."

Proof about how non-observant he is smacks into me hard and fast when he replies, "Yeah. Lucky." I didn't touch a sushi roll. His eagerness for a night on the town never gave me the chance. "If you change your mind—"

"I have your number." I peel out of his car before murmuring, "Good night, Brayden."

I slam his door shut, drowning out his uncaring farewell before galloping up the front stairs of Roxanne's grandparents' ranch with my stilettos dangling from my hand.

Brayden doesn't wait for me to push the key into the lock. He whizzes down the driveway like he has a hot date, leaving me searching for the light switch in pitch-black conditions.

I'm forced into my third coronary failure for the night when a deep voice inside the cabin grunts out, "I told you he doesn't deserve you."

Nadir switches on the lamp next to the single sofa chair he's sitting on before he stands. After taking in the shoes I dropped when he startled me, he heads to my half of the room. His walk is as arrogant as the haughty expression on his face, but it still does silly things to my insides.

Their frantic quivers are heard in my low tone. "You can't break into people's homes. It's against the law."

"The only unlawful thing that happened tonight was the fact that prick couldn't tell the difference between your screams of ecstasy and when you're in pain." Since I can't deny his claims, I remain quiet. "Has he ever gotten you off?"

"Yes," I reply, even with my head cautioning me against it. "Many times."

I would have gotten away with my snarky tone if I hadn't tacked on the last two words. They see Nadir storming across the room to pin me to the door I unlocked only seconds ago by my throat. "Many times... for the *last* time." He stares me dead set in the eyes while grunting out, "Dead men can't fuck anyone."

I swallow the brick his comment lodged in my throat before responding breathlessly, "You said you'd only kill him if he touched me. He didn't." I wouldn't even give Brayden a goodbye kiss because I was conscious Nadir could be watching.

Nadir times the throb of my pulse with his thumb and index finger before he shifts his focus to my mouth. "But he's touched you in the past, and for a man like me, that's a good enough excuse to kill him."

I yank my head away from him like I have some sense of control around him. "Then you better step into the gas chamber with him because you're now guilty of the same crime."

I'm anticipating for him to respond negatively to my comment, so you can picture my shock when he drags his thumb across my dry lips. It isn't a gentle rub—I don't think he knows how to be gentle—but there's no uncertainty his touch is full of lust. "Your sassy mouth will get you in trouble one day."

I'm startled by my boldness when I reply, "So I've been told."

Nadir doesn't seem bothered by my newfound attitude. The twitching of his top lip matches the mariachi beat of my clit when he tilts in so close, I'm reminded I am sans panties. The tension bristling between us is so perverse, he says the last thing I'm anticipating. "Get your ass into bed, angel, before I make you so bowlegged, you'll be bedridden for a week."

"I need—"

When he pushes his finger to my lips, my pussy convulses. I can smell my arousal on his skin.

Does that mean he didn't wash off my scent when I ran from him?

Does he want it there as clear as day for everyone to smell?

"Everything you need is on your bed." It's the fight of my life not to grind down when he wedges his knee between my clenching thighs. "Except me." His accent is more pronounced when he murmurs, "But that can change with a simple endorsement on a sheet of paper."

When he strays his eyes to the living room, I follow the direction of his gaze. The contract I left at The Commission is on the coffee table nestled between a two-seater sofa and two single chairs.

Although confused as to why we need a contract to get freaky, I'm not so daft to be aware of the right answer to his offer. I'll never go to heaven if I sign an official document announcing I ordered the murder of a fellow human being, so for that reason alone, I shake my head.

Nadir scoffs as if my denial is merely a delay tactic, but I feel the disappointment rumbling in his chest before he steps back, unpinning me from the wall.

After running his hand over his midnight black hair, fixing it into place, he locks his eyes with mine. "Bed. Now."

He doesn't need to tell me twice. I dip my chin, then race into the guest bedroom of Roxanne's nanna's home, once again needing space before I do something stupid.

My pace slows when I enter the outdated space. Nightwear has been laid out for me, and a bag of delicious-smelling food is sitting on the nightstand.

I fling my eyes from my favorite Mexican cuisine to the right when Nadir dumps a single sofa from the living room into the guest bedroom doorway. As he did earlier, he whips off his jacket, then removes the dress shirt hiding a dark blue wifebeater and an extensive collection of tattoos. Once he has them flung over the back of the worn sofa he moved as if it is weightless, he sits on it and balances his elbows on his knees.

"What are you doing?" I ask, genuinely confused.

He toes off his shoes, slouches back, then rakes his hooded eyes up my body. "I'll stay until you fall asleep."

My brows shoot up my face. He surely isn't so delusional he believes I can sleep with the eyes of a madman on me. That will induce nightmares, not eradicate them.

When I say that to him, he replies, "I either watch you fall asleep here or in *my* bed. Which would you prefer, angel?"

I realize his offer has nothing to do with me having a restful sleep and everything to do with ensuring I don't answer any of the numerous texts Brayden bombards my phone with every Saturday night when Brayden's first lot of texts make my phone on the bedside table vibrate like it's possessed. This is the first weekend we've spent apart since we became a couple, and it seems as if Nadir knows that.

"No," Nadir grunts out when I pace toward the attached bathroom, too tired to argue with a deranged man. "Food *then* bed. No shower."

A huff parts my lips. "I smell—"

"Like me. I am aware." When his reply freezes me, he tries to get my legs moving with a threat. "If you remove my scent, I'll have no choice but to replace it."

"You don't own me, Nadir."

I startle when he abruptly stands with a roar. I think his anger centers around my admission I'm not his. I'm horribly wrong. "Don't call me that!"

Although scared, I'm more curious than anything. "Why not? It's your name, isn't it?"

"Not here, it isn't," he spits out, his words seething. "You either call me Clover or sir."

I laugh about his last suggestion. "There's only one man I'll ever call sir, and he died when I was four."

Deadly black eyes stare at me when he snarls, "Then I guess we're settled on Clover, aren't we?"

Suddenly, more annoyed than scared, I march to the bed, fold down the bedding, then slip beneath the sheets.

The comforter has barely caressed my skin when Clover rips it away from me. "Food *then* bed. What is so hard for you to understand?"

"I understand you just fine, but I'm not hungry."

"I don't give a fuck if you're not hungry. You haven't eaten since breakfast."

My heart beats as loudly as Clover's boots stomp the carpet when he heads to the nightstand. I knew he was watching, but I had no clue it was for hours on end.

Once he's forcefully removed my dinner from the plastic bag it was delivered in, he shreds an *enmolada* in half, wraps the more generous serving of the two into a napkin, then hands it to me.

"Eat." My head barely moves an inch when he screams again, "*Eat!*"

Since his aggression removed a lot of the black mole sauce I hate, and I am both starving and scared, I give in to his over-bearing personality.

After accepting the greasy chicken and cheese concoction from his grasp, I take a dainty bite.

He watches me swallow every morsel of my half of the *enmo-lada*, the tightening of his jaw lessening with each mouthful.

"More. I want your stomach as full as your cunt will be when it's hugging my cock."

My stomach grumbles more in anticipation than fret when he peels off the lid of a bean-riddled soup with a dollop of guacamole on top. I'm not just excited to sample my favorite Mexican soup, I am also giddy at the prospect of Clover feeding me. He doesn't hand me the plastic spoon that came with the food. He digs it into the soup, scoops up a generous helping, then raises it to my mouth.

"Blow. It's hot."

I glance past the spoon when the front of his pants tightens in response to the circling of my lips. I'm not the only one finding this erotically enticing. His body is reacting to the odd tension bouncing between us in a similar manner to mine.

"Okay. Open up." When I do as demanded, his groan is as hearty as the one I release when the charro bean soup activates my tastebuds. The flavors are beyond comprehension, both yummy and spicy.

"More," he commands again before shoveling in another mouthful.

He continues to feed me until almost all the charro is gone, and the bulge in my stomach is as noticeable as the one in his pants.

"I can't," I murmur when he attempts to feed me another helping. I hold my hand over my mouth so I don't look like a pig while saying, "I'm full."

He arches a dark brow. "You're full?"

I raise my eyes to his so he can see the truth in them before nodding.

"Okay." He sets down the uneaten portion before he takes a step back. "Stand."

After breathing out my nerves, I slip off the bed. I feel him watching me, but I'm too scared to look up. I'm not afraid of him. I am petrified at how easily he convinces me that adultery is fine. Brayden may have been an ass today, but we're still very much a couple. The number of messages he sent while another man was feeding me is a sure-fire sign of this.

I'm given no choice but to return Clover's stare when he fists my hair to tug my head back. "I'll kill a man for looking at you as easily as I will kill him for guilting you into looking away."

His warning is brimming with underhanded threats, but it is also powerful and freeing. Guilt and shame are major triggers for me. I get embarrassed about how I was raised and where I was raised, then I feel guilty for being unappreciative of what I have.

The same can be said for my relationship with Brayden. I know I deserve better, and there are more negatives to our relationship than positives, but then I realize it could be so much worse. A lack of empathy is better than a man who threatens to kill me anytime I don't jump to his command.

It feels like years pass before Clover requests that I spin around. When I do so on a shaky pair of knees, ever so slowly, he lowers the zipper in my dress. The polyester material gathers around my bare feet a mere second before he shifts his focus to my bra.

A tinge of unwarranted jealousy fires through me when he undoes the three hooks that should be too tiny for his big fingers remarkably fast. Unlike my dress, he doesn't let my bra fall to the floor with a soundless woosh. He guides its fall, and the feathery float of his fingertips down my side boob causes goosebumps to break across my skin.

I chance a glance at his face when the budding of my nipples still his movements for the quickest second. He's towering over me, his body both powerful and lithe, but his eyes aren't on my breasts. They're on my lips, my flushed cheeks, then they meet my hooded gaze.

"Spin." His tone is more clipped than the one he used earlier. I'm positive he likes what he sees. He just doesn't want me knowing that.

After lowering my ragged breaths to ensure I don't pass out, I pivot around to face him. I wait for his eyes to drop, to drink in my naked form. They do no such thing. He continues to stare but not once does his focus shift from my face.

Within seconds, eyes so black they should reflect nothing but callousness suddenly seem soft and trustworthy. They expose the strength of desire. The potency of lust. They reveal even being in a relationship won't allow guilt to be your strongest emotion. I guess the dictionary got it right when they said lust is a powerful, addictive, and an almost overwhelming desire for something you know is bad for you.

Clover is bad news, but the way he took care of me tonight has me forgetting his undesirable qualities.

My heart overrules my rationally thinking head when he cups my cheek as I tried to do his at the dance club. He strokes my face with his thumb before he drops it to my top lip. My breezy pant dries the saliva on the tip of his thumb when its faintest dip into my mouth causes me to moan. I've never been looked at with so much desire. It's hypnotizing, and it has me wanting to act reckless, but before I can, Clover reminds me nothing happening is my choice.

He removes his gun from the back of his pants, places it on the bedside table, then commands me to my knees. "I fed you, so now you must pay for the privilege."

When I attempt to step away from him, angered that I thought he was taking care of me because he thought I was worth something, he stills the stomps of my feet by digging his thumb and index finger into my cheeks. He holds my face as firmly as he clutched my throat this morning. It is a terrifying yet stupidly arousing couple of seconds that has me torn between spitting in his face and kissing him.

I go for the former when he mutters, "I wasn't asking, angel. Get on your knees."

As he wipes my spit from his face, his eyes darken. I'm almost certain I've signed my death certificate, so you can picture my surprise when he says in a cool, calm manner, "You want this as much as me. I just need to show you how badly." My lungs heave with uncertainty when he undoes his belt and guides it through the loops. "If I have to force you, I will. I'm not a man who shies away from controversy."

I curse the selfish needs of my body when he guides me to the floor without further objection. I could blame the fact his gun is mere inches from my head, but that's a piss-poor excuse. Just like in the Blue Dragon's office, his dark aura stimulates carnal desires from me instead of fear.

Once I'm kneeling in front of him, he uses his belt to tie my hands behind my back. "Because you continue to push, the only part of you permitted to touch me tonight is your mouth. If you do as you are told, I may consider removing that clause tomorrow."

A shudder trickles down my spine when my hair is the next thing to be secured. He doesn't contain the blonde waves with an elastic. He uses his fist, his hold so firm, the roots of my hair tingle in the aftershocks of his tight grip.

"Don't worry, angel," Clover mutters when a shuddering breath escapes my lips in response to him lowering the zipper in his pants. "Lips as meaty as yours are far more valuable than a standard meal."

I don't get the chance to remind him I don't owe him a dime. I'm too busy gasping about the boing his cock does when he removes it from his trunks. It's long, girthy, and deserving of a standing ovation. If the veins feeding it weren't as angry as the expression that forever taints his face, I might have even gone as far as saying it's handsome.

My pussy clenches when Clover strokes his lengthened shaft with his hand three times before he nudges it toward my mouth. "Open up, angel. You *will* take every inch of me." He gives me a smug smirk when my lips part in response to the command in his tone, then he swipes his glistening crown across my lips. "What did I tell you?" I draw my lips over my teeth when he pushes his cock through them. "You want this as much as me."

Arousal dampens my pussy when he stuffs his cock deep inside my mouth with a forceful thrust.

"More," he grunts when he bottoms out at the back of my throat.

A mix of pain and pleasure shoots through me when I gag on his thickness and length. The odd combination is addictive, and it releases the moans I was endeavoring to hold back. My body is betraying me even more than my lust-filled heart. I'm supposed to be the victim. He's forcing me to suck his dick as payment for services I didn't request, yet my skin is on fire, and my insides are coiled tight.

When it dawns on me how stupid I'm being, I attempt to pull back from Clover's cock.

"No!" he screams before he rams my head forward, fully impaling himself inside my mouth. "You will choke on my cock before I'll ever let you deny it."

I cough and sputter before my eyes bulge out of my head. I'm almost certain I am about to be asphyxiated by his cock before the flaring of his nostrils when he watches salty black blobs slide down my cheeks reminds me there is more than one way to breathe.

"Good girl," Clover murmurs on a growl when I flatten my tongue so I can fit both his cock and tiny streams of air down my throat.

I keep my eyes locked on the twitch highlighting his clover tattoo when he rocks himself in and out of my mouth.

The longer I peer up at him, the less often he stabs my throat. He stuffs as much in as he can without making me gag before he slowly withdraws.

"Hollow those cheeks, angel. Show me how strong your sucks are."

His thumb rubs at the crease in my cheek when I do as instructed. It sends a current of pleasure to my pussy and convinces me I'm crazy.

I shouldn't be enjoying this, but I am.

Very much so.

I'm a filthy, dirty whore, and the acknowledgment of that on my face gives Clover the final push to find his release. As his hips still, he buries his cock deep into my mouth, then grunts when spurts of cum land on my tongue.

I swallow him down like the treacherous cheater I am, purring when he pulls out his cock with a pop before he's finished coming so he can coat my lips with his cum.

He rubs the warm, salty droplets into my parched mouth with his thumb before he tucks his half-mast cock into his trunks, yanks his pants up his stout thighs, then loosens the belt pinching my wrists. Once it falls to the floor with a soundless clatter, he lifts me in his arms, snatches up the duvet he ripped off the bed in a rage, then places me on the bed.

I stare at him in confusion when he stalks back to the chair he placed in the doorway as if it is doll furniture. Because he's tapping out a message on his cell phone, he doesn't spot my gawk for a couple of seconds, but when he does, his lips tug at the corners. "Sleep, angel. Tomorrow is going to be a big day."

Confident I'm dreaming, I roll onto my hip, then freeze my movements, hopeful my stillness will convince him I am asleep. He said earlier that he'd leave once I'm asleep, and since guilt is now my highest emotion, I'm praying he will keep his word.

As the seconds stretch to minutes, then the minutes stretch to hours, my eyelids grow heavy. I fight the weariness of my body. I warn it that the man watching over me can't be trusted when I'm awake, much less when I am asleep, but before I can comprehend the true danger rising around me, I fall into a restless slumber.

8

ESTELLE

I wake up startled and confused. Not only am I in a strange room, but foreign noises are also coming from outside. I could confuse them for a raccoon or squirrels being playful in the night if it weren't for the faintest sobs trickling through the crunches and grinds.

Forever curious, I remove the bedding cuddled around my body, then slip out of bed. My interests pique further when it dawns on me that I'm dressed in the nightwear that was laid out for me last night.

The hem of the cotton nightgown brushes my thighs as I quietly make my way outside of the guest bedroom. As I tiptoe toward the cracked open door at the back of the ranch, the tingle in the middle of my legs reminds me of the craziness that occurred before I drifted off to sleep.

The remembrance of my cheating ways could excuse the ruckus happening in my stomach, but it feels more perverse than that. Don't get me wrong. I feel horrible about what I've done to Brayden, and I plan to confess my sins at the earliest possible convenience, but the emotions bombarding me now aren't guilt-based. I'm more curious than empathetic.

I curse my curiosity to hell when it has me stumbling onto a scene more treacherous than any I've faced the past twenty-four hours. Aaron's murder was done and dusted by the time I showed up. These three assassinations are only partway through. One man lays dead at Clover's feet, the bullet wound between his eyes leaving no doubt as to how he was killed. A second man has the barrel of Clover's gun butted against his head, and a third is waiting at his left, crying and shaking.

I conceal myself in the shadows of the awning when Clover apparently senses my presence. He twists his torso to face me, momentarily revealing the professional-looking camera clutched in his hand.

My heart's flutters are felt low in my body when his lips tuck at one side for the quickest second before he devotes his focus back to the beaten man pleading innocence while kneeling at his feet.

He barely gets off half a promise to delete the offending images when Clover notches back the trigger of his gun, stealing his words with the deep embedment of a bullet into his brain.

As Clover's focus shifts to the third man, my hand shoots up to cover my squeal. I can't witness a murder and act nonchalant, but I'm also incapable of demanding my legs to move. I need to know what happens because I know these men's deaths are my fault despite my brain telling me otherwise.

The second man's promise to delete evidence hints as to why he's being punished, not to mention the snippet of lacy material dangling from Clover's pocket. He said he would hunt down the men who took risqué shots of me clambering out of Brayden's car. I didn't realize he was serious until now.

Over the frantic thump of my pulse in my ears, I hear Clover say, "Show me."

The camera Clover dumps onto the sloshy ground a second after removing the hard drive burrows deeper into the mud when the third man hands him a digital recorder with a long-range lens attached to the front. He scrolls through the digital archive of images before twisting back around to face me. "Come here, angel."

Although I'm positive he can't see me in the shadows of the night, I briskly shake my head. If I gain the ability to move my legs, you can be assured they'll only sprint in one direction—away from him.

I freeze like a statue when Clover snaps out, "I wasn't asking, angel. Come here." He doesn't solely command me to his side with a stern tone and deadly I'll-hurt-you eyes, he simply marches my way.

His murderous stomp gets my legs moving, but regretfully, not fast enough to evade him. His arm bands around my waist after only two shuddered strides, then his hot breaths batter my ear. "If you didn't want to watch, you would have stayed in bed."

It dawns on me that my sprint would have been a woeful waste of time when Clover spins me back around to face the only man left alive out of a trio of paparazzi. Brayden didn't bombard my phone with messages so soon after leaving because he missed me. The driver's side door of my car is partially open. The last time that happened, the battery drained of power, and Roxanne and I were stuck at the lake for almost twelve hours. Since Brayden was the only person we knew within a hundred-mile radius, we called him for help.

I freeze when it dawns on me that Clover isn't the only man who expects payment for every small deed he does. Even with Roxanne being with me, Brayden wanted his chivalry awarded upfront.

That weekend was our first real fight. We had only been dating a couple of weeks, so I was confident that was the end of us, but Brayden's groveling skills were more out of this world than predicted.

My focus returns to the present when the unnamed photographer stares at me with pleading eyes. I'm lost as to how he thinks I can help him until Clover thrusts his camera into my face. The photographs he snapped of me are surprisingly flattering, but the angle leaves nothing to be desired. It isn't exactly what you'd call an upskirt shot, but it's very risqué.

My breaths come out ragged when Clover breathes into my ear, "He thinks these images are okay. What do you think, angel?"

"Umm..." My first thoughts are to tell him I'm not a Playboy bunny, but then I realize that would see him murdered like his two companions, so I take another route. "They're okay. I don't mind them."

"You can have them. They are yours. Take the hard drive. No payment necessary," the paparazzi pushes out at the same time Clover responds, "You like them?"

I nod, preferring to lie without words. "They have an artsy feel to them. Roxanne would appreciate the fine lines and lighting angle." Roxanne is an artist, but she refuses to call herself one.

I think I have the wool pulled over Clover's eyes, but he seems to have a knack for reading my inner dialogue over my spoken words. With a shrug, he mutters, "I do not like them."

I don't get the chance to utter a syllable. With my body plastered to his, and his eyes locked on my face, he returns his gun to the unnamed man's head and fires one shot.

When droplets of the man's blood splatter on my cheeks, I scream bloody murder.

As my flight and fight mode activates, I whack my bare feet into Clover's shins before pushing away from him. The ground is sloshy from a sprinkling of rain we must have gotten when I was asleep, but the slippery conditions do little to slow me down.

Once I've crawled away from the slumped body of the man who was alive only seconds ago, I sprint for the street. The property is over ten acres in size, but it is nestled in the middle of Erkinsvale, so surely someone will hear my screams before Clover reaches me.

My prayers are left unanswered when Clover silences my cries for help by clamping his hand over my mouth. The meaty flesh on his palm tastes tangy even before I sink my teeth into it.

I'm anticipating my gnawing to see my brain matter sprayed across the rugged landscape like the three photographers, but Clover shifts my thoughts in another direction when he growls. It isn't a frustrated rumble. It's too filled with yearning to be confused as annoyance.

"Now we have matching marks," he mutters into the cool night air when he pulls his hand back to inspect the bite mark in the bottom left corner of his right palm.

My stomach flips when he uses the same hand to twist my head back to face him. He doesn't solely like that our bite marks are matching. He's loving the identical blood splatter on our faces as well. The furling of his lips reveals this, much less the thickness I feel getting thicker the longer he takes in my blood-smeared face.

"You're a sick fucking prick," I announce before I can stop myself.

"As are you, angel."

The moon reflects off his shiny white teeth when he sucks in a prolonged breath. A stranger could mistake his whiff as an appreciation for the crisp freshness of an early morning, but I can still taste his cum in my mouth, so we're no longer strangers.

He's sucking in the dampness not even the mud smeared from my knees to my thighs can overtake. Its odorous scent exposes I wasn't solely running in fear for my life. I was sprinting away from the prospect his protectiveness turns me on.

I don't think the men who photographed under my skirt should be killed for their stupidity, but what they did wasn't right, either. They should have gotten in trouble, but murder was too harsh of a punishment.

When I say that to Clover, he shrugs to announce his objection, then pivots on his heels to face the other way. I realize how silly it was for me to sprint in the dark when I spot half a dozen men standing over three deceased bodies. Although none of them are paying me an ounce of attention, the weapons strapped to their chest reveal they would have had no issues taking me down if ordered.

"Ensure they can't be found," Clover instructs when two armed goons place a blond-haired man into the trunk of a blacked-out sedan.

He waits for them to jerk up their chins in understanding before he breaks over the threshold I tiptoed past only moments ago. Not a peep seeps from his lips when he guides me through the compact layout. His lips only part when the scent of our combined smells fires in the air upon entrance. We didn't have sex, but you wouldn't know it from the smell lingering in the air. It's musky, raunchy, and one hundred percent assures me I'm going to hell.

After placing me onto the vanity in the bathroom, Clover moves around the confined space like he's been here before. He grabs a washcloth from the linen closet at the side, a towel from the rack straddling the toilet, and makeup remover wipes from a bag of recently purchased toiletries on my right.

Once he has everything he needs, he joins me back at the vanity. "Who would have known we'd reach almost two million by now."

My brows furrow, confused as to what he means. It doesn't loiter for long. The taillights of three dark sedans can be seen out the bathroom window. At five hundred thousand dollars per hit, he wrongfully believes I'm now indebted to him for one point nine million dollars.

"I didn't—"

He stuffs my denial down my throat by squashing his finger to my lips. I had always wondered if you could smell gunpowder residue. Although the vinegar scent is discreet, there's no denying it. Even without me witnessing him gunning down the first man, there's no doubt he killed him. There is too much gunpowder residue on his hands to discount, and it has me curious to discover how many times he fired his gun to track down the three men he did.

"How long were you gone?"

He lifts a makeup remover wipe to my cheek before locking his eyes with mine. "Not long. Why? Did you miss me?"

He continues removing blood from my face as if it's makeup when I ask, "Were they the only three?"

Although his silence scares me, it isn't potent enough to back away from my campaign. "Clover—"

"No. But since their deaths aren't on your hands, you do not owe me for them."

"I don't owe you for theirs, either," I reply while nudging my head outside.

He *tsks* me before muttering, "I'll be sure to remind you of that when I'm fucking you, and you are screaming for me to go harder. Faster. Begging for me to claim every inch of you."

My traitorous body responds positively to his threat instead of negatively, but I act as if it didn't. "You said I had twenty-four hours to make a decision."

"I changed my mind," he replies matter-of-factly. "You *had* twenty-four hours, then you circled my cock's head with those pouty lips of yours, and *everything* changed."

My lungs reel. I'm truly torn between being pissed off and turned on. "I sucked your dick because you *forced* me to."

When I attempt to slip off the vanity, he cages me with his thick arms, then brings his head to within an inch of my face. "Lie to me again and see what happens."

"I'm not lying. You had a gun and a threatening sneer—"

"And you were so fucking hungry for my cum, even now with the blood of three men on my hands and face, you can't stop recalling how good it tasted sliding down your throat."

When I shake my head, trying in vain to act like I have some sort of morals, he grips my throat and thrusts me back. His shove smacks my head into the mirror and forces my nightie to sit high on my thighs, but fear isn't the only emotion it causes.

Salaciousness is very much a part of our exchange.

"Stop pushing me, angel. I don't know how to hold back." He tightens his grip, bringing me to the point of asphyxiation before he eventually loosens it. "Killing is all I know. It is all I've ever craved." The hairs on the back of my neck prickle when he whispers in my ear, "But for some stupid reason, I want to make you scream my name more." He pulls back until our eyes align. "Don't remind me that there's more than one way I can achieve that because it will end with you being dead. Do you understand, angel?"

It's virtually impossible for me to nod with how hard he's gripping me, but I won't leave this room breathing if I don't, so I fight through the pain of his hold to bob my chin.

He smirks like there wasn't an ounce of hesitation to my reply before he nudges his head to the showerhead hanging above the bathtub. "I was hoping a washcloth would do, but you have more murkiness to you than first perceived." Not waiting to see the panicked flare darting through my eyes, he twists the faucet to full, then says, "Take it off."

As my chin dips in understanding for the second time, I slip off the vanity. My hands tremor when I lower them to the hem of my nightie so I can pull it over my head, but their brutal shake has nothing on the quake that hits my thighs when another command from Clover quickly chases its float to the floor. "Now me."

He balls his hands at his sides before he shifts on his feet so he faces me front-on. The flare of his nostrils soothes the jitters in my stomach. He isn't sucking down air to cool his body temperature, he's releasing the nerves I see in his eyes.

Steam from the scalding water floats around us when I raise my hands to the third button of his dress shirt. The top two are already undone, and his sleeves are rolled to his elbows.

My eyes don't know what to look at first when I peel his steam-damp shirt from his broad shoulders. His collection of tattoos is extensive, but no amount of ink can hide the numerous scars, knicks, and burn marks dotted throughout his torso and stomach. Most of the burn marks are round, but their circumference is too large to confuse them as cigarette burns, so I lean toward cigars.

"Now, my pants," Clover instructs when my fingertip gets within an inch of a circular burn on his left pec muscle. He doesn't exactly snap my hands away, but the warning in his eyes that I'm treading on foreign turf is enough to have me retreating.

Remembering his demand that I'm not allowed to touch him today smacks into me when I unlatch the buckle in his belt before guiding it through the loops. It's a long, heat-inspiring time that includes multiple flashbacks of his fat cock sliding in and out of my mouth.

I begin to wonder where he dumped his gun when the lowering of his trousers occurs without the clang of a semi-automatic weapon. I guess he doesn't need to weapon-up when he can make me jump to his every command with nothing but a sneer.

"Good girl," he praises on a purr when I bob down in front of him to remove his blood-splattered shoes.

My obedience both thickens his cock and instigates even more submissiveness. I want to please him. I don't know why. I'm merely relaying the starkly contrasting emotions I've been pummeled with the past twenty minutes.

He strokes my hair when I place his shoes to the side of the bathroom before he gestures for me to enter the shower before him.

"Wait!" he barks out before I've hooked one foot over the tub.

After adjusting the faucet so it sits between the hot and cold symbols, he checks the temperature with his elbow, then dips his chin, permitting me to continue answering his every whim.

I slant my head under the spray when he steps into the tub not long after me. I have to remind my lungs to breathe when he slackens the shudders raking through me by plastering his front to my back. He's so tall, his head sits above the showerhead, meaning his vision isn't impeded when he cleans the blood from my neck and the mud from my thighs with gentle strokes of his hands.

My head reminds my heart multiple times that we're showering to wash off evidence of three murders, but when his pinkie grazes skin closer to my pussy than my thigh, every caution is forgotten.

I'm once again lost in the throes of lust.

"Don't," I murmur on a faded breath when his hand moves from my thigh to my stomach.

The sweat beading on my neck from the amount of steam in a small space doubles when Clover growls in my ear, "Don't what, angel?"

I take a moment to ponder if he'd actually stop if I asked him before I finish my sentence like a hurricane couldn't stop him now. "Don't stop."

This time around, his growl is better than I could have imagined, and when it's chased by him cupping my pussy, its seductiveness is out of this world.

"Brace your foot on the tub. I'll make you come here before I have my way with you on the bed." When I do as asked, he drags my hair to one side of my neck before pushing between my shoulder blades. "Bend over. Ass in the air." His heated breaths float over my skin when he murmurs, "You follow instructions well when you stop being afraid about who is delivering them."

Goosebumps follow the trek his finger makes when he glides it over the bumps in my spine. They spread to every limb when the quickest crack fires in the air. He doesn't just slap his teeth imprints in my ass, he also slaps my pussy.

"I knew you were turned on. You're fucking soaked."

I almost blame the water gliding down my body for the wetness between my legs, but he notches his finger inside of me before I can, discrediting my lie before it leaves my mouth.

"Four deaths, two negotiations, and now I get to play with your soaking wet pussy for the second time in twenty-four hours. How did I get so lucky?"

I'm tempted to ask who his second negotiation was with but lose the chance when he plays with the wetness at the top of my pussy. He finds my clit in an instant, his rub-and-roll routine catastrophic to my senses. Pleasure shoots through me as my body responds to his touch like he wants me addicted by the end of the night.

"So fucking tight, angel. I bet it will hurt when I stuff my cock inside of you."

I'm too far gone to respond with worry about his accurate claim, so instead, I beg, "Please."

When my eyes lock with his over my shoulder, he pushes a second finger inside of me. He stuffs it in like he isn't facing an ounce of resistance before he tells me how fucking hot it makes him to hear me beg. "That word out of those lips…"

He lets his actions finalize his reply. He finger-fucks me and toys with my clit until I'm screaming his name and convulsing like the shower water ran cold hours ago.

I'm still riding the waves of pleasure when he pulls back the shower curtain, steps out of the tub, then carries me across the room. I land on the mattress with a thud, my wet hair as weighed down as the pressure Clover places on my stomach when I buck through the sensation of his mouth on my drenched pussy.

He drags his teeth over the hood of my clit before sucking it into his mouth. My head spirals when I'm blindsided by a second orgasm. I writhe against him, certain I'm seconds from dying but uncaring if it keeps his mouth on my soaked pussy.

Aftershocks of back-to-back orgasms rocket through me when he lifts my ass off the mattress so he can burrow his tongue deep inside of me. He pokes it in and out of me as if it is his cock before he demands me to ride his face.

"You will scream my name, angel. You're going to scream it so loud my men will expect another corpse when they return from burying those first three in the woods."

His words should disgust me. They should lessen the number of tingles in the lower half of my stomach, but I have no control over anything happening right now. Not me. Not the wave building in my core. Nothing.

"Give me what I fuckin' crave," Clover growls into my pussy before doubling the strokes of his tongue.

I try hard to hold back, to maintain some sort of control, but then his tongue hits my clit with a sharp stroke.

While screaming his brilliance into the crisp morning air, his name rips from my throat in a grunted roar.

He snickers about how quickly I fold under his demand before he clears evidence of my multiple climaxes from his face with a wipe of his hand, then he crawls up my spent body. "Knees up. You will take *all* of me, angel. I won't accept any less."

A shudder rolls through me when he drags the head of his thick cock through the wetness coating my pussy and thighs. His hips are so girthy, my thighs burn from being stretched so wide, but it has nothing on the pain that shreds through me when he lunges forward, dipping in the first four inches of his cock.

"Let me in, angel," he grunts before notching in another two inches.

As he fights past the squeezes of my pussy protesting about his painful invasion, he clamps his hand around my throat, then demands my eyes to his.

"You get off on this," he murmurs on a moan while rolling his hips upward ever so slowly. "The carnage. The pain. The murder." He rocks his hips with every word he speaks, impaling me deeper until he's almost fully seated. He can't fit all the way in. It isn't possible. "You've been seeking this type of upheaval your entire life."

When I shake my head, he punishes me for my lie by withdrawing his cock to the tip. Although his clutch on my throat remains firm, he stays perfectly still, unmoving and unspeaking.

It's the worse form of torture you can imagine, and I sing like a canary only seconds later. "Please. Take me. I need—" I stop, certain no amount of lust could have me spiraling this badly. It's an uncontrollable, wild encumbrance, but surely, its nuisance should be reserved for those deserving of the burden.

"Say it!" Clover screams before tightening his grip on my throat.

The desperation in his voice surges my desires to never-before-reached levels. "Please. Fuck me. Take me. I *need* you."

He lunges forward, stealing the words from my throat as readily as he pinches the air from my lungs. I scream through the pain of being stretched so wide, my inner muscles convulsing with an equal amount of pain and euphoria.

As he pins me to the mattress by my throat, Clover pumps into me over and over again. He fucks me like a wild animal, his speed, the flick of his hips, and the grunts coming out of his mouth are uncontrollable and blister-inspiring. I'm hot all over and almost certain our exchanges the past twenty-four hours won't just send me to hell. They've dropped me in the thick of it.

I am now as evil as him.

I suck in ragged breaths when he lowers his hand from my throat to my breast several blinding minutes later. When he gropes the bouncing globes of flesh, I notice my D cups look insignificant in comparison to his massive hands. I've always boasted that my breasts are more than a handful. I can't say that anymore.

When my head reels with lust, I attempt to tether myself down. My hands only get within an inch of Clover's back before he snatches them away, lifts them above my head, then secures them to the bed.

"No touching," he grunts before he uses his free hand to raise my ass from the bed.

He takes me harder and faster with every thrust, his cock pulsating with each moan that escapes my lips. Within minutes, my senses are heightened beyond reproach, and I'm begging for him to grant me my next orgasm like I'm unable to climax on my own.

Raw energy surges through us when his deadly black eyes lock with my baby blues. Something in them has altered. They're still as dark as death and filled with mayhem, but they also seem calm and adaptable to change.

In a sheer display of power, he releases my hands, lifts me from the mattress, and carries me across the room until my sweat-drenched back flattens against the window of my room and his hips piston, like exhaustion isn't fettering his features.

He fucks like a monster, furthering my belief that he isn't human. You can't look like him, protect like him, and fuck like him while also being a mere mortal. How is that fair to the human race?

With the perfect angle of Clover's pumps finding the sweet spot inside of me, my screams soon pierce my ears, and my body violently shakes. I call out his name over and over again while fighting the urge to sink my nails into his shoulders. I need to tether myself down before I float away. I feel like I'm about to fall. I am limp and lifeless, but one hundred percent certain I'll never experience something this euphoric ever again.

I fall headfirst into an earth-shuddering climax when Clover tugs me away from the window so quickly, I have no choice but to curl my arms around his sweat-slicked neck to ensure I don't fall.

Just my hands skimming over his heated skin doubles the size of the wave breaking in the lower half of my stomach. My orgasm is relentless. It barrels into me and splinters me into a million pieces. It takes me under so deep, even with Clover's cock throbbing through its own release, I am unable to fight the heaviness of my eyelids.

I pass out not long after Clover returns us to the mattress so he can sleep with his cock still inside of me and long before panic dawns that we didn't use protection.

9

———

ESTELLE

 jackknife into a half-seated position when the annoying buzz vibrates through my ears. My cell phone isn't solely responsible for my rude awakening. Someone is showering in the bathroom attached to the guest bedroom. Despite the numerous pleas of my morals, it isn't Brayden. Regardless of his healthy inheritance, he doesn't wear pricey, tailor-made suits. He prefers designer shirts paired with dark slacks or his favorite ripped jeans.

The layout of Roxanne's nanna's home is small, meaning I have no issue seeing the tailor markings on the pants I dumped onto the floor of the bathroom in the wee hours of this morning, not to mention the size of the man behind the faded shower curtain. Its see-through material reveals that the person showering needs to bend their legs to soak their head under the showerhead and that even if I hadn't made a horrendous mistake last night, a vivid imagination wouldn't be required to know he stuffs more than a big gun in his pants each morning.

I stop gawking at the detailed outline of Clover's cock when my cell phone commences hollering again. When its annoying ring causes Clover's shadowed frame to crowd the shower curtain, I snatch it off the bedside table, silence it, then snap my eyes shut.

My heart patters in my chest when I sense Clover's nearness only a second later. Even with him smelling freshly cleaned, the murkiness of his aura is still the most prominent aroma, not to mention the combined scent of our arousals.

His heated gaze heats my face for two-heart thrashing seconds before he spins on his heels and heads back to the shower. I pop open my eyes in just enough time to see the back of him before he pulls the shower curtain across the tub. The briefness of my gawk doesn't hinder the reality of it. The multiple circular burns, stab wounds, and scars covering his torso extend to the back half of his body as well.

The sight of them gurgles my stomach, but I lose the chance to unearth why its churns are more in sorrow than verification his victims fight back when my cell vibrates in my hand.

My emotions don't know which way to swing when I peer down at the screen. Not only is it midafternoon, meaning I slept for a ridiculously long time, but Brayden's message advises he's outside, waiting for me.

Brayden: *I figure you must have fallen asleep when you didn't reply to any of my messages last night. Don't worry, sweet cakes, I'll replace your car's battery after I drop you off at work.*

Shit! With everything that's happened, I completely forgot I'm rostered for an afternoon shift at The Commission today. Sunday is the busiest day of the week. Church-going wives are less suspicious of their husband's afternoon activities when they've endured an hour-long sermon by a local pastor only hours earlier.

My heart leaps into my throat when another message from Brayden pops up.

Brayden: *Are you coming out, or do I need to come inside and convince you to take the day off with my tongue?*

My thighs tremored when Clover issued a threat similar to that, but it sounds stupid coming from Brayden. He got angry about the paparazzi snapping my picture last night, but it had nothing to do with the almost pornographic material they obtained. He hated that my lacy thong stole the attention from him.

Even with my morals lost in the wind, I can't risk Brayden making true on his threat. He wouldn't leave Roxanne's grandparents' ranch alive, so after punching out a two-worded reply that says 'I'm coming,' I throw off the duvet, stuff my feet into the first pair of jeans I find, then pull a spicy-scented tank top over my head. It's far too big for me, but its sleeveless design won't be noticeable under the bulky hoodie I tug off a coat hanger just as the shower faucet switches off.

Confident I'm seconds from witnessing another assassination by a steaming-angry Arab, I bolt for the exit, uncaring that I leave my cell phone on the bed for Clover to find. His anger may lessen when he learns I didn't completely abandon him. I may have stolen the bike key he left on the bedside table that's littered with his belongings, but he'll have the means to call for help once he works out the passcode on my phone.

His cell phone and gun are the only missing items from his arsenal of goodies. A clip full of bills, his travel-size torture kit, a small black bead, and a Harley bike key were dumped on the nightstand, but I haven't spotted his cell phone nor his gun since the photographers' executions last night.

"Hey," Brayden greets with a broad grin when I slide into the passenger seat of his sports car. "Did you only just wake up?"

When he leans in to kiss me, I twist my head in just enough time to force his lips to land on my cheek. My brisk movements not only save him from having a bounty placed on his head, but it also thrusts mine into the line of sight of Clover's dagger-spearing gaze.

Even though he's standing on the porch butt naked, ringing wet, and brimming with rage, the only part of him that twitches when our eyes lock and hold is his cock. He's as pissed as fuck I'm fleeing him, but not even the knowledge I'm using Brayden to escape has him missing the parting of my lips when I take in his naked form for the second time.

Since my nerves were on edge last night, I wasn't sure if the lighting above our heads was misleading my findings or the drunkenness of lust, but now that there are more than three feet between us, I can confidently declare there isn't an ounce of fat on Clover's body. He's muscular, tattooed almost head to toe, and has the deadly stare of a murderer.

I check my mouth for spit when Brayden coughs, announcing I've failed to answer him. I stumble out a mumbled, "Yeah," before suggesting that he plant his foot to the floor. "You know what Mr. Monroe is like when I'm late. He won't let me leave until closing if you don't hurry."

It dawns on me that Clover's threats aren't idle when the lowering of Brayden's gas pedal sees him pushing off his feet to chase us down by foot. He isn't wearing shoes or a stitch of clothing, but he reaches us in a remarkably quick twelve seconds.

"What was that?" Brayden asks, panicked when the thump of Clover's fist on the trunk of his fancy car sounds like a bomb detonating.

"Nothing," I assure him before twisting the rearview mirror to block his view of Clover rolling across the mud-sloshed ground. He was close to ripping through the material of Brayden's soft top, but the jerking movements of Brayden's hand when he peered behind his shoulder flung Clover off. "It was just your car backfiring."

I don't know if it's the fright in my voice that sees Brayden entering the freeway without first checking for traffic or the image of Clover standing to his feet with an angry, I'm-going-to-kill-someone stare. Whatever it is, I'm grateful.

Brayden's life might not have been the only one that ended if Clover had caught up with us.

Mine may have perished as well.

It takes two miles for my heart rate to settle down, then an additional three for me to recall that Clover knows my place of employment. He killed the founder's son, so not only is Brayden taking the most direct route to our deaths, he's grinning while doing it.

"Where's your phone? I need to cancel my shift."

Before he can answer me, I spot it in the console of his car.

"Hey!" He tries to snatch it out of my grasp, peeved as hell I'm undertaking what he deems as an invasion of his privacy for a couple that's only been together for two months, but I twist away before he can. "Come on, Elle, this isn't fucking funny. You know how much I value my privacy." His words gurgle when neither my birthdate nor the day we got together unlock his phone. Not even my nickname spelled with numbers works.

I shouldn't be surprised. Brayden has always been selfish.

There's no uncertainty to my claim when the four digits of Brayden's birthday gains me access to his phone.

My mood is already reeling about his selfishness, so you can imagine how deterring it becomes when a risqué image pops up only a second later.

"It isn't as it seems," Brayden stammers when the rumbles in my chest escape my gaped mouth. "She was leaning in to whisper in my ear."

I have no clue what he's talking about, but there's no mistaking an image like this. Not only does it reveal that I am a cheater, it also exposes that I'm a liar. I told Brayden I refuse to swallow his cum because I don't like it, but in this picture that only one man could have taken, Clover's cum is both inside and outside of my mouth.

"Estelle!" Brayden shouts in shock when I glide down the window of his car and hook his phone into the marshland siding the road. Even if his phone survives the fall, it won't come out of its dunking in the inches of rainwater that ran off the road during recent downfalls. "Fuck."

He adjusts the rearview mirror so he can see behind us, but not once does he lower his speed. Even with panic my strongest emotion, I'm positive I am not the only one with incriminating evidence on his phone. That's why he continues our journey without saying another word. He even takes Exit 43 when requested despite it being in the opposite direction as to where we should be traveling.

Brayden only just parks out the front of the lake Roxanne and I were stranded at weeks ago before he blurts out a confession as if nothing that happened was his choice. "I don't know what you saw, but I can assure you it isn't as bad as it seems. I was drunk and high, and she was just... there." He gathers my hands in his like it will stop his face from wearing my anger before muttering, "It didn't mean anything. I was thinking about you the entire time."

I guess I should cut him some slack because not once did *he* enter my mind when I was with Clover.

"When?"

He rubs his thumb along the vein throbbing in my wrist, frustrating me more, before he gabbers out, "What color was the girl's hair in the photo you saw? That will tell me if it was last night or today."

"You've done this more than once?" I push out with a strangled breath.

I snatch my hand out of his hold when he grimaces. "It depends on what you classify as cheating."

"Doing *anything* sexual with *anyone* who isn't me is cheating, Brayden."

I swallow some of my anger when he mutters, "So letting a guy fuck you against a window for the world to see is cheating?"

The disappointment in his eyes exposes he isn't seeking clarification about his sexual exploits. He knows about mine with Clover.

"Who is he, Elle? And how long has it been going on?" He drags his hand under his nose like his earlier comment about being high was from a more potent narcotic than weed. "I take it a while since he followed us to my uncle's club."

As I shake my head, my heart pains from the rejection in his tone. "No. I only met him yesterday."

When Brayden scoffs like I'm lying, I try to cradle his hands like he did mine. He snatches them away before I can. "We dated for weeks before you'd let me touch you, but you expect me to believe you let him put his head between your legs after one fucking day!" His knuckles bust open when he pounds them against the steering wheel. "If he's so fucking great, why did you come out? Why didn't you just ignore my texts?"

"Because I wanted to tell you the truth."

"Bullshit, Elle. If you wanted to tell me the truth, you would have told me when I busted you with him in my uncle's office last night."

"Brayden..."

I should say more.

I need to say more.

I just can't.

Words only tumble from my mouth when the silence teeming between us shreds my heart to pieces. "I'm in trouble, Brayden. If I don't do what he wants, he will kill me."

Sprinklings of dirty blond hair fall into his pained eyes when he scoffs off my claim with a brisk head shake. "Elle..."

"It's the truth. He's a killer. I witnessed him murder three people last night. My life is in danger, Brayden, and so is y-yours."

My last word comes out with a quiver when Brayden brushes the back of his finger down the bruise in my neck. "Did he do this?"

"Yes. He's the man I was telling you about. The one who came to my apartment to kill me." *The one you told me I was acting out about.* "If I don't want him to kill me, I have to pay him his four-hundred-thousand-dollar fee." Although that isn't exactly the truth, trust isn't a strong point of mine right now. I'm lying to convince a liar he should believe me. Trust won't be on the agenda any time soon. "Can you help, Brayden? You know I wouldn't ask if it weren't important."

"Estelle..." He stops, breathes heavily out of his nose, then locks his eyes with mine. "You know I would if I could, but I don't have access to that type of money."

My mouth gapes as my eyes float over his three hundred-thousand-dollar ride.

"This is a lease. My name isn't even on the title." His clammy hand adds to the sweat slicking my skin when he places it high on my thigh. "People often think I'm rich, but I'm not. My parents are.

I won't get my inheritance until they die, so everything you see isn't mine."

As disappointment shoots through me, I freeze. I'm not disappointed with Brayden, for now. I'm frustrated that I stupidly thought he'd come to the plate for me. I'm not that type of girl. Excluding Clover's wish to rid the world of people he believes have done me wrong, there's hardly anyone in my corner. It's been Roxanne and me against the world for years, and I don't even know if she is safe anymore.

"Estelle..." Brayden blubbers out with a sigh when I rapidly swipe at the silly blobs sliding down my cheeks. "Surely, it can't be that bad."

"It is, Brayden! Why is that so hard for you to understand?"

My neck is bruised, my feet are cut up, and he knows my best friend is working with the Petretti crew, yet he still thinks I'm being dramatic.

Clover was right, he doesn't deserve me.

"Come on, Elle," Brayden pushes out in a hurry when I throw open his car door and peel out of the leather seat. I'm so angry, the sweat slicking my body acts as if it is glue. I'd be trapped if Clover's attention hadn't made me slightly addicted to pain. "You need to cut me some slack. I've never had to deal with anything like this before."

I whip around so fast my hair slaps my face. "And you think I have?" I don't know what shocks me more, his lack of response or the confirmation on his face. "Being poor doesn't automatically make you a bad person, Brayden. For the most part, it keeps us out of trouble because we don't have to constantly second-guess someone's motives." My eyes bounce between his. "That's why you turned up this morning, wasn't it? It was a test."

"No! It wasn't a test." When I glare at him, calling bullshit, the truth finally comes out. "I wanted to prove that sexual promiscuity doesn't matter when it comes to soul mates and that I'm not above forgiving someone for their mistakes when I love them."

I hate myself for my silence, but it can't be helped.

We've never exchanged those words before.

Not once.

"Say something, Elle. Anything."

Although what I say next isn't exactly what he wants to hear, it has to be better than more silence. "You love me?"

"Yes," he replies with a childish dimple-blemished grin. "I just had no fucking clue how much until I thought I was losing you." I stand frozen in shock when he bridges the gap between us while murmuring, "We can't let him win, Elle." It feels wrong that most of his confession centers around wanting to remain top dog than actually taking care of me, but I've wanted to hear those words from a man for years, so I'm a little stumped on how to reply. "I don't have access to that type of money, but if you're willing to think outside the box, I know a way we can get it."

The 'we' part of his comment lowers my agitation, and since there are over thirteen miles between Clover and me, I can finally think rationally. I nod when he looks at me with pleading eyes instead of belittling ones rather than shaking my head as my heart is begging.

It doubles the amorous glint Brayden's eyes are rarely without. "Come on. The quicker we get this wrapped up, the faster we can move on with our lives."

Not speaking another word, he wraps his arm around my shoulders and guides me back to his car. Although we still have a lot to discuss, I let him lead the way. I'm not a damsel in distress, but tell me one girl who doesn't want to be saved from the beast?

While ignoring my inner voice screaming '*you,*' I slide into the passenger seat of Brayden's car before slamming shut the door, praying I can close this chapter of my life just as swiftly.

10

CLOVER

"Not a word."

Galib's lips lift like not an ounce of disdain was projected in my snapped comment before he pops open the back passenger door of his pimped-out SUV. He waits for me to slide in before asking my plans for my Harley Davidson custom V Rod. "What do you want to do with your bike?"

"Leave it. I'll come back and collect it."

Galib's smile doubles, but he doesn't announce that he knows the real reason I'm leaving my two hundred-thousand-dollar ride at the side of a ranch worth half its value. He isn't stupid. He likes his intestines inside his body, and I'm too riled to leave them there if he pisses me off.

I should have killed Estelle when she gave me what I wanted last night, but regretfully her sass draws me in even more than her pouty lips, tight cunt, and peachy ass. I work with cartel associations across the globe—Mexicans, Italians, Greeks, and even the Bratva. If there's a mess to take care of, I'm the man for the job, but today I was left blindsided by a feisty little hellion and her rat of a boyfriend.

I didn't think the prick would be game enough to go against me. He wilted like a picked flower when he spotted me under the awning of Roxanne's grandparents' estate. I've had many men run from me the past decade and a half. Rarely do they show back up breathing only hours later.

I must be off my game. I blame Dimitri. By not killing him, I made myself appear weak to my competitors. I've struggled to fix the injustice the past two years, but it will take more than merciless killings to do that.

A massacre is needed, and I know just the man to start it on.

As my blood thickens with the urge to kill, I sling my eyes to Galib. "Have you had any sightings yet?"

He swallows before shaking his head. "His cell phone was last pinged near Exit 40. Men are combing the area."

"What about his car. Does it have a LoJack system?"

My jaw tightens when he shakes his head for the second time.

When he hears the sigh I couldn't hold in, he says, "They'll pop up, Clover... eventually."

"It's the eventual part I'm worried about. You know how men with small cocks operate. They have something to prove since they can't man up in the bedroom."

Air whizzes out of Galib's nose when he confirms I'm on the money with a huff. Men like Brayden Katz crave the limelight because clothes aren't an optional requirement.

They wither when placed under a true spotlight.

I lick my dry lips, growling when the taste of Estelle's cunt fleetingly hardens my cock. I thought fucking her face would be the highlight of my night. I was dead wrong.

Her tight little cunt is as tasty as her peachy ass.

The desire for another helping is heard in my tone when I

instruct, "Make sure Idris relays everything directly to me. I don't want anyone moving in but me. Estelle will be punished, but only by me. I'll kill anyone who dares to touch her."

Galib's dark brow raises in surprise before he eventually dips his chin. "I understand."

I return my eyes to the window in just enough time to witness the driver pull into the dusty lot of an industrial building on the outskirts of Hopeton. We've arrived at my first appointment for today with twenty minutes to spare.

Although my orders are not to kill the investment banker who pocketed half of the 1.8% deficit he unearthed in Dimitri's cooked books, I don't see myself holding back. I have excess energy to burn—adrenaline I had planned to exert on Estelle before she slid into the car of a man who will be dead by the end of the week.

"Before you go..." The piqued curiosity in Galib's tone slows my exit from his vehicle.

"What is this?" I ask when he hands me a typed note.

Excluding the occasional one-off clients I pick up on the dark web, this is usually how I correspond with vigilantes too scared to take matters into their own hands. Details about the target are shared through Galib, my handler, money is exchanged by untraceable wire transfers, then everything is shredded, leaving no evidence but an inactive cell phone number and shredded ink reams from an ancient typewriter.

The reason behind Dimitri keeping his girl locked up twenty-four-seven comes to light when Galib discloses, "It's a bounty for Roxanne Grace. Three million for kidnap, seven point six for her head."

I won't lie. My interests are apparent. Although this isn't the first time I've seen a bounty on Roxanne's head, the bid was nowhere near this high. I haven't seen figures this high since Dimitri's wife was kidnapped while eight months pregnant with his daughter. A standard hit can be arranged for under one hundred thousand these days. My fee is five times that because I calculate the value of the kill more than my target's wealth. If the death of your father sees you set to inherit a five-million-dollar fortune, you can sure as fuck be guaranteed I'm not going to risk life behind bars for a measly eighty thousand. Furthermore, low tenders get you sloppy work. Evidence will be left, and eventually, it will lead the authorities back to you.

If you don't want that, hire a professional.

I'm as qualified as they get, and just like the two-million-dollar bounty on Dimitri's head three years ago, something smells off with this tender. Roxanne Grace is Estelle's best friend. She has no money, no inheritance, and absolutely no influence in the mafia world whatsoever, so why the fuck does anyone want her dead?

I don't need a good reason to kill someone, but I do need something. A pissy attitude. An outstanding debt. Hell, I've even been hired by wives wanting to teach their cheating spouses a lesson. But this—this has nothing on it. That's an immediate red flag for me. I've been caught out before by assignments like this. I won't make the same mistake twice.

"Thank them for their offer but tell them I'm not taking on any new clients at the moment."

If Dimitri is aware of this offer, my little black book will be full for the next several months, anyway. His wish for anarchy will keep me occupied. For what it misses, I'm sure Estelle's plump lips and tasty cunt can pick up the slack.

"Nad—"

I cut off Galib's interruption with an evil-pronged sideways glare. It's been a few months since I've reminded him who he works for. Perhaps he needs a refresher. "I said no."

The last time he convinced me to accept a tender saw me almost slicing his ear off with a blunt scalpel. I've never accepted payment for a job I did not complete, and the reminder of the rules it now forces me to follow pisses me off to no end.

"Dimitri may not be my friend, but I respect him enough not to mess with him." Galib is unaware of the unique bond I have with Dimitri because he hasn't attended a single meeting we've had in the past two years. All of Dimitri's tenders are handled in person by me. "And I suggest you rethink any objections you have before you possibly lose more than an *unrequired* chunk of cartilage."

I don't need to lower my eyes to know his dick is shriveling away. I hear it in his threatful swallow. "Very well. I will be back to collect you in an hour." He shoves a recently replenished torture kit my way before raising his eyes to mine. "I thought it would be best to avoid cross-contamination."

His reminder of my short yet memorable twenty minutes with Estelle in the office of the Blue Dragon itches the faintest grin onto my mouth. It isn't enough to ensure Galib his slip-up has been forgotten, but it does see him breathing for the first time in thirty seconds.

"Come back in two hours. I plan to take my time with Mr. Tomas."

Before Estelle, I killed for pleasure and fucked for fulfillment.

One night with her flipped everything on its head.

I could hang bodies from bridges across multiple states, yet I doubt the feared respect it would gain me would be close to the fiery burn her sass lit in my stomach.

Estelle Armstead wasn't the first tender I failed to cash, but I can guarantee you, she will be the last.

11

ESTELLE

The underbelly of the Blue Dragon is completely different from its top half. The same tangy mix of sex and sexuality is in the air, but the pungent smell has nothing to do with sweaty bodies bumping and grinding on the dance floor and everything to do with sex.

The attendees at the early festivities are wearing masks, but that's the only strips of clothing they're wearing. There also doesn't appear to be a no-touch policy. There are fewer hands visible than there are hidden.

A chill skates down my spine when Brayden directs me toward an office at the back of the sex-scented space. Even with all my cards laid on the table, butterflies still wreak havoc with my stomach. I've heard rumors his uncle balances his multiple businesses on the crest of legitimate and illegal, but I had no proof until now.

Just before we reach the door at the end of a long hallway, Brayden drops his eyes to mine. He's been holding my hand the past forty minutes, so I'm aware of how sky-high his body temperature is, but his gaze is cool and impassive when he says, "Let me do all the talking."

I nod. Never in my life did I think I'd have to ask a stranger for a dollar, much less four hundred thousand of them, so I'm fine with him taking the reins. I'd probably mumble like an idiot before fleeing his uncle's sex club without a dime to my name.

The warmness flooding the room from the vent above my head does little to settle my goosebumps when we enter his uncle's office. The door latches behind us. I'm locked in with nowhere to run, and Marc isn't the only man around his desk. There are half a dozen of them.

When the men whose ages range from mid-thirties to late sixties drag their sullied eyes down my body, I wish I had taken more time to grill Brayden on his plan. I'm not so stupid to believe a man who barely knows me would lend me four hundred thousand without some sort of stipulations attached to the loan, but I was hopeful a ton of interest would be on the line, not my body.

My heart rate drops when a gentleman with a seedy mustache asks, "How many men?"

Brayden pipes up before I can, but he doesn't seek clarification to the man's question as I was planning. He reminds me why I have more than a three-date rule. "Number is undisclosed, but I can assure you her cunt is tight."

My eyes rocket to Marc when he asks, "Is she clean?"

"Yes," Brayden answers with a bob of his chin. "She had a full workup only two weeks ago." He fails to mention it was because he had a weird-looking wart on the side of his groin. "It came back all clear."

"Good," his uncle replies as his eyes rake my body.

When a man with dark sideburns and mismatched eyes stands from his seat, I release the parking brake and attempt to make a run for it. I barely get two steps away when Brayden snatches up my wrist.

"It's okay, Elle," he assures me, unaware I'd rather face Clover's wrath than spend a single minute with *any* of the men in this room—including him. "They won't touch you. They just like to inspect the merchandise before the sale."

Inspect the merchandise before sale?

What the fuck?

I pull away when a man attempts to sniff my hair before locking my panicked eyes with Brayden. "I can't do this," I blubber out, my voice barely a whisper.

He hinders my attempt to flee for the second time, but instead of tugging on my wrist, he cups my cheeks, then lowers his forehead to mine. "It's a one-time deal, Elle. One night. That's it. Then we can move on with our lives without worrying about anything that has happened the past twenty-four hours."

I dance my eyes between his like we're not being circled by hungry sharks. "They don't want to pay me four hundred thousand dollars to play Scrabble with them, Brayden. Do you understand that isn't what they want?"

I don't know what shocks me more, his reply or the fact he's fine sharing his girlfriend with another man. "I know. But as I said, it's a one-time-only deal. It isn't like you haven't already done the same for less."

My palm hurts as much as my heart when I slap him hard across the face. I don't care who the hell he thinks he is, I will not be disrespected in such a manner. "I'm. Not. Doing. This."

A man with massive biceps thwarts my plan to flee with my head held high and my morals intact. He shakes his head, denying my numerous silent pleas for him to move out of the doorway before he nudges his head to the table Brayden's uncle is now standing behind.

The red imprint my scorn left on Brayden's face roused the spectators enough for Marc to sign his side of our agreement without the slightest quiver to his signature.

When he tilts his gold pen my way, I shake my head. It doubles the redness lining his cheeks. "I thought you said this was a done deal," he snaps out, his eyes focused on his only living nephew.

"It is," Brayden replies, acting as if things aren't as dire as they seem. "She's just being tenacious. Her spitfire stubbornness is what drew me to her. I'm sure it will be the same for your bidders."

I attempt to slap him for the second time, but before I can, I'm forced to the table by the goon who blocked my exit. He doesn't march me to the table with a firm grip on my elbow. He tears chunks of hair out of my head when he fists the locks Brayden made sure were secured in a high ponytail.

When he forcefully places me into a chair across from Marc, I retaliate to his violence with an elbow to his groin. He desperately wants to hit me, I can see the urge in his eyes, but before he can, Marc orders him away.

"She won't fetch nowhere near as much if she's marked." Ignoring the dismissing snicker of the elderly man at our side with silver hair, Marc once again thrusts his pen my way. "Sign... or I'll let them share you now instead of waiting for them to lodge their bids first."

Bids?

Jesus.

When my chin tucks in close to my chest, the words Clover spoke when I refused to look at him smack into me.

"I'll kill a man for looking at you as easily as I will kill him for guilting you into looking away."

Although it's completely wrong of me to hedge all my bets on his dominating personality rearing its ugly head, I don't have any other choice. Either I sign Marc's contract and pray Clover finds me before my auction occurs or answer the silent pleas from the men circling me.

They're hoping I won't sign so Marc will be forced to follow through with his threat. One is so eager he's already stroking himself through his pants. I don't know if he's turned on by the gun butted to my temple or Brayden's confirmation that I'll be worth the coin they're going to hand over on my behalf.

His comment fills me with so much anger, I secretly hope I find him before Clover does. He'll soon learn the real reason I never swallowed his spunk, and I'll grin while doing it.

12

CLOVER

I hold my finger in the air, instructing Galib to wait before I spin back around to face Mr. Tomas. His head is hanging at an odd angle, and his body is wearing almost as many nicks and scars as mine, yet he's still breathing.

It's been a fun hour and twenty minutes.

The hiss of a man on the verge of death fills my ears when I place a perfectly constructed cut to a vein in Mr. Tomas's groin. It isn't a vital artery, but it will weaken him enough even if he finds the will to live, any joy he could possibly have will be waned.

During my somewhat manic torture regime, I discovered the reason for Mr. Tomas's embezzling ways. He likes his women young, too young to be legal. That comes at a cost men in standard nine-to-five jobs can't afford.

To him, he wasn't doing anything wrong. He might have been stealing, but since the money went from one Petretti member to another, he thought he'd never be prosecuted for his insolence.

It's unfortunate for him Dimitri didn't reach the same conclusion. When I told him where his money was going, he switched his tender from a shakedown to a hit. Now, not only have I dispersed some of the annoyance heating my veins, I've also pocketed a cool half a million dollars for an hour's worth of work.

As I said before, it's been a good day.

After admiring my handiwork for another thirty seconds, I crank my neck back to face Galib. The sullen expression on his face makes sense when he announces he's located Estelle. Her resurrection isn't responsible for his surly mood, though. It's where she was found that has him reeling. "She's at the Blue Dragon, sir."

I peel back the latex glove covering my watch to check the time. My jaw tightens when I notice it's late in the afternoon. Last I heard, Marc Harris was planning to run two operations out of the Blue Dragon. The first is a dance club where Dimitri's crew has the rights for the distribution of narcotics and weapons, and the second is a sex club.

Although Dimitri previously supplied Marc with an array of women for pre-opening entertainment, Marc went without his services this time around. Rumors around town are that he's sourcing his women from other entities, who force women into the sex trafficking trade instead of coercing them with money, fancy cars, and the promise of a john with no next of kin and one foot in the grave.

"Do you have footage?"

Galib's Adam's apple bobs up and down before he dips his chin.

I thank him with a stern nod before accepting the towel and packet of makeup- removing wipes he's holding out. They work better than baby wipes. They don't have the talcum powder scent and are drenched with enough chemicals to remove blood.

"Spin," I order when it dawns on me that I'm without the navy-blue wife beater I usually wear under my dress shirt. It was removed from the floor where I left it when my scroll through the dark web for images of Estelle's panties had me so angry, I was sweating like a pig.

Once Galib does as told, I undo the remaining three buttons on my dress shirt, then replace it with a freshly laundered one. Usually I shower after a kill, but since my priorities are elsewhere, I've changed things up today.

"Okay," I mutter when I have my shirt buttoned up to the collar.

Galib has been part of my team for years, but he has no clue as to the number of scars on my body. Not even the women I've fucked are aware of their existence. Up until last night, I only ever fucked in a dark room. The fiery burn in Estelle's eyes had me switching things up. She has the face of an angel and the body of a goddess, but her eyes are as evilly wicked as the black blood in my veins.

After dumping my shirt, the baggies from my feet, and my hair net into the raging bonfire in the middle of the warehouse, I follow Galib outside before wordlessly demanding for him to cough up the goods. He's just about to hand over a tablet when the sound of a man choking to death freezes his hand partway across. Mr. Tomas has decided to swing himself off the stool his tippytoes have been precariously balancing on the past hour and a half. He'd rather not live than live without a functioning cock. Can't say as I blame him.

I wait for his body to stop spasming in the aftershocks of asphyxiation before snatching the tablet out of Galib's hand and continuing our walk. A new type of excitement heats my blood when a video commences playing of Estelle. She's been walked through the underbelly of the Blue Dragon. Although I'm already itching to kill Brayden, the wish doubles when I notice his hand is curled around Estelle's. That's classified as touching, and I very much look forward to explaining that to him.

"Find out who that is," I request when Estelle's slip past a man with burnt orange hair and fogged glasses is done with a prolonged gawk of her face. His dick is buried in the cunt of a busty blonde, and his ass is being plowed by a guy with more hair on his chest than his head, yet he can't take his eyes off Estelle.

Eye-fucking is very much a no-go term in my contracts as well.

"Where's the rest of the footage?" I tap on the video, cautious I may have paused it during my stomps. When my jabs do nothing but replay it from the start, I snap my eyes to Galib. "That's it? That's all you got."

A panicked flare darts through his eyes, and his lips twitch, but before a syllable escapes his mouth, we're interrupted by an accented voice from our side. "There are no cameras in Marc's office. I made the recommendation while investing in his latest business adventure."

Col Petretti smiles a smug grin I'd give anything to increase with a scalpel before he slides out the back of his new Range Rover. His bones are too frail and weak to maneuver in and out of a standard-size car, so he upgraded his fleet a couple of months back.

I should have known he was one of the silent shareholders in the Blue Dragon. There isn't a trade that involves sex within a hundred-mile radius of Hopeton that he doesn't dabble in. The wrinkles on his face make him appear as old as dirt, but he isn't so old he'd let the prime pick be auctioned without first sampling the merchandise.

"If you're here to conduct a safety check on your clientele, I'm afraid to tell you you're too late. His conscience got the better of him."

I return Col's smirk, more than happy for him to know how

much I despise him. I'm confident he wouldn't have any doubts if I disclosed he's the sole reason I didn't kill his son.

I had a father just like him—a tyrant of a man who saw his children as profit margins instead of human beings. He didn't just hate his daughters, though. His sons were treated as badly.

I thought I had finally escaped his madness when he contracted me to another man. I had no fucking clue he was a saint compared to a man as evil as Mr. Latif.

My insides bare the markings of my father's abuse.

The ones on my body solely belong to Mr. Latif.

Col drifts his eyes from Mr. Tomas hanging from a beam in the middle of the warehouse to me. "It looks as if you took your time with him. Why was that, Nadir? Did you have excess energy to burn."

Galib isn't the only one who steps between Col and me when I attempt to respond to the taunt in his tone, so does Ezra James, the Governor of Mafia Law.

As much as this pisses me off to admit, my bond with Dimitri isn't what is protecting Col from my wrath.

Rules are.

Rules that Ezra governs across the globe.

Despite what people believe, Mafia sanctions aren't solely run in first-world countries. They're dotted throughout the globe and stretch as far as the United Arab Emirates.

Mr. Latif is the head of the UAE chapter, and my title as his 'son' means my actions are umbrellaed under his entity. I cannot break the rules, and the reminder makes me the most unhinged I've ever been.

I don't just spit on the gym bag of cash Ezra dumps at my feet, I toss it into Col's chest. "Payment has already been transferred."

"This isn't restitution for Mr. Tomas, although I will admit your high pricing makes sense." Col shifts on his feet to face me, his grin still prominent. "It's for an earlier contract. One you didn't ensure was endorsed before carrying out the tender as documented."

My nostrils flare when he removes a seven-page document from the breast pocket of his suit jacket. I know the document he's holding before he peels back the first page. It's the only contract I printed from a standard computer. I was in a hurry, so I didn't have time to wait for Galib to type up my contract on the typewriters we generally use.

It's the contract between Estelle and me. The one I left pinned to the refrigerator at the ranch so she couldn't miss it when she got home. I crossed out the four-hundred-thousand-dollar payment and adjusted it to one point four million. I'm not a man known for praise, but the taste of her cunt and its tight squeezes when she coerced me out of the pits of hell deserved recognition.

Underhandedly telling her one night between the sheets with her is worth a cool four hundred thousand was the only thing I could come up with at short notice.

"Although your alterations to the contract were done before endorsement by the client, any changes must be approved by both the client and consultant," Ezra advises, stepping closer. "Since that did not occur, the original amount cited is the amount owed." After removing the gym bag I tossed into Col's chest from his hand, Ezra returns it to my feet. "Please consider payment rendered in full for Ms. Estelle Armstead."

It's the fight of my life to hide my chuckle. It rumbles in my chest for the next several seconds. I am amused as fuck they think a measly four hundred thousand will keep me away from Estelle. She's fair game, and I have every intention of forcing her juices onto my cock at the next available opportunity.

I imagine a scalpel being slashed across Col's throat when he says, "Any further negotiations with Ms. Armstead must be done through her handler."

Confident I knew who funded Estelle's payment, I spit out, "Marc Harris has no mafia standings, so not only can I kill him for his ill assumption that he means something in this town, I can also force him to watch Ms. Armstead suck my dick without handing over a dime."

My focus shifts from Col to Ezra when Ezra discloses, "Marc is not Estelle's handler. Col is."

I snatch the document out of his hand that has Estelle's name scrolled across the bottom. It explicitly states that she is now owned by Pet, Inc. a subsidiary under Col's command.

"Estelle was already contracted to me. That makes this contract null and void."

"Her contract with you was unsigned—"

"Yet, you're fucking paying for it!" I scream in Ezra's face while struggling not to gut him where he stands.

I kill for hire because I don't have to hold back. My every whim for carnage is answered day in and day out. It was a job molded for me so I'd never be neutered by the bureaucratic bullshit that almost cost me my life. I can't do that today, and just the knowledge that I have to hold back has me wanting to massacre an entire family.

"Payment was made in good faith."

I toss the contract into Ezra's face, both shutting him up and adding an inch papercut to the unruffled stubble on his chin. Then, I turn to face Col. "Name your price."

I don't even need a second to realize I fell straight into his trap. Just showing an interest in having Estelle's tight cunt squeeze my cock again tripled her asking price.

Col removes a business card from his wallet. "You can find out tomorrow night."

I shake my head. "*Tonight.* Her auction is to be held tonight."

Ezra scoffs. "Tonight is *not* feasible."

"Tonight, or I'll—"

"You'll what, Nadir?" Col interrupts, his tone a cross between piqued and angry. My interest in Estelle has him keen to learn just how tight her cunt is, but he's frustrated because he knows his auctions rarely reach reserve when he tests the merchandise before the bidders arrive. Not even soft cocks desperate enough to purchase a woman want one that's already broken. "Learn how deep the Latif's ties run? From what I heard, you're on your final leg. You shouldn't push it."

His silent confirmation that he's been in contact with my family doubles my determination to find a way to kill him. It may take a week, it may take a year, but as long as the result doesn't alter, I'm willing to wait it out.

After taking a moment to relish my rare silence, Col mutters, "Bring cash. If you want her event brought forward, the least you can do is ensure there's no paper trail." He clicks his fingers at Ezra two times like their ranking isn't almost on par before he climbs into his idling Range Rover.

Although not a word spills from Ezra's mouth, I see the silent apologies in his eyes. I understand his hands are tied and that he merely governs the rules, he doesn't create them, but it doesn't make my wish to kill him any less.

I'm so desperate for carnage, I accept two unclaimed tenders before instructing Galib to withdraw every penny in my account.

"What shall I tell Mr. Latif if he inquires about the withdrawals?"

I yank Galib's lackey out of the driver's seat of his car by the collar of his shirt before sliding behind the steering wheel and dumping Estelle's contract with Col's entity onto the passenger seat. "Tell him Dicks Sporting Goods had a sale so I stocked up on hunting rifles."

"And Estelle?"

Her name alone shatters my concentration. It also thickens my cock, but I'm unsure if that's in remembrance of the events last night or verification that tonight's auction will only end one of two ways.

She'll either be a possession I'll keep chained to my bed until I grow bored or another victim on my already extensive kill tally.

Both outcomes are perfectly acceptable for a man as merciless as me.

13

ESTELLE

"*D*on't touch me."

When I kick out, the goons surrounding me secure my legs to the makeup artist chair they strapped my torso to an hour ago.

They don't just stop at my legs, though. They end my verbal fight as well.

"I fuckin' hate you," I mumble through the industrial tape slapped over my mouth while glaring at Brayden sitting across the room. He's punching messages on his phone like his arrogance isn't undoing two months' worth of wooing.

I freeze when a disturbing notion enters my head. He wasn't wooing me. He was grooming me in private, then, not only will his name be missing from the suspects' list when I'm found in a shallow grave, he can deflect any commentary about me not being 'skilled' enough for this industry.

Such as now. When the woman who's been prettying me up the past hour says, "You do realize she'll fetch more if I plump up her lips with filler before the auction."

Brayden replies, "Believe me, her lips are plenty plump. They're the first thing every man notices about her. Them and her rocking tits."

My eyes snap from the blonde to Marc when he assures, "It's fine, Alice. Just do what you can. I have a feeling she'll break sale records this evening even without makeup." He angles his head so his flopped hair doesn't hinder his perusal of my body. "They like them feisty."

I'd bare teeth at him if my mouth wasn't sealed shut with tape. Furthermore, my sinuses have always given me issues, so I have to concentrate my efforts on not passing out. I can't trust the people circling me when I'm awake, so the last thing I want is to be in a room with them while I'm unconscious.

"What have you got hiding under here?" the blonde murmurs more to herself than me while dragging my sweater over my head.

My nostrils flare to suck down some deep breaths when the sleeveless shirt I threw on in a hurry leaves nothing to the imagination. It's like when I go to sleep in a spaghetti strap top. More of my boobs are outside my shirt than in it when I wake.

"Wait," April instructs when her assistant moves toward a rack of clothing at the side of the room. "This could work."

She demands the tape around my legs and torso be cut. When the goons do as requested, she plucks me from my seat. I'm lost as to where she's going with this until she unbuttons the zipper in my jeans. After folding the dark blue material across itself, she tucks the ends into my jeans then refastens the fly. Instead of it hanging limply off my body, it hugs my curves while showing a teasing amount of side boob.

"Perfect," croons an accented voice from the side of the room. It's the same elderly man who's been eyeballing proceedings for the past several hours. Anyone would swear he's going to benefit from my sale as much as Marc.

When he realizes he's caught my stink eye, he stands from his chair and paces across the room. His haughty approach makes my stomach gurgle. He has the worst aura to date. Even a part-time community college student knows bad news when she sees it.

He's as bad as it gets.

The scent of garlic and tomatoes filters into my nose when he stops to stand in front of me. "I've been waiting for a chance to get back the millions I've paid him over the years, and today could very well be that chance." He grips my face as hard as Clover did when I lied to him, but his is done in a cruel, undermining manner. "Let's hope whoever buys you is too impatient to ruin your cunt to take you home. I'd consider a discount just to watch the light in your eyes be extinguished." He smiles about the whitening of my gills before he locks his lust-filled eyes with Alice. "Leave the tape on her mouth. They'll bid more knowing we had to subdue her."

With that, he releases my face from his terrifying hold before he exits the room without so much of a backward glance.

Only twenty minutes later, I'm guided out the same door, except my exit isn't done via my own free will. I'm thrown over the shoulder of a goon like my fists aren't beating into him, and everything I see is upside down.

The atmosphere in the underbelly of the Blue Dragon is starkly contradicting to what it was only hours ago. It stills reeks of sex and depravity, but the couches, tables, and cushioned areas once filled with naked, grinding bodies sit empty. There are no groping hands, fondling couples, or teasing trios. Women with black hooded capes line the corridor, and the pungent scent of fear has rid the air of oxygen.

"Commence the auction with her. Fresh meat always attracts higher bids." I can't see who's talking, but I'm reasonably sure it's the elderly man with the Italian accent. "Then go in order of newness to the market. We only get a handful of rotations before the stock becomes old."

The emptiness of my stomach does little to ease the nausea rolling through it. He said his comment like some of the auctions tonight aren't one-off travesties, that they'll occur time and time again until the bids dry up.

It dawns on me that it is the case when I'm placed on my feet at the front of a long line. Although, half the face of the woman standing next to me is covered with a cloak, I'm sure I've seen her before. Roxanne and I wrongly bickered about her a handful of times the past year when she was spotted on the arm of a man double her age at the premieres Brayden attended. We thought she was a gold digger. Now I feel guilty.

I don't know what compels me to reach for her hand, but the instant a black hooded cape is draped over my head, instincts overtake me. We hold hands for the next several minutes, our grip tightening the more murmurings of a boisterous crowd sound out of the door we're lined up in front of.

When it's time for proceedings to begin, I have to be dragged away from her. Our immediate connection should be odd, but considering the circumstances, I guess it isn't. Most people's true selves don't come out until a crisis. Look at Brayden, for example. I thought he'd be the man I'd run to in a crisis. In reality, he's the monster I should have run from.

Pain rockets through my neck when the goon marching me through a blackened door shoves my head down. "Keep your head low until I say so."

An eerie feeling causes goosebumps to break across my skin when I'm forced into a room that smells of liquor and cigars. There aren't as many feet peeking through the bottom of my cloak as anticipated. I can only see three pairs of black boots.

I realize I have the situation all wrong when a spotlight highlights the pads of my feet a mere second before my cloak is ripped off and my head is yanked back by the goon pushing me around. I'm not standing amongst the men wanting to bid on me, I'm standing above them on a glossy stage with a real-life auctioneer at my side. The rest of the women are waiting in the queue behind me. We're being run through like cattle at a stockyard.

When the auctioneer commences bidding at ten thousand dollars, I peer past the blinding lights highlighting every flaw of my body. Although most of the crowd's faces are concealed like the women waiting to be auctioned, there are a handful I recognize. Clover's is the most notable, but a gentleman in his fifties with burnt orange hair and an unconcealed face deserves a mention. I can't recall where I've seen him, but I'm certain it's been on more than one occasion. He's older than the men I usually associate with, but he's the perfect age for the clientele at The Commission.

I snap my eyes back to Clover when the unnamed man accepts the auctioneer's opening bid. He has kind eyes, but today has taught me not to judge a book by its cover.

The pleading in my eyes doubles when Clover fails to lodge a bid no matter how much I silently beg. Tenders come in from all sides of the room, but he remains tightlipped and not once does his paddle twitch.

I stare at him in silent begging when the auction sails past the reserve price Marc bartered with his associates earlier this evening. I get he's pissed about the way I fled and that he wrongly believes I already owe him close to two million dollars, but why show up if he has no intention to bid?

When the auctioneer bangs down his gavel, the gurgle of my stomach is scarcely heard over the ruckus of the crowd when Clover moves into a prime spot for the next auction. I fetched an eye-watering amount that makes sense of the college students selling their virginities to fund their school expenses, but to the bidders in this room, the auction following mine is now more enticing thanks to Clover's interest.

It's obvious everyone in the room knows who he is, and when he opens the bid for a petite blonde with bright green eyes at one hundred thousand, the awe in the spectators' eyes augments.

As I'm led off the stage by the same man who forced me onto it, Clover continues increasing his bids until the auction tiptoes into the two-million-dollar range. The amount on offer silences the group hanging off Clover's every word and drops my mouth enough that if I had a mustache, I wouldn't anymore.

My auction ended at one point seven million, so Clover could have afforded to purchase me if he wanted to. He just didn't.

I stop fighting the goon at the same time the man who won me arrives at the auctioneer's table to fork over the exorbitant amount he paid for me. He looks innocent enough. If he hadn't bid on me in an underground sex trafficking ring, I could have easily excused him as a father arriving to collect his child from Sunday school.

My eyes bounce between the unnamed man and the elderly gent helming the auction when they greet by exchanging a handshake. "Pleasure to do business with you again, Winston."

"The pleasure is mine, Col. It always is." Winston's accent is unique, but it has a sleazy edge to it that makes my skin crawl. "I'd like the same preference as previous purchases."

Col angles his head before dipping his chin. "Twenty percent on resale. Scars must remain on her body. If you damage her face, no refunds will be given."

"That's fine," Winston replies with a grin. "I'm a sadist, not a narcissist." He hands over identification before dumping a duffle bag full of cash onto the table separating him from Col. "Her return will be in six weeks." He scans his eyes over my body. "Perhaps eight. She seems bratty enough to warrant longer training."

My heart tells me to run, but my head keeps my feet rooted to the floor. Even if I wanted to flee, I wouldn't get far. Winston is standing at my left, Clover and his newly purchased sex slave are at my right, Col is blocking my front, and his juiced-up goon is guarding the back.

I literally have nowhere to run.

After jotting down details of Winston's sale into an ancient-looking ledger, Col hands him a business card before waving his hand across his body. "A suite is set out as per your requirements."

The excited flare darting through Col's eyes disperses when Winston replies, "Not today. Beginners need a nurturing environment to break in the first time. Perhaps we can return later this week." He shifts on his feet so he faces Clover head-on. Although his eyes are for Clover, his words are for the stunning blonde standing motionless at his side. Her frozen state is understandable. She's standing next to men craving for her to step out of line. If she budges an inch in the wrong direction, she'll be in a world of hurt. "Be good, little one, and remember what I taught you."

With money more important to him than exchanges between clientele, Col ushers us on so he can commence Clover's transaction.

Since I'm being called to Winston's side like a dog, I only catch a portion of what Clover says to Col, but it leaves no misunderstandings as to why he didn't bid on me. "I've been waiting for Andria to be returned to market for years now. A change-up was required because who knows when she'll be available again."

I'm so stunned by his comment. I don't voice a protest when the tape on my mouth is removed before I'm bundled into the back of a classic Rolls Royce. Words won't save me, and although the Armsteads were bred to do anything necessary as a means to survive, aching up for a fight with men carrying guns seems like a stupid thing to do.

"Where are you taking me?"

I wait and wait and wait for Winston to answer me.

If his response were my only lifeline, I'd be dead by now.

"My sale was not of my own free will, so anything you're planning to do to me is illegal and will be prosecuted to the full extent—"

Winston ends my warning with a brutal backhanded slap. My head flings to the side with so much force, I spot Clover entering the suites Col pointed out earlier. He isn't alone. Andria is following behind him, but instead of walking, she's on all fours, being led into the dark space like an animal. Her collar is studded, there's a gold clover dangling in the middle of it, and her lead is made from the same black leather material of Clover's belt.

I comprehend not all Winston's aggression is for me when I notice the direction of his narrowed gaze. I'm not the only one who has spotted Clover and Andria's retreat. Winston waits for them to enter the first suite marked private before he signals for his driver to go.

Although frightened, the next forty minutes whizz by in a nanosecond. I want to say that time flew by because I was busy staring at a single headlight in the darkness, but that would be a lie. We haven't had a single vehicle behind us the last fifteen miles. Nothing but acres upon acres of trees surround us.

I shift my eyes from a long driveway to Winston when he hands me a cape similar to the one I wore at the auction. "Place this on. You are not to address the staff or look at them. If you need something, ask me. If I deem it a necessity, I will consider supplying it. Bathroom breaks are to be on the hour. If it is fifteen minutes past, you will wait until the following hour. You will shower morning and night and after any play sessions. Legs and underarm hair are to be shaved every day. Your vagina will be waxed first thing tomorrow morning. If you are here long enough for an additional appointment, it will be booked by me."

He continues rambling off rules on how I am to dress, act, and speak around him. I am only to call him sir, meals will be supplied to my room three times a day, and I am to eat everything offered, including anything I do not like, and although I will be confined to my room for twenty-three out of the twenty-four hours of a day, I am only to spend eight hours maximum in my bed.

"Personal hygiene and peak physical fitness are a necessary requirement for all my little ones. If you don't maintain the high standard as stated in the dossier in your room, physical punishment will be administrated. Do you understand?"

His jaw tightens the longer it takes for me to respond. "Yes, I understand."

My fight-and-flight mode has kicked in, but a quick sweep of the area exposes I have more chances of stumbling onto a coyote than a savior this far out of town. I'm also barefoot, which is ideal for sprinting but not in woodlands.

I'll devise a new plan once my mind stops reeling, but for now, I follow Winston up a set of extensive stairs. It was clear from the amount he paid for me that money isn't an issue for him, but the number of polished shoes I see on our walk authenticates my claims, not to mention the sparkling carved marble my feet are tapping on.

"Atticus will take you to your room. I'll fetch you shortly for our first session."

Blonde hair falls from my face like a waterfall when my eyes snap to Winston's. "Can we start my training tomorrow? It's very late. I'm tired."

I step out of the firing line when he raises his hand for the second time tonight. He caught me unaware in the back of his Rolls Royce because Clover was in the vicinity.

It won't happen a second time.

"Disobedience must be immediately rectified." The chill in

Winston's voice doesn't solely immobilize me. The women surrounding us also freeze like statues.

Excluding a couple of raunchy books I've read that mention brats, I don't have any knowledge on the BDSM lifestyle, but that won't stop me from saying their responses don't seem normal. It's as if they'll be punished along with me.

After a quick swallow, I say, "I wasn't disobeying you. I was merely offering you a suggestion since I didn't shave this morning. I don't want to disappoint you our first time together."

I think my ploy has worked until he replies, "Very well," but am proven wrong when he adds, "I will have Cecille place a razor and shaving cream in the playroom." A flare that frightens the living hell out of me darts through his eyes when he whispers, "I look very much forward to shaving you, little one. Let's hope you're a squirmer."

Preferring to risk death in the woods than be hacked up by a psycho, I push Winston away from me with a grunt, then sprint for the door I shadowed him through only moments ago.

I make it through the threshold and down three dozen stairs before my campaign is ended by a broad-chested man. He doesn't impede my steps with his large frame, nor does he throw his fist into my face as my flinching eyes are predicting, he jabs a needle into my neck.

It must be a sedative as it immediately pulls my legs out from beneath me. As the world blurs around me, the goon returns me to his master's feet by my hair. Excluding the wrenching of my hair from my scalp, I don't feel anything. My legs and arms are too numb to feel something as insignificant as pain.

Winston pats the goon's hair like he's a good puppy before he drops his hate-filled eyes to mine. I can barely see him through the haze hindering my vision. I feel drunk, sick, and a headache is already forming behind my temples.

"Go to sleep, little one," Winston murmurs. "Everything will be ready for you when you wake."

When the heavy weight of sleep beckons me to it, I try to fight. My chances of surviving are already low, and I don't see them improving if I fall asleep, but before my brain gets the chance to protest that, darkness wins.

14

ESTELLE

The first thing my eyes land on upon opening is a man stroking his cock in the corner of the room. He's wearing a mask that covers one-half of his face. The other half is concealed with white paint. It's a mask similar to the one worn in *Phantom of the Opera*, but it has silver engravings all over it.

Its pattern continues with the rest of his outfit—*if you can call it that*. The bowtie and open vest combination he's wearing doesn't hide the fact he's pantless. None of the men surrounding me are wearing anything below the waist, and there are at least a dozen of them.

"Ah... there she is. Sleeping Beauty finally wakes."

When a man in a full black mask drags his hand down my cheek, I attempt to yank away from him. His mask hides his identity, but his voice is very distinct.

Winston looks desperate to punish me, but my inability to deny his touch sees him holding back. I thought it was vulnerability making me feel naked. I had no clue not a stitch of clothing covers my body.

If that isn't already bad enough, I'm fixed to a leather seat that's suspended from the ceiling. The movements of my arms, legs, torso, thighs, and head are limited because of the thick leather straps holding me hostage to the swing, and even if I wanted to tell Winston off, I couldn't. I'm gagged with one of those red ball gags I've only ever seen in the windows of sex shops.

"Don't be modest, little one," Winston murmurs as he runs his hand up the pink skin on my inner thigh. "Despite your lie, I ensured you're well presented for my guests before strapping you in. Your skin is as soft as a baby's bottom." He quivers out a breath when he drags the back of his hand down my bare vagina. "I'd let you experience the sensation if you knew how to follow the rules." He sighs like he's disappointed, even with contentment being the most obvious feature on his face. "Alas, you still have a lot to learn."

I growl through the gag when he brushes his hand down my pussy for the second time. His touch disgusts me, but it isn't the sole cause of my panic. Most of it centers around Winston signaling for the first man in the line to step forward.

The young man doesn't take his eyes off Winston nor his hand from his cock until instructed, and even then, the dribble of pre-cum seeping from his uncut dick drips to the floor like a leaky tap.

"Remember, little one, gentle touches until she proves she wants otherwise."

A scream rips through my gag when the masked man dips his chin. His head bob thrusts his face into the light of the chandelier above his head. He's years younger than Winston. I'm not talking six or seven. I mean *decades* younger. He'd be lucky to be eighteen.

"Please don't," I try to scream through the gag when Winston yanks on a steel chain at his side to hoist me closer to the masked teen's face. "I'll do what you want. I'll listen." Being sexually assaulted is already horrendous, but it will be ten times worse being a forced participant in a sexual assault. This man's eyes are hazy. Nothing he's doing is via his choice. It is against his will as much as it is mine. "Please, sir, I'm begging you!"

When my murmur sounds more like words than sobs, Winston holds his index finger in the air. It immediately suspends the teen's mouth an inch from my pussy, and I breathe for the first time in what feels like minutes.

After ordering the teen to rejoin the line, Winston tugs the ball gag out of my mouth, then moves to stand in front of me. "What did you say, little one?"

I wet my lips the best I can with my bone-dry tongue, swallow twice, then prepare to repeat my sentence, but a ruckus in the foyer of Winston's home steals his devotion before I can. I can't see the person doubling the output of my heart, but since his arrival increases the scent of murder and desecration, I immediately know who he is.

A dry mouth is a thing of the past when Clover enters the room weaponed up and ready to fight. A black balaclava covers most of his face, but portions of the clover tattoo on his cheek are visible in the eye cutout.

Just like last night, he kills the last three men in the line with direct-kill shots to the head. When their slump to the floor announces their deaths before the vision of the guns in Clover's hands, two men race his way while another two bolt for the exit.

A bullet in the back is a fitting death for the cowards too scared to fight, but Clover uses a hands-on approach for the men in front of him. He slices a knife across the jugular of one before he drops it to the second man's cock.

I hear Winston's swallow more than I see it when the man's penis flops onto the floor a mere second before Clover blows his brains out.

After kicking a third man to the side with a hard boot to the sternum, he pops two bullets into his stomach before wedging a final one into his skull.

Every muscle in my body pulls taut when he shifts his focus to the only man not wearing a full mask. It's the teen who stood at my side only moments ago, the one who is as innocent as me.

"No, no, no," I scream on repeat, my voice suddenly found again. "He's an innocent. He didn't do anything wrong."

It dawns on me that Clover is a killer in all forms of the word when he forces the teen onto his knees before he slits his throat while staring straight at me. There's no remorse in his eyes. No hesitation. He killed him all the while imagining he was killing me.

"If you hadn't run, he'd still be alive." He waits for me to absorb the sheer anger in his voice before he slings his deadly black eyes to Winston. "Knees. *Now.*"

When he shakes his head, stupidly believing he can ignore Clover's directive, Clover forces him to obey by kneecapping him. Winston's howls hide my frantic gasps when Clover reverts his focus back to me. He doesn't immediately free me from captivity as hoped. While staring into my eyes, he drags his knife from my throat to the apex of my pussy. It leaves a trail of blood from the men he massacred and has my thighs fighting against the restraints bounding me so I can press them together.

He doesn't push on the blade with enough pressure to draw blood, but the darkness in his eyes exposes he's struggling to hold back. He's as angry at me as he is Winston, and the knowledge makes my breaths more needy than panicked.

"What did I tell you, angel?" he asks after removing his balaclava so he can take in my peaked nipples and hued skin without hindrance. "You crave carnage."

In quicker than I can blink, he pulls a second revolver out of his black coveralls, points it at Winston's head, then fires once.

When Winston's blood splatters my face, torso, and stomach, my first instinct is to scream. The blood of a dead man is on me. I should be crying bloody murder, but instead, I watch in fascination at the lightening of Clover's dark eyes when he rubs Winston's blood into my cheek.

He smears it across my face before shifting his eyes to my breasts. Considering we're in a room full of dead people, I should be turned off by the yearning in his hooded gaze, not thinking up ways to make it last forever.

Perhaps Roxanne is right. Maybe I do pick men I know are toxic because I'd rather have a drama-filled life than one not worth living.

I push my inane thoughts to the back of my mind when Clover says, "Next time you run, angel—"

"I'll run to you," I interrupt, certain they're the only words he wants to hear.

Clover grunts as if he isn't turned on by my submissiveness like Winston would have been before he finalizes his sentence, "The next time you run, angel... I'll kill you." Once again, there's no hesitation in his voice. His words are one hundred percent truthful. "Do you understand? Or shall I drag Brayden in here so you comprehend the severity of my threat?"

"I understand," I murmur, certain I can't face more carnage in this one day.

Faceless men were hard enough. Although Brayden is a dick, I don't think I could stomach witnessing the murder of a man I know, both personally and sexually.

"Good." After a final prolonged glance of my body, Clover slices his knife through the leather holding me hostage, then assists me to my feet. His scent that's both familiar and massacre-fueled engulfs me when he undoes the top three buttons in the all-black coveralls he is wearing to expose his navy-blue wifebeater underneath. It's the same style and size as the one I threw on before racing toward my death. How do I know this? The hemline reaches the same spot on my body it did before April prettied it up when he pulls it over my head, and the same risqué amount of side boob is exposed.

"Come in," Clover says once he's satisfied I'm covered.

After smirking about my wide-eyed response, he shifts on his feet to face the door he burst through with guns blazing only minutes ago. My heart rages out of control when a man with inky black hair enters the room. His angry sneer isn't solely responsible for the patters of my heart, though. It's the woman trailing him. The blonde from the auction. The one I had an immediate connection with but am now insanely jealous of.

She crosses the room like it isn't dotted with bodies, her steps fast yet as smooth as silk. When she reaches Clover's side, he pets her hair before he addresses the man with the midnight black hair. "Take Estelle back to the ranch. I will stay with Andria until the exchange occurs."

The craving for more violence smacks into me hard and fast when his lackey yanks me away from Clover at the same time he demands Andria to her knees.

As I'm walked out of the space reeking of death, Andria immediately jumps to Clover's command, both eager to please and willing to submit.

"Good girl," Clover praises her before running his hand down her silky hair for the second time. Once he has the kinks flattened out, he twists her faultless locks around his fist then lifts his lusty eyes to mine. "Remember how this feels the next time you want to run into the arms of another man."

Just before he's plucked from my vision by a rough yank to my arm, Andria's hands move to the fourth button in Clover's overalls.

The image of her kneeling before him, preparing to remove his cock makes me so sick to my stomach, I physically dry retch. The man I thought I was falling in love with only last week is sitting in the back of an SUV, sobbing like a child, yet I fight to go back to the man who has tortured me more than he's nurtured me.

I must be insane.

15

ESTELLE

I'm still fighting to get out of the dark-haired man's hold five miles later. My thrashing only loses steam when Brayden mumbles on a sob, "He made me kill my uncle. H-He made me hold a gun to his head and pull the trigger." He locks his traumatized eyes with mine. "W-What am I supposed to tell my mother? Uncle Marc was her only sibling. Their parents died years ago. She has no one left."

I almost feel sorry for him, then I remember his uncle is a monster.

Correction. *Was* a monster.

"You should be more concerned about what they're going to do to you than the painless, non-dramatic way your uncle died." When Brayden's eyes snap to mine, stunned by the vengeance fueling my high tone, I ask, "Do you really think you're alive because killing your uncle is atonement for your crimes?" When hope flares through his eyes, I *pfft* him. "*Puh-leaze*, Brayden. I was sold to a psychopath for the minor charge of infidelity, so how bad do you think the punishment will be for forcing a hired hitman to part with over two million dollars for a woman when he could have hundreds kneeling before him without handing over a penny!"

I freeze as the entirety of my comment smacks into me.

Clover doesn't have to pay for women like Andria to please him, so why did he?

My breathing stills even more when I recall the direction of Clover's eyes when Winston and I were ushered away. He wasn't staring at Andria or me. Not even Col had his utmost devotion. He was peering at the ledger that had Winston's personal details scribbled across the worn paper. He was unearthing my location without neither Col nor Winston having any idea.

"Who's in the suite at the Blue Dragon?"

Brayden looks confused by my question, the armed goons look disinterested, but that doesn't mean it goes unanswered. It merely arrives from the last place I'd ever expect. It comes from the speaker at my side. From the *exact* voice that cautioned me about going to the police two days ago. "As far as Col is concerned, Clover is there with his recently purchased asset."

"That wouldn't work," I advise the uniquely accented voice. "Col hinted that he likes to watch. He would have realized by now that it isn't Clover in his assigned room."

I hear him snicker before he asks, "Are you sure you haven't done this line of work before?" When I respond to humor in his voice with a huff, he adds, "Col does like to watch. That's why Clover picked a room with surveillance cameras instead of two-way mirrors. It also has a desk smack bang in the middle of it."

It takes me longer than I care to admit to put two and two together, but when I do, my stomach gurgles. "What footage are you playing?" Clover's comment to Col gave no indication he's purchased Andria previously, but that doesn't mean he hasn't. He's very clever at being deceptive.

I don't know whether to be relieved or panicked when a familiar beg for more sounds down the line. They're not the ones I released at Roxanne's grandparents' ranch. They could barely afford to feed themselves each week, let alone install surveillance cameras so high-end Clover's comment about wanting to see Brayden grind against my ass sounds as if he's sitting directly behind me.

"How do you think I knew you were with him?" Brayden asks, his voice a cross between a wail and fury. "Half the club heard your screams that night from the surveillance monitors behind the bar. I looked like a fucking idiot."

"Brayden..."

He fills the void in my reply with an angst-filled statement. "I fucking loved you, Elle. I wanted a life with you, then you hurt me."

"You let your uncle *sell* me! He fucking *sold* me like a piece of meat!"

"Only because I knew *exactly* who was purchasing you. My uncle organized for Winston to be a decoy. He was meant to push up the purchase price, then forfeit the sale after the auction. Once his purchase was refunded, and he was handed a share of the payment my uncle receives from Col for hosting the sales, he was meant to sign you over to me."

"That isn't what happened, Brayden. That isn't *close* to the events that occurred tonight."

"I know." He rips his hands through his hair, pulling some of it out in the process. "I don't know what happened. We had every-thing worked out. My uncle and I sat up for hours this morning..." His words slow as his pupils dilate. After sucking in some big breaths, he locks his wide eyes with mine. "We discussed every-thing in my uncle's upstairs office. We plotted it right in front of the fucking cameras. Oh my god, I'm an idiot."

He's as good at groveling as he is at giving head, so I'm unsure which side of the fence I should be on when he murmurs, "I'm so sorry, Elle. I knew what we were planning would hurt you, but I thought it was our only option." The goon with dark hair forcefully pushes him back into his seat when he attempts to scoot closer to me. Although it darkens his light eyes with annoyance, it barely touches the remorse in them when he says, "You know everything I said was just a ploy, right? I had to convince Col I was selling you because I had lost interest. He usually only purchases virgins, so I had to assure him you were worth the initial purchase price. That was the money we used to pay off Clover. You don't owe him anything anymore. I freed you."

I'm going to blame the sedative Winston's goon gave me earlier tonight for the disappointment roaring through me. I don't feel free. I feel more trapped than I ever have.

Needing answers, I ask, "What are you saying, Brayden? That someone got to Winston after you?"

He bobs his chin before he once again attempts to scoot to the edge of his chair. It is lucky I'm efficient in lip reading when he's stopped for the second time. *"Winston's son was in the foyer when Clover stormed in. He didn't attempt to stop him. That makes me wonder if this was a hit. Now the Petrettis get two payments instead of one. Col keeps the money Winston paid for you, and Clover gets payment for killing him."* He rolls his eyes. *"They made a killing tonight—literally."*

"No. That can't be true."

I want to say more. I just can't. I'm too confused to form sentences. Even if everything he said is true, why did Clover purchase Andria? Where does she fall into this grand scheme of manipulation and lies? Clover purchased her to save me, didn't he?

The hits keep coming when I recall the last words Clover

spoke before I was yanked away from him. *'I will stay with Andria until the exchange occurs.'*

"Who is Clover handing Andria to? Who *actually* purchased her?"

When silence comes at me from all angles, I realize Brayden's theory is more factual than deceitful. I've been conned into believing Clover is my savior when in reality, he's the monster from my nightmares who only saved me for profit.

Not thinking, I use Clover's goon's distraction to my advantage. After snatching his gun from the back of his trousers, I butt it to his head before he knows what's coming. "Tell them to pull over." When he has the audacity to chuckle, I flick off the safety on the tang, cock back the hammer, then compress the trigger enough the scent of his heated skin soon overtakes the fear leeching out of Brayden's pores. "My daddy is a hunter, so you should believe me when I say your brain is two millimeters from being splattered on the headrest in front of you." I inch back the trigger a little more. "Now one millimeter."

"Okay. Okay. Calm down."

I see the shudder of his heart in his hand when he signals for the driver to pull over. It doubles when I nudge my head to the nature strip siding the road. "Now get out. *All* of you." When the driver places the gearstick into neutral before doing as instructed, I drift my eyes to Brayden. "Do you know how to drive a stick?"

When he jerks up his chin, I alter my plan for the third time tonight. "Climb into the driver's seat." I wait for him to slot behind the steering wheel before devoting my attention back to Clover's goon. He isn't eager to leave me alone with Brayden, and in all honesty, it makes me worried I'm making a horrible mistake, but as my daddy likes to say, better the devil you know than the one you don't. "Out."

"Ms. Armste—"

"Out!" I repeat, screaming.

With his nostrils pumping and his fists balled, he slides to the far side of the cab and pops open the door. "He will find you," he warns before stepping out.

It's wrong of me to say I'm hopeful, so I keep my mouth shut.

16

ESTELLE

"It isn't just your cell phone you need to dump, Brayden. Your smartwatch and Fitbit also need to go. Pretty much anything capable of tracking."

Acting ignorant to his whiny groan, I dash around a dumpster protruding over the footpath like my feet are protected by the thick-soled shoes Brayden is wearing. Not only are my feet bare, I'm also freezing. Clover's sleeveless shirt is the equivalent of a dress, but it's chilly out, so shouldn't a man living with regrets offer his coat to the girl he wronged?

Not Brayden. That isn't the way he operates. He's worse than a beheaded chook when it comes to responding to a crisis and more selfish than anyone I've ever met. Every deed that's been put into play tonight has been actioned by me. I suggested we dump the SUV a couple of miles out before hitchhiking a ride so our movements can't be tracked, and I used Clover's shirt to remove evidence that we were in Clover's car.

All Brayden's done is whine about how much walking we did

before spotting an interstate tagged truck, then suggested I flash my tits to guarantee he'd stop.

Thankfully, neither my disheveled appearance nor a lack of flaunting my assets hindered our efforts to find a ride. The very first truck I hooked my thumb at pulled over. Although he wasn't impressed when Brayden jumped into the cab with me, mercifully, the one thing Brayden does understand is bribery.

The wad of cash he handed the driver made his annoyance a thing of the past. While stuffing the bundle of money into the front of his rugby shorts, his eyes lit up like a Christmas tree. The heat they projected kept the chill to a minimum during our twenty-mile trip to Hopeton.

Recollection of our time in the truck reminds me that there are more ways to be tracked than communication devices. "You should also use cash as often as possible and make sure any contact with your friends and family is done discreetly."

Brayden stops walking before he cranks his neck my way. "I know somewhere we can get cash. *Lots* of it."

As his eyes pop out of his head, he snatches up my wrist, then races down the sidewalk like my feet aren't still cut up. I apologize on repeat to the people he bumps us into. He snarls at them like they're in the wrong.

"No!" I yank my hand out of his grip and take a step back, my eyes never leaving the Blue Dragon. "I'm not going in there. You fooled me once, Brayden. It won't happen again. I'm *never* going back there."

"I swear to God, I won't let anyone hurt you, Elle." When I shrug off his claims, he tries another angle. "Besides, you have that..." he nudges his head to the gun I'm still clutching like it belongs in my hands, "... and you know how to use it. We're also only going to my uncle's upstairs office. You've been there. You know it's safe."

I almost blurt out that I only consider it safe because Clover took me there, but the removal of his jacket renders me silent. I can feel my body shuddering, but I didn't know they were visible until he drapes his jacket over my shoulders.

I realize Brayden isn't the only fool in this alleyway when he murmurs, "Mike won't let you in the door if he sees that..." he once again nudges his head at my gun, "... so its best we cover it up." He raises his eyes to my face. "Unless you'd rather give it to me."

I hit him with my biggest stink eye to date. There's only one way he'll ever touch any part on my gun—when I pop a bullet between his brows.

When my inner monologue sounds more appealing than disgusting, I ask, "How much money are we talking?"

Brayden twist his lips. "Two or three..."

"Thousand?" I fill in when the excitement in his voice has me missing the last half of his statement.

While grinning a full-tooth smile, he shuffles on his feet and rubs his hands together. "Millions, baby."

My eyes bulge. "Your uncle has two million dollars in his safe!" That's enough to fund three lifelong escapes, let alone my pathetic little one.

Brayden clamps his hand over my mouth before straying his eyes to the people mingling outside the club, desperate for an invitation to the festivities inside. Once he's confident my shriek didn't gain us unwanted attention, he drops his hand, then says, "With opening night a hit, and..."

"The auctions he held earlier tonight bringing in a lot of coin?" I finalize, aware his pause this time around isn't genuine like his first.

He nods his head. "His safe is overflowing, and the bank doesn't open until Monday."

When he arches a brow, wordlessly requesting my thoughts, I take a minute to ponder. There are a lot of people lingering both inside and outside of the club, and I am weaponed up like Armageddon is about to start, so I guess there's no harm in trying to fund our escape with money Brayden is entitled to. He was Marc's sole beneficiary.

Brayden looks like he wants to kiss me when I gabber out, "In and out. No pussyfooting around."

"Deal." He squeezes my hand before fiddling with the collar of his jacket. I appreciate his endeavors to make me look presentable until he shifts his focus to my hair. His mini-makeover isn't for my benefit. It's about him like it always is.

When my anger reaches boiling point, I pull away from him before gesturing for Brayden to go first. He isn't much taller than me, but if his uncle's men have a shoot-to-kill order, my chances of survival will be greatly improved just from using him as a shield.

"It's okay," Brayden assures me when he feels the leaping of my pulse when he joins our hands. "Your safe and protected. I won't let anything happen to you."

Unlike when we entered the Blue Dragon opening night, Brayden doesn't release my hand when the bouncer ushers us into the club without needing to join the line. He holds on tight, his grip never loosening even when approached by women dying for the chance to talk to him.

"Get the lock," he suggests when we enter Marc's office unscathed.

When I do as asked, he moves for a safe hidden under Marc's desk. His uncle must have shared the combination with him because he commences filling a gym bag with bundles upon bundles of cash in less than two seconds.

"What did I tell you, Elle, plenty for us to live off."

His 'us' comment stumps me. I would have left him with

Clover's goons if I knew how to drive a stick because there is no 'us.'

There hasn't been since he organized for his uncle to auction me.

When I say that to Brayden, his eyes pop up from the over-stuffed bag. "But this was the plan all along, Elle. Me and you, sipping cocktails in Belize with a fuck ton of money."

I don't know if he's delusional or insane, but if it weren't for Clover, there would be no me. Winston would have either chipped at my personality until there was nothing left but a shell of a woman, or I would have because I'd rather not exist than spend a single moment with a man who doesn't like me for who I am.

"I can't do this. Not just because it's with you but because it's wrong." I point to the bag of cash. "That's blood money, meaning it isn't the solution to our problems, it's the cause of it."

Brayden glares at me like I have two heads before he brushes off my concern with a nasty snarl. His arrogance strengthens my belief that I've made the right choice. Running won't solve anything. It won't unmuddle the confusion that forever bombards me when Clover is in my vicinity, and it won't assure me Roxanne's safety is Dimitri's utmost priority.

She's my best friend—*my only friend*—so there's no way I can leave her. And don't get me started on the twisting of my stomach when I add Clover into the mix, or I'll be tempted to check myself into a psychiatric hospital. He's bad news, but isn't everyone who forces you to look outside the bubble you're living in?

Brayden shouts my name when I fling open the door of his uncle's office, but since he's too busy stuffing bundles of Benjamin Franklins into his bag like he refuses to leave a single bill behind, I walk out the doors and onto the sidewalk without interference, suddenly mindful Brayden was a lesson, not my forever.

17

ESTELLE

"Are you sure you'll be okay?" The kind man who let me ride the bus for free strays his eyes to Roxanne's grandparents' ranch before shifting them back to me. "It's dark out, and there are coyotes around these parts. I don't want you getting hurt."

I smile, confident coyotes are the least of my problems. "There are too many beasts hiding in the woodlands for the coyotes to worry about little ol' me. I'll be fine." After leaning over to press a kiss on James's cheek, I whisper, "Thank you, James. You've given me faith that gentlemen do still exist."

I take a moment to relish his flushed cheeks before dipping my chin in thanks to Doris for the umpteenth time for the knitted socks she gave me to keep my feet warm, then I gallop down the bus's stairs. Like a true knight in shining armor, James waits for me to wave him off from the porch of Roxanne's grandparents' ranch before he continues delivering his customers to multiple destinations on the East Coast.

A tinge of insecurity plagues me when I push down the handle on the front door. Coming back here is very much unhinged and dangerous, but I truly don't believe Clover wants to kill me. He massacred over a dozen men. If he wanted me dead, wouldn't he have done it then?

There has to be more to his plan than he's letting on, and I'm hoping the three hours we spent apart tonight has reared his domineering personality enough to force the truth from him. I hardly know him, so this could be foolish for me to say, but he seems more honest when his controlling traits are on full display.

My heart patters in my chest a million miles an hour when the door pops open with a creak. My eyes instinctively shoot to the chair Clover was seated in when I arrived home from the dance club. I won't lie. I'm disappointed when I discover it's empty, but mercifully, my letdown doesn't linger for long. A lamp on the side table is switched on, and an envelope with my name scribbled across the front is balancing against the aged material.

I remind my lungs to breathe when I pace across the room to snatch up the plain white envelope. I tear it open with a vengeance, gasping when I spot what's inside. The photograph is of poor quality, but there's no doubt the woman being spooned by a large brute of a man is Roxanne. I'd recognize her anywhere. Her ruddy lips are undeniable, much less the faint scar running down her forehead. It's nowhere as visible now as it was when she walked out of our apartment with a spring in her step weeks ago, but it's still distinguishable.

A squeak pops from my mouth when a heavily accented voice advises, "If you do as asked and follow the rules, no harm will come to you or your friend." Even with his accent oddly similar to Clover's, I know it isn't him—regrettably. It's the man I aimed a gun at hours ago. "As per your new contract, you are to reside here until instructed otherwise. We have announced your resignation to your employer, and we're in the process of removing your details from scheduled events."

The stranger's dark eyes pop up from the contract he's reading when I ask, "Events? What events?"

Although that shouldn't be the first question I ask, it was the easiest of the three rolling around in my head, so I went for it. Furthermore, I was popular in school, but invitations to parties stopped landing in my Messenger app when our senior year ended, so I have no clue what he's on about.

The unnamed man appears displeased by my interruption, but he answers my question nonetheless. "Parties Winston had planned to take you to." He hands me a gilded invitation for an event a little over six weeks away. "Although Winston can no longer attend this event." He chuckles as if humored by the loss of life. "We've kept your name on the guestlist for now."

"Why?" I ask, truly confused.

This time around, he acts as if I never interrupted him. "You will be collected the night before the event at ten o'clock sharp. You are to wear this to ensure no one sees you." He hands me a cloak similar to the one I wore in Winston's house, but the inside is lined with a strange silver material. "If you don't, you will be punished."

The thumps of my heart are heard in my reply, "By whom?"

His smirk tells me everything I need to know.

It stupidly doubles the output of my heart and pulls my knees inward.

After drinking in my silent response in the correct manner, the stranger murmurs, "Sleep well, Ms. Armstead. Your nightwear has been laid out for you, and supper is on the bedside table."

He's halfway out the door when uncalled-for jealousy impedes his brisk strides. "Why didn't Clover tell me this himself? If he plans to punish me for acting out, why are you here in his place?"

I hate his smirk this time around. It guts me even more than witnessing Brayden's betrayal firsthand and angers me to the point I remember why I left Brayden with a bag of cash that won't buy him half my morals. "Tell *Nadir* he can shove his deal up his ass."

Although panicked my hotheadedness could cause trouble for Roxanne, I have no real reason to fret. Clover's picture is grainy because, as he said himself, Dimitri has Roxanne's security so tightly locked up, not even he can reach her.

"Loyalty can't be bought, Mr..."

I leave my statement open for him to fill in, which he does remarkably fast. "You can call me Galib."

His refusal to disclose his family name has me on the back foot but not enough to harness my sass. "Loyalty can't be bought, Galib, and neither the fuck can I. I thought Nadir was aware of that since he *failed to bid on me last night*." My words get faster and louder the more I talk. "Why did he do that? Why did he let that horrible man take me! Was it for her? Did he choose Andria over me?"

I hate myself for my last two questions.

I truly hate myself.

This is supposed to be about me deserving better, not unwarranted jealousy because a man I hardly know ranked me second.

Too frustrated about my absurdity to act like the responsible adult I'm meant to be, I dump the satin cape on the floor, give Galib a two-fingered salute, then pivot on my heels and storm toward the guest bedroom at the back of the ranch. "While telling Nadir what he can do with his contract, be sure to tell him to go fuck himself as well."

"I will pass on your messages, Ms. Armstead." There's a hint of cheekiness to Galib's response, but it hardly exceeds the warning in his deep timbre when he asks, "But can I also offer some advice of my own?" I freeze when he reaches the end of his question, but

I don't spin around. I don't want him to see my flushed cheeks when he murmurs, "If you wanted to spark a reaction out of *Nadir*..." he says his name with the same vicious edge I used, "... you should have sat next to the truck driver. Then perhaps he may have died for doing something more tenacious than staring at the swell of your bosoms." He waits for me to swallow in shock before he repeats, "Sleep well, Ms. Armstead. It's been a big day."

I remain frozen halfway between the living room and the guest bedroom for the next several minutes, unmoving and speaking. The only time my legs get with the program is when my brain announces I need far more than a long soak in a tub to remove the murkiness of my day.

I need alcohol—lots of it!

Roxanne's grandma wasn't wealthy, but when you're desperate to escape, even boxed wine will do.

After checking the use-by date, I pour a generous serving of Cantine Povero Dolcetto into a coffee mug, then toss it back as if it is water. It's sour, which isn't surprising considering it went out of date last month, but it pacifies the adrenaline surging through my veins from watching Clover take down a dozen men with an army of one.

It was... *god.* I don't have the words to adequately express it. He was a monster, but not the type you think of when someone says they've had a nightmare. It was too erotic for that.

Too panty-wetting.

Frustrated by my inner monologue, I guzzle down half a box of wine in under an hour. It sloshes in my empty stomach when I refill my cup before trudging to the bathroom.

While waiting for the tub to fill, I sip on the tarty wine, hopeful it will have me acting ignorant to Clover's scent lingering in the air. It's so masculine and strong, I'm shocked he sent his lackey to do his dirty work. I thought he'd be too dominant to do that.

My brittle laugh echoes in the cool morning air when I realize wine didn't improve my idiocies. As if Clover would leave Andria for me. She's so gorgeous, she comes with a two-million-dollar price tag.

While groaning about the insolent fool I've portrayed the past two days, I place my mug onto the edge of the tub, then dip my toes into the water to check the temperature. The knots of a hard day unkink in my neck when the heavily warm water forces a moan to part my lips.

When an accented voice murmurs, "Did Galib not warn you what would happen if you started without me?" I spin around so fast, the wine in my stomach rushes to my head, making me woozy.

Clover's shoulder is propped on the doorway of the bathroom. He's changed since I last saw him. His black suit is back, but the jacket has been removed, and the top three buttons of his dress shirt are undone. His hair is wet and dripping, showing he recently showered, but the veins in his arms are pumping like he's endured multiple vigorous activities for the past four hours.

Just the thought of what he could have been up to frustrates me to no end. "Why did you shower? Were you extra sweaty after an intense 'workout?'" I air quote my last word to ensure he can't mistake what I'm referencing. I'm no fool. I'm aware his expression has nothing to do with the massacre he undertook and everything to do with his recently acquired asset. His face is relaxed like his every whim has been fulfilled. "I take it Andria was worth her price tag."

His smirk is equally evil and pleased. "Stop badgering me, angel. I am not the one on trial."

He steps closer to me, forcing me to take a gigantic step back. Although he scares me, it isn't the only emotion I feel when in his presence, so I need to maintain distance to keep a rational head.

I flatten my back to the wall when he asks, "What did I say would happen if you were to run from me again?"

I settle the flutters his clipped tone caused the lower half of my stomach before replying, "I didn't run..."

He steals my words from my throat with a brutal grip on my face before he arches his big brooding body over mine. "What did I say would happen if you were to run from me again?" he repeats, his voice becoming louder.

His heated breaths batter my cheek when I murmur, "I didn't run."

He crowds in even closer, stealing more than my senses. "What did I say would happen—"

"I didn't *run!*" I interrupt, shouting. "I tried to force you to chase me. That's *completely* different. Wanting someone to chase you isn't close to running."

My cheeks burn when he coerces my eyes to his. He's holding me so roughly, my cheeks will wear the marks of his fingers for days, yet my body responds positively to his aggression instead of negatively. "You wanted me to chase you? Is that why you told Galib to tell me to go fuck myself?"

My head shakes, but my heart betrays my mind with words. "Yes." As my eyes bounce between his, words I shouldn't speak flow from my mouth. "Then... when you were with her... I wanted you to chase me *then*. But you didn't. You stayed with her." Nothing but angst is heard in my tone when I ask, "Why did you bid on her, Clover? Was it to save me?"

The last bit of hope I'm clutching sails out the window when he replies, "I bid on her because unlike you, she's obedient and does as told."

I don't know where my hand comes from. One minute, it's pinned at my side. The next minute, it's smashing across Clover's cheek. I slap him so hard it's still echoing around the confined space when I gabber out, "Did she..." It's a fight to get the words out of my mouth. "Did you..." After giving my head a stern talking to, I shout, "Did she suck your cock? Did you let her touch you like that?"

When he answers me with an arrogant smirk, I bang my fists on his chest. I get in three or four solid whacks before he snatches them up, spins me around, then uses his body to crowd me against the wall.

"Don't fucking touch me!" I scream when his hand slides from my collarbone to the apex of my pussy. "You have no right to touch me."

"Are you sure about that, angel?" he growls into my ear after cupping my pussy. "You're dripping for me."

Anger and desire wash over me when he notches two fingers inside of me. I clamp down my inner muscles, but nothing keeps him out. He is right. I am wet for him, and he's using the dampness to his advantage.

As the tip of his middle finger rubs my G-spot, his thumb finds my clit. After circling the nervy bud two times, he whispers in my ear, "Stop fighting me, and I'll let you come. Only the good girls who listen get to come."

"Did you say that to her?" I snap out before I can stop myself. "Did you let her *come...*"

My last word occurs with a quiver. I want to hate this man. I want to despise him with every sense of my being, but when he staggers back to brace his backside on the rim of the tub, then curls me over his knees to spank me, all rational thinking ceases to exist.

Pain blasts through me when he spanks three times in rapid succession, then mini explosives detonate in my core when he slaps my clit with the same intensity.

As I soar toward the clouds of orgasmic bliss, I'm not thinking about who did what and who hurt who. I'm on the Grand Express racing through climax station, uncaring about anything or anyone.

I'm so consumed by the greatest orgasm I've ever had that the sound of Clover's zipper lowering doesn't cause the slightest bit of fear to encroach me. I want him to claim me, to make me his. I've wanted it since day one. I was just too scared to admit it.

After adjusting me until I am straddled on his lap, he pulls his big cock out of his pants, then braces it against my heated pussy. When he coats himself in my wetness, I could continue to argue. But right now, my desire to remove the murderous glint in his eyes is greater than my wish to discover if I've been played for a fool again.

Brayden wasn't the first man to do me wrong. I've yet to have a single faithful boyfriend or bed companion. The call of Tinder is too loud these days, and monogamy seems to be a thing of the past.

When anger rises in me for the second time, Clover coerces my eyes to his by clutching my hair in a determined hold. My lungs labor through a choking breath when he reads the pained expression on my face as no one else ever has. "One more thought of him tonight will see your ass as red as the bullet hole I plan to burrow between his eyes for hurting you." When confusion fetters my features, he smirks a dangerous grin. "You didn't help Brayden escape, angel. You sentenced him to hell by responding *exactly* how I knew you would."

I lose the chance to seek clarification as to what he's on about when he fills me with one ardent thrust. As a scream shreds from my throat, my nails dig into the muscles hiding under his dress shirt. He's so impatient to have me, he hasn't removed an article of clothing. The fact he isn't concerned about me making a mess on his pants doubles the tingles reforming in my core. Brayden walked out of my apartment cleaner than he entered it. He even went as far as brushing his teeth in the middle of the night to ensure any remnants of our time together were removed before he went home.

Their differences see me asking a question I shouldn't express in the midst of fucking. "Did you kill the truck driver?"

"Yes," Clover responds without pause for thought. As he continues pounding into me, he raises his eyes from my over-stuffed pussy to my face. "He looked at you like Joshua did when Winston summoned him to your side. He didn't see you. He saw a piece of meat, a chunk of steak he could consume then spit out as if it was worthless."

"Joshua wasn't a monster. He was scared—"

"No!" His roar is felt all the way to his cock. "He was not scared. He was struggling to contain himself. To follow orders. He was not scared about anything *except* the desire to watch you take your last breath." It's the fight of my life not to fall into orgasmic bliss when he whispers, "He wanted to hurt you, so I hurt him first."

Incapable of arguing with the truth in his eyes, I shift my focus to a man I know without a doubt wouldn't have hurt me even if ordered. "What about the bus driver, James? Did you kill him?"

Clover's jaw twitches before he pushes out the briefest, "No." The smile inching my lips higher sags a little when he adds, "But I won't hesitate next time, angel. Anyone you put between us will be dead. Do you understand?"

When I nod, he steals my ability to continue asking questions by sealing his lips over mine. Sparks of pleasure shoot through my body when he plunges his tongue into my mouth in rhythm to the jerking movements of his hips.

While kissing me senseless, he fucks me like a wild animal. His speed is relentless, and it soon has my mind empty of a single thought that doesn't involve him.

Within seconds of his mouth leaving mine, the tub's rim no

longer holds our combined weight. Clover's grip on my ass as he repeatedly impales me is the only thing stopping me from falling to the floor.

The sheer power he displays while driving me to the brink causes my senses to overload. I moan into the steam-filled space before begging for him to take me harder. Faster. To make me come like I've never come before.

Loud, recurring poundings bounce around the bathroom for the next several minutes. He uses every muscle in his body to drive me wild. He consumes every inch of me. I'm screaming and incoherent, then the most blistering orgasm takes hold.

I free my nails from his shoulders before arching back with a moan. With Clover's grip on my nape and hip holding me steady, I float halfway between the floor and the ceiling while shuddering through an uproar too powerful for this world. The sensation is amazing, and I don't care who hears it.

Strings of words topple from my mouth. I wouldn't be able to repeat a single one if requested. I have no clue what I'm saying. I don't even realize I'm being moved until the softness of bedding caresses my back.

Clover's finger strokes my bloomed cheek, drawing my focus to his face before he lowers his eyes to an area of my body that feels instantly hollow when he withdraws his fat cock. A new type of fire sparks in my stomach when he uses my arousal glistening on his veiny shaft to glide it in and out of his circled hand, but I'm confused as to why he's offloading his cum onto my stomach and breasts instead of inside of me. What changed between now and two nights ago when we fucked without protection?

I still when a horrid thought enters my head.

"Don't," whips out of Clover's mouth before a single thought tainting my mind can be articulated.

While staring at me with warning-filled eyes, he rubs his cum into my stomach, breasts, and neck before he raises his hand to my face. A moan I can't hold back ripples my lips when he drags his thumb across my bottom lip before he dips it into my mouth.

"Suck."

I do as demanded, only stopping when the faintest beep of a horn sounds in the distance. It stiffens Clover's thighs as well as my inability to deny him hardens his cock.

After glancing out the window, he returns his eyes to mine. They're darker than they were moments ago, filled with anguish.

The taste of our combined arousals lingers in the wake of his touch when he steps back from the bed so he can tuck his now deflating cock into his pants.

After yanking up the zipper like it isn't damp, he straightens his shirt, then moves for the jacket he tossed over a tall stack of drawers. Worry that I've done something wrong stops littering my thoughts with negativity when he freezes partway out the door. He doesn't peer back at me sprawled across the mattress covered in his cum. He mutters one word, "Wait," before he leaves without so much of a backward glance.

I am too stunned to move. I'm not even sure I am breathing, then the rumble of a motorbike launches my feet into action. As I snatch up the bedding like I have the funds to have them dry-cleaned, I charge toward the window Clover pinned me to, certain that is the direction the rumble is coming from.

To begin with, the situation seems innocent enough. Clover is taking guardianship of a bike he owns. Then the back door of a dark SUV pops open, and a flurry of blonde enters the frame. Andria has also showered since I last saw her. Her wet hair is twisted off her face in a side-styled braid, but it's her makeup-free face that makes her early morning bathing routine obvious. Not an ounce of red lipstick remains on her mouth, and I was too blinded by lust to thoroughly inspect Clover for lipstick smears.

I sink away from the window when Clover glances my way to ensure his farce isn't being witnessed. Only once he's confident I'm still in bed, weighed down with sexual exhaustion, does he extend his hand in offering to Andria.

He assists her onto the back of his bike, drags her forward until her pussy heats his lower back, then shoots off down the driveway like a bat out of hell.

I race for the bathroom just as quickly, disgusted my insecurities once again have me confusing lust as love.

18

ESTELLE

I scrubbed my skin so raw in the shower, even now, two days later, it still looks sun-kissed. I've played the events of that day on repeat the past forty-eight hours. Every word spoken has been thoroughly scrutinized, yet I am still at a loss as to what happened. My mind is so muddled, I'm beginning to wonder if anything that occurred the past four days is real. I have the surveillance photograph of Roxanne pinned to the refrigerator, and Clover's navy wifebeater is in the laundry hamper, but everything still seems so surreal.

I'm so certain I am dreaming, I've tossed on gym clothes and done my makeup as if the humidity won't melt it off my face the first two miles of my run.

A run won't unscramble the confusion muddling my mind, but it will do wonders for my self-worth. Exercise has always been a go-to pick-me-up for me. It keeps my thoughts fresh while also reminding me that I'm stronger than perceived.

You can knock me down, but I guarantee I will *always* get back up.

With classic heavy metal blaring out of the twenty-dollar 'air pods' I purchased for Roxanne and me two years ago, I stuff a dated iPod down the front of my borrowed yoga pants, and then gallop down the front stairs of the porch.

It's early, but the dew point is refreshing to both my lungs and soul. Within half a dozen strides, the heaviness on my chest slackens, and the fog in my head begins to lift.

The swiftness of the benefits associated with exercise sees me pumping my legs faster. I sprint down the driveway of Roxanne's grandparents' estate as eager to pound the asphalt as I am to smash my fist into Clover's nose.

I am so hyped with adrenaline I'm tempted to test out some martial arts moves I learned last year on a brute of a man who blocks my exit with his large frame. The only reason I don't is because an angry sneer isn't backing up his campaign to slow me down. An assault rifle is.

After tugging the pods out of my ears, I raise my hands in the air, then take a step back. "W-Who are you?"

I watch a lot of crime shows, but I'm not skilled in weapons manufacturing. However, I don't need to say the gun he's holding looks oddly similar to the one the goon had when he ushered me on and off the stage during my auction.

The knowledge that Marc's associates could be looking for me is why I've remained hidden the past two days.

That, and the fact I was too embarrassed to show my face.

I got played by two men in one day.

Not even a five-dollar prostitute has odds that low.

Ignoring my question, the stranger replies, "Turn around and go back inside."

"I'm not doing anything that will get me in trouble. I am just going for a ru—"

"Turn around and go back inside," he repeats, his accent deepening. It doesn't have the same Arabic twang as Clover and Galib's. It's clearly Italian and thick enough to convince me he's a recent visitor to the states. "Now."

"You can't tell me what to do…" My words trail off when a shimmer of red captures my attention.

As I stand frozen in shock, a red dot rolls up my body and over my face before it settles on a portion of my thrusting chest that's near my heart. Even a crime-show novice would recognize the dot as the mark of a sniper. Considering the man's gun in front of me is facing the ground, it doesn't take me long to understand that there's more than one shooter.

The knowledge has me backing down in an instant. "Okay. I'll go."

As I spin around, my lungs beat my ribs like I completed a five-mile run. The snapping twigs and faint murmurings I heard the past couple of nights now make sense. These men didn't just show up. They've been here as long as me.

Confident I know the land better than Clover, I make my way back to the cabin before darting down the narrow slip between the front porch and an open barn. A back road borders this property, and hardly anyone knows about it. The locals use it when they want to enter and exit Hopeton undetected.

"Ugh!" I squeal in frustration when a man wearing a camouflage jumpsuit steps out of the bushland before I'm anywhere near the boundary fence. He shakes his head at me before nudging his head to the cabin.

"I just want to go for a damn run!" I push out with a handful more curse words. "And get supplies." By supplies, I mean the bottles of wine I had planned to pretend were weights the last two miles of my run. I have fourteen dollars in my purse and no sense that crushed grapes aren't food.

My stomps back to the cabin are loud, but they don't drown

out the man's response to my tantrum. "What type of supplies do you need?"

I whip around to face him so fast, my ponytail slaps me in the face. "Umm..." *Come on, brain, you drank boxed wine the past two days, not champagne. You shouldn't be this slow.* "Milk, bread, and butter." When he whips out his phone to jot down my order, I add items any man under sixty would be embarrassed to purchase, hopeful it will see him extending an invitation for me to go to town with him. "Flow cups, tampons, and antibacterial cream for down there..." I point to my crotch. "Also, if you could tell them the rash now has more pus-filled heads than dry ones, that would be great. I could need another ointment for that."

If there was an ounce of lust in his eyes, there isn't now. He looks at me as if I have a second head before he gestures to a man on the roof of the barn to join us.

"*How many of you are there*?" I murmur to myself when he climbs down a rickety ladder and swaggers our way. The gun he leaves mounted on a stand is facing west. The dot on my chest came from the north. That means he can't be the same sniper who lit up my chest only minutes ago.

"What's up?" goon two queries, his voice undeniably southern. I imagine him chewing on a long piece of straw when his mouth curves at one side while he reads the list goon number one jotted down. "You need *all* of this?"

"Yep," I reply without the slightest stutter. I'm not a fan of lying, but I know how to do it when it benefits me. That's why I flirted with all the old guys at The Commission. They didn't need to see my tits to stuff dollar bills into the waistband of my shimmery booty pants.

Goon two twists his fat lips. "You've got a rash?"

"Uh-huh," I answer again with utmost honesty.

He cocks a brow before gliding his eyes down my body. "Where?"

"On her—"

Goon two stuffs goon number one's words back into the back of his throat by slicing his hand through the air. "I want her to tell me." He steps closer to me." Where's your rash, Miss Pretty?"

I wet my lips, hopeful some spit will ease out another lie before pointing to my crotch. "Down there."

Hot air blows wisps of hair off my face when he whistles out, "You have a rash down there?" When I nod, he asks, "Then, why haven't you taken care of it the past couple of days?"

I spread my hand across my hips. "I have."

The pegs of his teeth blind me when he grins a full-tooth smile. "Nah, you haven't. You wash up real good morning and night in the shower, and you lather yourself in moisturizer each night before bed, but not once have I seen you touch yourself down there when you're not in the shower, and we both know ointments like that don't work if they're washed straight off."

"You've been watching me?" I bark out when the truth dawns on me. "Clover will have your head for that."

He drags his teeth over his bottom lip before he shuffles side to side. "Nah, he won't, because we both know he's far too busy plowing Ms. Andria to worry about Miss Pretty mistaking the concept of a one-night stand."

I slap him, and I slap him hard. The connection of my palm to his cheek burns my hand, but it has nothing on the fury that scorches my veins from his confirmation Clover's time is occupied doing *exactly* what I thought he's doing. Or should I say 'who' he's doing? "I hope you don't kiss your momma with that filthy mouth."

The expression on his face would have you convinced I complimented him. He loves that he forced me to retaliate just as much as I loathe the warning he gives his associate when I spin on my heels and head back to the cabin like I have a shotgun under my bed. "You've got to watch the feisty ones, Rich. They'll steal cupid's bow and stab you in the heart the instant the money pit runs dry." I glance over my shoulder when his voice changes in both pitch and accent when he adds, "Where you going, Rich?"

My skyrocketing blood pressure gets a moment of reprieve when goon number one hooks his leg over a dirt bike while saying, "To get 'Miss Pretty's supplies." His blue eyes dazzle in the morning sun when he locks them with me. "Is there anything else you need?"

When I shake my head, he smiles, kicks over the bike, pulls back the throttle, then disappears in a cloud of dust.

An hour later, he startles me when he enters the kitchen via the attached laundry. His steps are so lithe, I didn't hear him climb the squeaky back porch stairs.

He smirks when he spots the knife I weaponed up with, his smile doubling as he mutters, "Couldn't find cupid's bow?"

I give it my best shot not to return his smile. I hold out for not even three seconds. "No, so I went for the next best thing."

When he places milk, bread, butter, flow cups, and tampons onto the kitchen counter, I dump the knife into the sink. I wish I had the gall to cut him down like his associate's earlier comment did my ego. I just don't.

"They didn't have the regular tampons you girls seem to love, so I got you the slim ones. Hopefully, they won't conjure up too many memories of Kai when you use them." I'm lost to who he's talking about until he jerks his chin to the open barn attached to the cabin. "He has little-dick-man vibes all over him."

"Is that how he knows I moisturize before bed? Is he a perv?" The ranch has plenty of natural lighting, but I haven't opened a curtain in days. I wasn't just hiding my face. I was hiding from the world.

Rich places the milk into the refrigerator before pivoting around to face me. "Nah. He's scared enough to jump on cue, so there's no way he'd overstep a mark for a quick peek."

"Then how does he know my routine?"

His chest rises and falls three times before he blurts out, "Infrared. It shows where you are and what you're doing without the full invasion of surveillance cameras. That's how I know you wash your hair in warm water before you give it a final rinse with the cold."

"It stops the frizz."

"Huh?" he asks, either confused by my comment or shocked we're engaging in a conversation that has nothing to do with the fact I'm being held hostage in a home by armed goons.

"The cold water. My mom says it stops the frizz by contracting the hair follicles. I'm not sure if it's true, but..." I hold out my hair that doesn't have any flyaway hairs even with the humidity being high today.

Rich folds his arms in front of his chest, showcasing that the hairs on his arms are the same coloring as his hair—golden blond. "Your mom sounds like a smart woman." I nod, agreeing with him. If she hadn't had me at such a young age, she could have been anyone she wanted to be. "Where is she?"

I glance out the kitchen window like the drapes are open. "Still here, where she's always been." Although it feels odd confessing to a stranger, it also feels freeing. "She has a nice plot under a tree in a cemetery not too far from here. My dad splashed out on a double plot in case addiction takes him early too."

"Drugs?"

I shake my head. "Alcohol." My sigh is silent when he strays his eyes to the empty wine boxes overflowing from the bin. "That's wine. It doesn't count."

"Everything counts, Estelle."

I huff at him. "Says the guy who terrorizes women for a living."

"I don't terrorize women," he responds without flinching. "Unless they like that kind of thing."

I shouldn't laugh. His comment isn't even funny, but I can't hold it back, so I set it free. When it increases the cockiness on Rich's face, I attempt to knock his ego down a peg or two. "You're an ass."

My rile doesn't have the effect I was aiming for. "So I've been told..." he pauses, screws up his face, then shrugs, "... more than once." After hitting me with a frisky wink, he paces to the door. "Let me know if you need anything else."

His swagger falters when I mutter, "You forgot the antibacterial cream."

As he spins around to face me, he rubs his hands together. "The pharmacist suggested a more thorough inspection of your wounds." His grin is blinding. "I told him we're not that close just yet." He winks for the second time before he slips out of the door like my mouth isn't hanging open.

I'm not dim when it comes to dating. He just hit on me, not only proving you don't look as shit as you feel, but also that Kai was more on the money than I care to admit. I'm being held against my will, but I'm beginning to wonder if the order came from Clover. Surely, not even a hired goon would be stupid enough to put himself in the sights of a hitman.

I guess you don't need to fear death when you already know where you'll end up.

Hell isn't scary when you were born to live there.

Several hours later, my eyes pop up from my cell phone screen. It's charged and sitting on the kitchen windowsill that once was the perfect spot to get reception, yet not a single bar is present. It's like the equipment spying on me is hogging all the internet coverage.

"Do they have blockers up?"

Rich freezes, draws his brows together, then hesitantly shakes his head. "Not as far as I am aware."

"Then why can't I get reception?" He doesn't answer my question. I don't give him the chance. His cheeks are white, so unearthing the cause of his fear is more pressing than having the ability to aimlessly scroll my Facebook wall like anyone on my friends list would go against mafia men to free me from captivity. "Why are you so white?"

I feel the blood in my cheeks drain when he answers, "You have a visitor."

"Who?"

He signals for me to join him on the front patio. "It's best to show you."

My first instinct is to run, then I realize I won't get far with a sniper in the back, two at the front, and one on the roof. And that's just the men I've seen. There could be more.

I'm also harboring a lot of pent-up anger. So much so, if my unexpected caller is Clover, I hope he brought backup.

The determination on my face fades when the sports car gliding down the driveway headlights flash three times.

"That's your cue to go."

"Go?" I repeat while shooting my wide eyes to Rich. "I can leave?"

He laughs like I told him the difference between a golf player in and out of the bedroom. "No. The heat receptors aren't as receptive out there, so your hook-up can be done in private."

My throat becomes scratchy when I read his comment in the wrong manner. "I'm not fucking someone in the woodlands."

Rich stops me from returning inside by grabbing my elbow. "You're not fucking anyone... well, I don't think you are." Hope floods color back into his cheeks. "Are you into girls?"

Ignoring the urge to whack him in the stomach, I shake my head.

He barges me with his shoulder, exposing I could have hit him and not faced punishment for it. "Can't blame a guy for asking. I'd sign on for a year of abstinence just to see you and Roxie make out for five minutes."

He isn't the first guy to claim that, but I don't respond how I usually do. I'm too stunned by his underhanded confession that my visitor is Roxanne to pop my knee into his groin. I reach the bottom of the stairs before his playful chuckle exposes he wasn't overly truthful with his comment before sprinting down the driveway.

I can't see anything, the headlights of the sports car are hindering my vision, and I'm most likely sprinting toward my death, but my pace doesn't wane in the slightest. Roxanne has been my friend for an eternity, so if anyone can help me wade through the nonsense swarming me the past four days, it will be her.

"Estelle," I hear Roxanne breathe out a mere second before her shadow blocks the headlights' blinding rays long enough, I see the face of the man seated behind the steering wheel. It's the man from the photograph on the refrigerator. The one who spooned Roxanne like the scar running down her forehead was caused by angst instead of a head injury.

I realize that could be the case when I spot Roxanne's tear-stained face in the second leading to our bodies' brutal collision. Her scar isn't as red and angry as it once was. If she weren't fighting to release the tears welling in her eyes, it would be barely noticeable.

She loses her battle when my relieved sigh that she's safe rumbles up my chest, but mercifully, Florida's bipolar weather gives us a perfect excuse for the wetness on our cheeks. The heavy downpour soaks us head to toe in under a minute, and the winds whipping in from the coast covers the chill that rolls down my spine when Dimitri's exit is quickly followed by the cracking of twigs in the distance.

"Come on. Let's get you inside before you catch pneumonia."

As I guide a shuddering Roxanne up the stairs of her family ranch, I stray my eyes across the cabin, seeking Rich.

He's nowhere to be found.

"You know about the snipers?" Roxanne half-queries half-advises when I spin around to roll down the blind on the front bi-fold doors.

Nodding, I pivot back around. "There are also heat sensors, so I suggest turning on the shower long before getting undressed." I arch a brow when the confusion on Roxanne's face switches to fury. "What?" I peer behind me, suddenly panicked my scan of the room had me missing Rich. He isn't the largest man in the group, but he also isn't tiny, so I'll be shocked if I misplaced him.

When I fail to find what has Roxanne's attention so rapt, I shift my eyes back to her. "Do I have something on my face?"

"Your neck..." I have more understanding of the term pocket

rocket when she crosses the room at the speed of light. "What the hell happened?"

Shame burns my cheeks when she yanks back my hair to expose the grab marks Clover left when he pinned me to the wall, the bed, and when he stopped me from falling to the ground when my float into ecstasy had me stupidly believing I could fly.

I fix my hair back into place while murmuring, "It's nothing. I fell asleep on the couch. The armrest dug in. It will go away in a day or two."

She doesn't buy my lie for even a second. "That isn't nothing, Estelle." As she paces out her frustration, she reminds me that Clover's introduction into my life was because he was paid to hurt me. "He said he only sent him to scare you. That he ordered him not to touch you." She freezes, cranks her head my way, then thrusts her hand at my neck. "How is that not touching you!" Anger rises in her face as she balls her fists. "Fuck him and his stupid ideas. I'm not playing his mind games anymore."

"Roxanne..." I try to stop her storm out, but her shortness has nothing on her determination when she's riled up. She is out the door in under a second, and even quicker than that, a red dot highlights her chest.

"What the fuck?" she murmurs in shock, the mark of a sniper even more undeniable since it's been done in the darkness of a cloudy night. "They're here to protect us, to ensure Dimitri doesn't have to hand over a dime." I'm lost as to what she's referencing. It's for the best. I don't need words to answer her next question. I merely need to shake my head. "Aren't they?"

19

ESTELLE

Two weeks later...

"This is bullshit. I can't believe he's doing this." Roxanne slams the refrigerator door shut, her angst at an all-time high since the food in the refrigerator is as outdated as the rest of her family home. "He let that imbecile hurt you to force me to eat, then put an eye-watering amount of capital on the line to ensure my safety, yet here we are, growing penicillin in a fridge that's older than me!"

Her whine when she flops onto a chair around the two-seater dinette hurts my heart as much as the giggle that leaves her mouth. Her moods have been as teetering as a rollercoaster the past couple of days.

When she spots my concerned watch, she murmurs, "There's something wrong with me. How can't there be? One minute, I'm laughing. The next minute, I am crying. I'm all over the fucking shop."

"There's nothing wrong with you. You're just emotional," I reply, pacing closer to her. "And that's okay. You went through quite the ordeal. If it were me, I would have been in a loonie hospital by now."

We've talked a lot the past two weeks, but since my four days in hell weren't close to the inferno Roxanne was forced to walk through the past couple of weeks, I haven't mentioned my exchanges with Clover after I fled our apartment or how I was sold to a man who misunderstood true D/s relationships. My father is alive, and although my mother has passed, her death didn't stain anyone's hands but her own. I wasn't forced to hold a gun to her head in the room where my father laid bludgeoned.

My parents raised me the best they could, but even if they had disrespected me the way Roxanne's parents did her, I still would have struggled to endure what she did the day an ultimatum from Dimitri saw Roxanne's father take his own life.

Confident food will always be the best cure for a broken heart, I ask, "Would you like me to cook you something? We've got left-over bananas from the bunch Rich bought last week and plenty of flour. Even without maple syrup, banana pancakes *always* hit the spot."

For the first time in weeks, something more than tears form in Roxanne's eyes. "Would you mind? I'm starving."

"I wouldn't have asked if I did." After bumping her with my hip, I gather up the ingredients required, groaning when I realize I'm missing one vital component. "We're out of eggs. I forgot we used them in the fried rice last night."

As my mind flicks through a ton of recipes in my head, seeking what I can use as an alternative for eggs, Roxanne suggests, "Could you ask Rich to get us some eggs? He seems *real* eager to help you."

"Don't go there, Roxanne." Her waggling brows are my fault. I told her I ended things with Brayden two weeks before the 'Clover' incident because he wasn't giving me what I needed. With the channels on the outdated television sporadic, and our cell service basically non-existent, she's reverted to her old favorable form of entertainment. She is trying to play matchmaker. "And in case you've forgotten, he's one of the men holding us hostage. That means he isn't a good guy, Roxie."

"Eh." She shrugs. "He brought you chocolates when you had your period last week. To me, that makes him a good guy."

I toss the bag of flour at her head, laughing when it makes her hair more Snow White blonde than golden. "If you hadn't spent weeks surrounded by mafia men, I doubt you'd say that." When guilt creeps into my veins about her pensive look, I pull my hair into a messy bun. "All right. I'll let you toss me to the wolves. Who wants steak for dinner?"

As Roxanne's eyes pop out of her head, she holds her hand in the air. "Me! Me! Me!"

Her girly squeal is still ringing in my ears when I throw on my big girl panties—figuratively—then dart through the laundry room attached to the kitchen. I race down the steps of the back porch like my heart isn't racing a million miles an hour, my speed only slowing when Kai tells me to get my ass inside.

When I flip him the bird, the caution in his tone grows. "I won't tell you again, Miss Pretty. Get your ass inside."

"I want to talk to Rich, and from the whisperings I've heard in the woodlands the past two weeks, you're not the boss of him." I want to add, *or me*, but Clover stole more than my sanity when he disappeared on his bike with a pretty blonde draped over his back. He took my sass right along with him.

I hear Kai adjust the scope on his assault rifle when Rich pops out of the bushes. With his eyes locked on me, he signals for Kai to stand down before asking, "What's up?"

His friendly smile makes the cool morning not so cold. "Our supplies are getting low, so I was wondering if you could pick us up a couple of things."

My voice is barely a whisper, but Kai still hears me. He tells Rich I'm playing him for a fool before warning him that messing with me will have his dick on a stake by the end of the week.

I brush off his comment with a bit of wit. "Not according to you, already dickless Kai. Remember... he's too busy plowing Ms. Andria to worry about little ol' me mistaking the conditions of a one-night stand." I narrow my eyes when he howls like a wolf before shifting my focus back to Rich. "Can you help us out? There will be a big chunk of steak with your name on it if you can."

He takes a moment to drink in my best pleading expression before he jerks up his chin. I'm so excited weeks of captivity hasn't dampened my ability to make men weak at the knees, I squeal before curling my arms around his neck to hug him tight. "Thank you so much. We truly appreciate your help."

Rich's cheeks are the color of beets when I pull back. It doubles the strange flow of electricity crackling between us, but I act ignorant when he yanks his phone out of his pocket and hands it to me. "Jot down everything you need in the Notes app. I'll swing by the market after my shift and get what you need. I should be back right around dinner time."

"Thank you, Rich. That will be perfect."

After punching in an array of products into his phone, I hand it back to him, smile like my dinner invitation is about more than fixing Roxanne's heart, then spin on my heels and skip back inside.

"I told you he had the hots for you," Roxanne murmurs when I flatten my back on the door that separates the laundry room from the kitchen to breathe through the uncontrollable nerves fluttering in my stomach. My endeavors are pointless when Roxanne adds on, "And what was this I heard about a one-night stand?"

As my pupils dilate to the size of saucers, I swallow to relieve my suddenly dry throat while also racking my brain for a lie that isn't necessarily a lie.

20

CLOVER

My eyes stray from a shady stack of evidence when Galib enters my home office. Corruption like this is why men on both sides of the evidence hire me. They can't trust me any more than the law, but I sure as fuck won't run off with their money before getting the job done. Some assignments take less than an hour to complete while others can take days. The one I'm currently overseeing could stretch into months if I'm not careful. But no matter the length of time, at the end of the assignment, the target will be dead, and I'll be well compensated for both my time and skill set.

When Galib signals that he'd like to speak to me in private, I raise my finger in the air, requesting a minute. This negotiation sitting in front is in the two-million-dollar range. For that amount, I'd usually have the recently drafted contract signed before the ink dries, but with current arrangements stretching my time thin, I need to be more vigilant with upcoming projects.

If it were a standard hit, I'd slot it into my calendar like an afternoon fuck session.

Since it isn't, I advise my procurer that I need more time to consider a decision.

"Make one now, or I'll take my business elsewhere." The pixelated image hiding my contact's face like he's a key witness for an imperative CIA case flickers in rhythm to the voice modifier he's using to alter his tone.

I lean in close to the camera in my computer, ensuring he can see the absolute honesty in my eyes when I reply, "That's your choice to make, Mr. McGee, but I can assure you not only will my competitors refuse your tender upon discovering my organization has blacklisted you, but they may also accept the bounty I intend to put on your head if you don't change your tone this very instant."

No amount of voice manipulation can soften the panicked gasps of a man whose life is now hanging by a thread. Our proposal didn't commence with the exchange of salutations. I know who he is because I'm not a man who works with cowards. If you want to hide your identity from me, I am not the hired hitman you're seeking.

"I-I can give you until the end of the week."

I smirk at his assumption he thinks he's in charge before announcing, "You'll have an answer by the end of the month. If you move before then, the next broadcast you'll air will be your final breath when I hang you from the Baccarat chandelier behind your left shoulder with your intestines hanging out of your belly button. They're not made to withstand more than one hundred and forty pounds, but I'm sure the industrial wiring you had installed in your basement last month will do the trick."

I take a moment to drink in his threatening swallow when he realizes I know more about him than his username for the dark web before disconnecting our connection. It has been a long, tedious couple of weeks that I see growing wearier when Galib answers the silent question beaming out of me with a brisk shake of his head. "Nothing yet. I'm sure it won't be too much longer."

When my groan of frustration comes out as a vicious roar, I'm reminded that Andria is kneeling at my side with her head bowed and her hands resting on her thighs. She didn't squeak in fear—she's far too obedient to ever do such a thing—but the quickening of her breaths caused the faintest rustle to her blonde locks.

Her hair is a couple of shades lighter than Estelle's, but the length and volume are the same. If I excluded her lack of rebellion, I could pretend Estelle is kneeling before me instead of a submissive trained to do *everything* her master requests. Nothing is off-limits with Andria. She'd rather obey than disappoint. Her submissiveness is why I purchased her.

As I pet Andria's head in recognition of her continued obedience, I shift my focus back to Galib, suddenly aware he interrupted me, not the other way around. "What is it?"

Conscious I am rarely of sound mind when the itch to kill is thrumming through my veins, he places a single surveillance image onto my desk, then takes a step back. A squeak ripples through Andria's lips when my fists ball from taking in an image so clear, you'd have no idea it was captured from space. Estelle's arms are curled around a man with golden blond hair and a massive fucking target on his back.

Andria's chin sinks deeper when I release her hair from my rueful grip so I can take in the photograph with more diligence. It appears innocent enough until I realize the man Estelle is embracing has his eyes closed, and his hands are a mere inch from her ass. He isn't returning her embrace, he's imagining it occurring again and again and again, with less clothing each time.

Not on my fucking watch.

"Who is he?" The sternness of my words return Andria's breaths from frightened to excited. She makes the ideal sub because she isn't scared of being pushed to the brink. Estelle is the same. When she stops worrying about who's giving orders, she follows commands well, but since her brattiness hardens my cock more than her submissive qualities, I don't push her as hard as Andria's previous masters obviously have.

The fight for control can be as gratifying as having it handed over willingly.

When Galib sets down a copy of a driver's license for a Richie Gold along with a second set of photographs, I stand to my feet.

My blood is so hot with vengeance, I won't charge Estelle for Richie's death.

I'll do it for fun, and I'll smile while doing it.

"Come, little one," I say with a grunt while making my way to the door.

Like the good sub she is, Andria falls into step behind me without a peep seeping from her lips. Let's see how long she remains silent when people believe she's the cause of a public execution.

21

ESTELLE

Several hours later, when the creak of a door opening sounds into the living room, Roxanne's eyes pop up from a box of hair dye we found in the bathroom cabinet of my room. Unlike the boxes of wine I went through in an embarrassingly fast two days and almost all the food in the pantry, there's no expiration date for hair dye.

For the first time in two hours, a grin tugs at my lips when the recollection of what our guest is bringing for dinner shoots an excited glint through Roxanne's eyes. She's been a little reserved since I admitted I've had multiple interactions with Clover after Dimitri ordered him to our apartment.

If I know her as well as I think I do, she understandably mistook the quivering of my words during story time. I've never shown an interest in a dominant personality before, so it's understandable she reached that decision. I could have corrected her somewhat inaccurate philosophy, but since I need to unmuddle my confusion to do that, I haven't.

I will, just not until I have the answers I'm seeking.

When the flare brightening Roxanne's eyes dampens, I swing my eyes in the direction she's facing. Our guest isn't who we're anticipating. It's a grumpy, meaner version of Rich, and although he's arrived with supplies, there's no way the slim bag he's holding is plumped out with generous cuts of steak.

"Where's Rich?" I ask, my tone equally pissed and worried.

Kai mumbles something under his breath while marching across the room to dump a bag of groceries onto the counter like his aggression won't ruin the perishable items inside. The anger making his face as unappealing as his attitude amplifies when he drinks in the food lining the pantry shelves. "I fucking told him your shit would lead him to trouble," he murmurs with a sneer.

"Hardly any of that food is in date," I reply, aware I shouldn't play his games but too over his attitude to care. I'm not a piece of shit, so why am I letting him treat me as if I am. "It was purchased by Roxanne's grandmother before she passed away. That was over a year ago."

He scoffs at me before hitting me with a nasty sneer. It snaps my last nerve. After leaping out of my chair, I cross the warped wood floors at the speed of a bullet. I don't care that he ruined food he didn't pay for. I'm pissed as fuck he thinks he has the right to disrespect me. I haven't spoken to my father in over a year because he called Roxanne a whore after she spent a couple of hours in lockup for a crime she didn't commit, so I'm not going to let some punk-ass treat me as if I'm worthless.

"What's your issue? I didn't do a single thing to you, yet you hated me on sight." I hit him where it hurts when I ask, "Do I look like her?"

"Like who?" he barks out, falling straight into my trap.

I fan a hand across my cocked hip. "The woman who knew she

deserved better than the shitty life you attempted to hand her." He scoffs again, but I'm not buying his act. He's a woeful liar just like Brayden. "Perhaps if you treated her with a little bit of respect, she wouldn't have left you."

"If you touch her, it will be the last thing you *ever* do," Roxanne warns when Kai steps up to me like he'd give anything to slap the sass off my face.

Her caution dampens the murderous gleam in his eyes, but it doesn't alter the angst in his words when he says, "That's sweet coming from the girl who's collecting murders like little black dresses." His reply stumps me until he leans in close and whispers, "Do you want to know where Rich is..." Although he isn't technically asking a question, he's pausing for dramatics, so I nod. "He's in a ditch, where your boyfriend put him because you couldn't keep your hands to yourself." As the blood drains from my face, he murmurs, "I gave him a week. They didn't even give him to the end of the day. So, congratulations, Miss Pretty, you can add another victim to your ever-growing tally."

My chin quivers as his confession rings on repeat in my ears.

Rich is dead.

My actions killed him.

When Kai uses my shocked silence to make an unscathed getaway, I slide down the wall of the living room, then cradle my throbbing skull in my hands. My head is swirling with so many emotions, I don't hear a word Roxanne speaks when she endeavors to pull me out of the debilitating panic attack Kai's confession forced on me.

"I invited him to dinner," I blubber through the painful sobs wreaking havoc with my body. "And gave him an innocent hug to thank him for his help. That shouldn't have gotten him killed. He didn't deserve to die for that."

As I rock through the pain tearing me in two, Roxanne pulls

my soaked face into her chest, then whispers soothing words in my ear. She promises me that there will be more to Rich's death than a dinner invitation, and that it is in no way my fault, having no clue that Clover killed a man because he did something as simple as look at my breasts through a shirt.

22

———

ESTELLE

Two weeks later...

The past two weeks passed in a blur. Rich's death hit me harder than I thought possible. I mourned a man I hardly knew more than I grieved the death of my mother. It isn't that I was in love with Rich or hopeful he was the missing piece I've been seeking since I was sixteen, it's the guilt I can't let go of. He was killed because I put my unrequired needs before his safety. It was stupid of me to do, and I've learned from my mistake.

Even now, weeks after we ran out of milk, neither Roxanne nor I have requested supplies from the men holding us captive. The meals we prepare with the almost expired food in the pantry are bland and lacking nutrients, but it could be worse.

We could be dead like Rich.

In a way, his punishment makes sense. His murder scared Roxanne and me enough we haven't been tempted not to toe the line the past two weeks.

We've steered well clear of it.

I want to say that makes us smart, but I feel too spineless to believe that. Rapunzel wasn't locked away to keep her safe, she was abused and manipulated by the ugly old witch. Kind of like how Roxanne is being treated by Dimitri.

And if I were honest, how Clover is treating me.

I would stop it from occurring if I had any clue how to do that without more bloodshed. Since I don't, I continue staring at the moonless sky out of a window that doesn't have bars but very much feels like it does.

A rare grin tugs at my lips when Roxanne murmurs, "If you're summoning the berries to your mouth with your mythical powers, let me assure you, they're more potent than a bad boy and one hundred percent capable of killing you." She bumps me with her hip before she joins me by the window. "I'll ask Kai to grab us some things tomorrow. I doubt he'll be happy about my request, but he might do it since it came from me."

Hearing her underhanded confirmation that Kai has an issue with me, I say, "I don't know what that guy's problem is. He's hated me from the get-go."

I stray my eyes to Roxanne's when she murmurs, "You intimidate him. Men don't like when women do that." She sighs. "Why do you think we're stuck here?"

"Because your boyfriend is a controlling misogynist who also happens to have a really nice cock."

Her hip bump this time around nearly sails me across the room. She's mindful I'm playing but also aware my comment is true. My incarceration has nothing to do with ensuring I'm not sold to another maniac who grossly neglected the terms associated with an exchange of power in D/s relationships and everything to do with Roxanne's new beau not wanting her to be lonely when he locked her in a dungeon so his enemies can't find her.

If I weren't so devastated about Clover's lack of contact over the past four weeks, I would commend Dimitri on his efforts to keep Roxanne safe. No man I know would put thirty-million dollars on the line to protect a woman they don't care about. I couldn't even get a measly four-hundred thousand from Brayden.

Alas, I guess that's what you get when you want to be an independent woman. Perhaps if I weren't such a stickler for paying my half when he first started sniffing around, he wouldn't have been so stingy when I needed him the most.

I pause, grinding my back molars when Roxanne murmurs, "I thought the battery in your car went dead weeks ago?"

"It did." I peer at the patch of dirt where my car sat untouched the past month, gasping when nothing but wilted weeds remain in its wake. "Where the hell did my car go?"

Roxanne doesn't answer me with words. She points to the slice of independence I saved my butt off for senior year that's barely visible in a barn at the back of the property. "Do you think they drove it there or pushed it?"

I shrug, truly unsure. Cars come and go all the time, but since it's usually the men dotted throughout the landscape arriving or leaving from a shift, I never paid them much attention. Shift changes occur like clockwork two times a day. I catch the occasional one, like the one occurring now, but other than that, I steer clear of the windows.

I don't tease myself by gazing outside like Roxanne has the past four weeks. She was with Dimitri long enough to sense his presence. I knew Clover for two days. If that isn't a flashing warning about future disappointment, I don't know what is.

"There's a way we can find out." I eyeball Roxanne with suspicion when she snatches her nanna's bowling bag from the bottom of the closet, then I smile like a loon when she says, "Do you remember how we snuck out our senior year?" When I nod, she adds, "We could do the same now."

I wish her comment were true, but unfortunately, it isn't. "We can't. They have heat sensors on us." I choke on my last word when she pulls her nanna's canister of homemade deep heat out of her bowling bag. Before she passed, her nanna was booked in for two knee reconstructions. With her pain higher than the medication her doctor prescribed, she got inventive. Her deep heat felt like a soldering iron was burning through my skin when she rubbed it on an old sports injury I got while playing softball in high school.

"All we need to do to cheat the infrared is mimic the heat of our bodies." After checking that the guards are still mingling in the driveway, Roxanne digs one of the bowling balls out of the bag, gloves up like she's about to give someone's rectum an inspection, then lathers one side of the weighted ball with the deep heat.

"We're insane even considering this." Although I'm cautioning Roxanne about the trouble we're racing toward, I commence stuffing the winter clothing her grandma ensured she was never without even with us living in Florida under the bedding.

A chuckle rumbles in my chest when Roxanne says, "I hope the heat sensors don't take in symmetry. We're all boobs and no legs."

I *pfft* her. "They'll be too busy wondering what we're doing in the same bed to worry about missing bits from our waists down." She slaps me in the face with a pillow when I murmur, "They'll probably stroke one out."

We stop giggling like schoolgirls when the male voices in the distance grow louder. The shift change is over, and the men holding us hostage are heading back to their stations.

"We're going to get in so much trouble for this," I whisper as I follow Roxanne's sprint for the back door.

The fact the punishment for our disobedience can only be handed to Roxanne and me doubles the length of my strides. We make it to my car in under ten seconds, breathless and red-faced but smiling like we're outrunning her grandfather chasing us down with a waggling shoe in his hand instead of an assault rifle.

"Say a prayer."

I wait for Roxanne's teeth to graze her bottom lip with anticipation before stuffing my key into the ignition and turning it over. My eyes bulge when the engine roars to life after the first twist. I tested the battery over half a dozen times before Roxanne arrived at the ranch. It was so flat, the ignition didn't even make the clicking noise it did when we got stranded at the lake.

With my heart in my throat and my eyes locked on a stream of idling SUVs that are concealing the mosquito buzz noises of my engine, I place the transmission into drive, then slowly pull away from the property we've been held hostage at the past four weeks.

"Holy shit," Roxanne murmurs when we make it onto the back street without a single red dot highlighting our bodies. "We did it. It actually worked."

I smile as large as she does until we reach a T-intersection at the end of the street. Although our first thoughts should be to get as far away from the ranch as possible, we both know that isn't feasible. We literally have nowhere else to go. We were on the verge of being evicted before we stopped paying rent, my father would need to beg Roxanne for forgiveness before I'd ever consider asking him for help, and I don't see Mr. Monroe being overly obliging to a request for an advance since I haven't arrived for a shift in over four weeks.

After switching on my headlights so Roxanne can see the minimal choices in front of us, I place my life in her hands by asking, "Which way?"

Her green eyes stray to mine. They're wide and full of apprehension. "I have no clue. I didn't think that far ahead." After a couple of seconds of deliberation, she murmurs, "We could get some food so we don't have to ask Kai for help." She stops me from signaling right before murmuring, "Do you have any cash? If we use a card, we will be tracked."

"Umm..." I scrummage through my handbag that's so rarely used, dust conceals its fake designer lining. "I have seventeen dollars, a handful of buttons, and a peanut M&M."

"Estelle," Roxanne pushes out with a groan when I shove the M&M into my mouth and crunch through it with my teeth. "That could be laced with germs."

I purse my lips and shrug. "Then I guess it's lucky we have penicillin growing in the fridge, isn't it?" My eyes bulge for the second time when remembering the last time I got scowled at for eating candy left in the bottom of my bag. "Check the glove compartment. Brayden left his watch in there when we went skinny dipping in the lake." The memory of our time together shouldn't warm my heart, but for some stupid reason, it does. Brayden was an ass, but there were a handful of times he made me feel like I was worth something.

"Bingo!" Roxanne shouts while dangling Brayden's Rolex in the air.

I signal right. "Pawnshop, it is!"

When we enter a pawnshop in the middle of Hopeton, we represent shady drug dealers to a T. The hoods on our sweaters are up, and our chins are balancing on our chests. If that isn't bad enough, I hand the pawnbroker a watch with 'for my darling son' engraved on the back.

"Hock or sell?" he asks after checking the watch for a serial number.

"Sell," Roxanne answers at the same time I say, "Hock."

I twist to face Roxanne before murmuring, "I don't want Karma biting my ass." *Clover's teeth hurt enough. I don't want to consider how painful Karma's gnaw will be.*

She peers at me like she heard my inner monologue before explaining her apprehension. "If we hock it, he'll need details for the loan. If we sell—"

"We can take the cash and run." I groan, knowing what needs to be done but hating that it's our only option.

After shifting my focus back to the pawnbroker, I mutter, "Sell, please."

Guilt about the bad deed I'm doing flies out the window when the broker lowballs me with a ridiculous offer. "Twenty dollars."

"*Twenty dollars*?" I choke out. "That's a three-thousand-dollar watch!"

He peers past my shoulder to ensure we're alone before replying, "That I won't be able to sell here since it doesn't belong to you."

Although he has a point, his offer is still way too low to accept. "We need more than twenty dollars. That won't even get us half a bag of groceries."

My stomach gurgles more than my words when Roxanne tugs off the Celtic ring she inherited when her grandma passed and places it onto the glass separating us from another man attempting to railroad us. "How much for this?"

"No, Roxanne. I can't let you sell it. You love that ring."

She acts tough, but I hear the quiver in her words when she whispers, "We need food, and I don't know about you, but I really don't want to ask Dimitri's men for help." Her eyes float over the invisible bruises only she can see on my neck before she murmurs,

"Look what happened the last time he did that." My heart pains when she pushes her ring to the pawnbroker's side of the counter. "How much?"

"To pawn. We're not selling it." I don't care if I have to hand over identification. Roxanne's name is on every database in the country. No one is looking for me—not even the man who demanded me to wait for him.

I have more understanding about Clover's line of work when the pawnbroker insults us for the second time in under a minute. "I'll give you thirty for both. Twenty for the watch. Ten dollars for the ring." He bounces his eyes between us, grinning when he spots our shocked expressions. Roxanne's ring was estimated to be worth over seven hundred dollars in the asset summary statement attached to her nanna's will, so his excuse that he's lowballing us for selling stolen merchandise is full of shit. He's just being an asshole. "Take it or leave it."

I'm about to knock his attitude back to next week, but before I can, Roxanne says, "We'll take it."

"Roxie..." Anything I'm planning to say traps in my throat when she snatches up the three crumbled ten-dollar bills the pawnbroker dumps on our side of the glass cabinet, stuffs them into the pocket of her sweater, then hightails it outside.

After filling in the paperwork to ensure I can get her ring back at the next available opportunity, I chase after her. "Even hocked, your ring is worth way more than ten dollars," I gabber out once I join her on the sidewalk. "It's sentimental value alone makes it priceless."

"You wouldn't say that if you knew how it came into my custody."

Her disheartened tone pulls my brows together in confusion. "Anything in your nanna's possession when she passed went to you. Right?"

I feel about the size of an ant when Roxanne says with a sniffle, "That's right. Including the ring my mother lost when she forced her car off the road."

"What?" I'm too shocked to say more than that. Roxanne's mother has always been a little unhinged, but surely, I'm mistaking what she's trying to say.

Roxanne waves her hand at the pawnshop on our right. "Smith couldn't find any video proof, but my mother's ring proves she was in the car with my nanna when she crashed." I wrap her up in a firm hug when a sob rips from her throat. It causes an avalanche of questions to spill from her mouth that I don't have an answer for almost all of them. "If she was in the car with her, why was she found alone, Estelle? Why wasn't anyone with her when she died? Why did she have to die alone like no one loved her?"

"I don't know," I whisper, unable to find the words to explain the cruelness that lives deep inside some people. That's one of the reasons I wanted to become a crime scene investigator, so I could put away the actual bad guys. "I wish I could give you answers, but I truly don't know what they are."

With her confession putting a dampener on our newfound freedom, I load her into the passenger seat of my car, use some of the thirty dollars to buy eggs, milk, bread, and butter from a corner store, then return to the ranch, where we sit half a mile up, waiting for the next shift change to occur so we can sneak back into our mandatory yet highly unjustified confinement.

23

ESTELLE

Two weeks later…

In the two weeks following our initial escape, Roxanne and I worked through her grief about her mother's betrayal with hours of conversations and the occasional trip or two outside the bland walls of her grandparents' ranch.

Two times, we went to the local grocer to replace the basic necessities we once took for granted. The rest of the time, we pretended we weren't birds trapped in a windowless box. We stargazed at Bronte's Peak, made sand angels in the crystal white beach below, and one day, I gave Roxanne a tour of Erkinsvale like she hadn't lived a majority of her life there.

We even detoured past my father's house to see if he was home. He wasn't, but his pretty new wife was. She yelled at me to stay away like I was the cause of his drinking problem before she followed my car down the road with a broom in her hand.

The men who watch us morning, noon, and night are either

oblivious to our adventures outside these walls or ordered not to respond. My intuition points to the former, but my head tells me not to be so stupid.

The longer they watch us, the more carefree they're becoming. Kai didn't even knock the other day when he hand-delivered the mail Erkinsvale's bipolar weather almost ruined. He dumped it on the entryway table, grunted when he thought I was devouring peanut butter by the spoonful when in reality, I was scrounging up leftovers so I could add flavor to the slice of toast Roxanne and I were about to share for breakfast, then stormed out.

His rudeness, along with Clover's absence the past six weeks, had me itching to devise a better way to piss him off, so you can imagine how bad the desire became when his delivery not only announced we had been evicted from our apartment as suspected, but also that our friend Claudia's final appeal for the custody of her son had been denied.

Claudia and Roxanne met when they were hospitalized together in the criminal wing of Erkinsvale Private Hospital. Roxanne was under arrest for the suspected murder of her ex-boyfriend, Eddie Cordova. She 'allegedly' tortured him for hours on end *after* he ran her over with his car—*twice!*

As you can imagine, it only took a first-year defense attorney to have those charges squashed, but regretfully, Claudia wasn't as lucky as Roxanne. Even with witnesses coming forward to say her abusive piece-of-shit of a husband had his hand on the steering wheel in the lead up to their crash, she was sentenced to three years in jail. That already ridiculous verdict was plumped out to seven when her right to appeal landed her before a judge known for harsher sentences.

Claudia was seven months pregnant when she was sentenced to Wallens Ridge State Penitentiary. She gave birth to her son six weeks later in a cold and unsterile room, and she hasn't laid eyes on him ever since.

Although there isn't much Roxanne and I can do to help her, sometimes all a woman needs is a shoulder to lean on and an ear to listen. Roxanne and I are that crutch for Claudia. Before we were forced into our own unfair incarceration, we visited her every month, encouraged her multiple endeavors to win custody of her son, and smuggled in Snickers candy bars like they were narcotics. It wasn't much, but it kept Claudia's hopes up—hopes that were dashed when we didn't arrive for our monthly visit last month.

Claudia's letter was full of understanding. She said she looked forward to living vicariously through us when we share stories about what we've been up to the past couple of weeks, but there was a lot of sadness hidden amongst her words as well. Her final request to have her son housed with her was denied by the warden, and all hopes were lost about presenting new evidence in her case. She's innocent yet incarcerated at the worst prison this side of the hemisphere.

The unfairness of both her imprisonment and ours saw Roxanne and me plotting a plan I'm confident will ruin us, but I'm too tired to care. If Dimitri cares for Roxanne as I suspect, it's time for him to stop hiding his feelings by locking her away. If he wants to protect her, he needs to man up and do it himself.

"Shit! We're out of the good stuff." Roxanne's eyes pop up from the bowling bag to me when I toss the empty deep heat canister on the mattress. After flopping onto the lumpy bedding, I groan. "I knew there was a reason I was hoarding our last ten dollars." I roll over to peer at her with sorrow-filled eyes. "I'm sorry. I stuffed up."

"It isn't your fault. I'm the one who got us stuck here." Before I can correct her, she cocks her hip, then arches a brow. "Actually, this isn't my fault. *None* of this is my fault. It's *his*."

She hasn't referred to Dimitri by name for the past two weeks.

She isn't just angry our sneak outs didn't poke the green monster on his shoulders. She's also as mad as hell she hasn't detected his presence at the front of the property the past two weeks.

Clover must have given him some pointers on how to stay discreet.

I want to tell Roxanne she deserves better than a man she has to goad to interact with her, but then I realize I'm no better than her. Clover tried to kill me, and he murdered men directly in front of me, but without fail, just before I fall asleep, his dark and tormented eyes invade my thoughts every single night. They spellbind me and have me recalling how much I miss him, so I can only imagine how bad it is for Roxanne, considering she was in Dimitri's realm far longer than I was in Clover's.

I force my stupidity to the back of my mind when Roxanne says, "You know what? If Claudia weren't counting on us, I'd drive to Dimitri's home right now to give him a piece of my mind. *He* freed me *after* clipping my wings. That's crap! I'm not putting up with his shit anymore. *He* can't treat me like this..." She pauses to get her emotions in check before swinging her watering eyes to mine. "Fill up the tub. I don't care if I have to run a gauntlet, we're going to see Claudia."

After giving her my best get-him-girl look, I race into the bathroom to fill the tub with scalding hot water. When the water reaches the halfway mark, Roxanne hooks the bowling balls into the tub like they're weightless. I get an idea of her plan when she rotates the ball that floats to ensure both sides reach the same level of hotness.

"For this to work, we'll need to be quick. They won't stay warm for long once we remove them from the tub."

When Roxanne nods, agreeing with me, I collect everything we need for a five-hour drive before peering out the window to check the shift change is still occurring. "Not yet," I murmur to

Roxanne when she risks being burned to remove the sunken ball from the tub. "They're talking to a dude I haven't seen before."

I scoot over so Roxanne can peer out the slim window when she joins me near the foggy glass. "That's Smith. What's he doing here?"

Since she seems to be summarizing more than asking a question, instead of answering her, I ask one of my own. "Do you think he's here to beef up security?"

We were pretty blasé with our last escape.

We didn't even stuff our beds with fake bodies.

Roxanne's headshake lasts for barely a nanosecond. Her wavering moods the past couple of weeks aren't responsible for her backpedal. It's the group of men piling out of Smith's rusty white van.

Confident Dimitri is finally responding as Roxanne has hoped, I shove her jacket into her chest, then snatch up my car keys. "We need to leave before we lose the chance."

With the bowling balls left bobbing in the bathtub and my heart rate soaring to a record high, I follow Roxanne out the back door. We only just clear the first barn when gravel being stomped under boots sounds through our ears. Mercifully, the crunching is spaced far enough apart, I'm positive we're not being chased. Although I don't see that still being the case when Kai climbs his ladder.

In less than a second, he's halfway up the brittle wood, his climb unhindered by his third double shift this week. I don't know his schedule because I watch him as closely as he watches me, but because he announces his arrival each shift like he's a king arriving for his coronation. He's so up himself, I look forward to hearing him talk his way out of how we escaped under his watch. Even if the bowling ball trick had worked, we would never be back in time for the next shift change. Our sneak out tonight *will* be busted, and I'm more excited by the prospect than scared.

Halfway across the overgrown land, Roxanne suddenly stops running. As her nose screws up, she throws a hand over her mouth. Her cheeks are white, and her top lip is housing a sweat mustache.

"What's the matter?"

Her stomach makes a peculiar noise when she murmurs, "I don't feel very good." I step back when she burps. It's vomit-free. However, it doesn't smell that way. "I told you eggs aren't meant to smell like that."

"The eggs were fine. I ate them, and I'm not sick." My last word comes out with a quiver when a familiar voice breaks through the silence surrounding us. Kai is ensuring we're aware he's doing a double shift by rooster calling from his station on the barn roof. He usually does the same thing every morning when the clock strikes six. "You have five seconds to pick between staying or going, Roxie." The first thing Kai does after scaring the living daylights out of us is log into the infrared cameras monitoring our every move. "Five... four... three..."

"We're going." She gags so violently, even my stomach feels swishy before she groans out, "I just need a minute."

"We don't have a minute, Roxie. We don't even have thirty seconds."

With her index finger held in the air, she burps for the second time, and just like magic, it fixes everything. As quickly as her nausea arrived, it vanishes, and the natural coloring of her cheeks return.

"You good?" I ask, highly suspicious about her quick recovery.

She swishes her tongue around her mouth before pursing her lips. "Yeah. I feel great."

I don't know whether to laugh or groan about her bubbly

response. Her moods have been a wild ride the past few weeks, so I do both while sprinting for my car like its gas tank isn't as empty as our stomachs.

"We will detour to Ravenshoe for gas. There aren't as many homeless people there so they may be more obliging to beggars." It shames me to admit we have to beg for money, but for once, I can say with the utmost certainty that the circumstances behind our poorness isn't our fault. I had a job. I lost it because I was thrust into a dark and demented world that spat me back out in under forty-eight hours.

As her head bobs up and down, Roxanne fixes her belt into place. "Wait..." With her eyes locked on the SUVs we eyeball every escape, she shallows her breathing. "Now."

I twist the key in the ignition in sync with the driver of the lead SUV. When my engine roars to life on the first turn, I inwardly tap dance. I don't know who meddled with my car when it sat vacant in a field, but they must have mechanical knowledge. It purrs like a kitty every single time I drive it.

It's kind of like how my body hummed whenever Clover was in its vicinity.

"What is it?" Roxanne asks forty miles out of Ravenshoe.

A handful of locals were generous enough with their donations I could have purchased half a tank of gas, but one nice motorist offered to fill our tank without accepting a dime of our donations. He said he understood what it's like to struggle, which was shocking considering he was driving a sports car I've only ever seen on the cover of a glossy magazine.

He wouldn't give me his details so I could send him money

once I got back on my feet. He simply made me promise to ensure I pass on the same generosity to someone less fortunate once I'm able to.

His gray eyes twinkled in the moonlight when I promised to do exactly that.

Roxanne's brow sits as high as her voice when she asks, "Are we being tailed?"

After taking in the single, circular headlight I noticed thirty miles ago for the hundredth time, I dip my chin. "I think so."

As Roxanne makes her watch undeniably noticeable, I signal to take the next off-ramp. We're meant to stay on the freeway until we reach Wallens Ridge State Penitentiary, but I'm so eager to discover if the motorbike is following us, I'll face an unrequired detour.

My pulse thuds in my ears when the motorcyclist signals to exit not long after me.

Testing a theory, I flick off my blinker, then flatten the gas pedal to the floor.

Roxanne's eyes return to mine when the blinking orange light behind us disappears not long after the rider follows us past the exit. He didn't turn off. He's still behind us. "Who do we know in Dimitri's crew who rides a motorbike?"

Clover immediately pops into my head, but before my excitement can get away on me, the motorcyclist merges into the passing lane, zips past us in a blur of light, then cuts us off so he can take the next exit ramp at a speed too fast to be safe.

"He must have had his off-ramps mixed up." Roxanne's sigh when she sinks back into her seat is a combination of disappointment and relief.

After taking a moment to settle my skyrocketing blood pressure, I say, "You look tired. Why don't you catch a couple of z's while I drive? We'll swap halfway."

Roxanne tries to stifle a yawn. Her attempts are woeful. She's so exhausted, she looks on the verge of collapse while asking, "Are you sure you're okay to drive? Visiting hours don't start until nine, so we could pull over at a truck stop and get some sleep."

I brush off her offer with a shake of my head. "I'm too hyped with adrenaline to sleep." I'm not lying. I thought Clover was tailing us. The thrumming it caused my body will keep me awake for hours.

When Roxanne hears my comment as intended, playfully, she laughs before running her hand down my forearm. "Wake me if you need me."

She's out cold before my head gets in two bobs.

24

ESTELLE

Although my earlier comment about my eyelids being propped open with adrenaline was in jest, it's proven accurate without uncertainty when I pull into the dusty lot of Wallens Ridge four and a half hours later. We lost around forty minutes begging for gas money at Ravenshoe, but with traffic light due to the early hour, only an extra twenty minutes was tacked onto our usual driving time.

I doubt I could say the same if I had answered a single demand of my bladder the past thirty miles. I've been busting to use the bathroom since we cruised through Kumbia, but since I didn't want to wake Roxanne, I continued as if all the restrooms were closed.

When I switch off the engine, Roxanne's eyes slowly flutter open. "What happened to waking me?" she asks after taking in the barbwire-topped fence of a maximum-security prison. "We were supposed to swap places halfway."

"You looked tired, so I let you sleep. Shoot me." I grimace when the need to pee becomes physically painful. "I doubt a bullet wound would be more painful than an almost overflowing bladder."

Concern I could get arrested for indecent exposure doesn't enter my mind when I stuff a handful of tissues into the pocket of my jeans, then peel out of the driver's seat. I waddle to a grassy patch in the far corner of the property like a pregnant lady shuffling to the restrooms after an ultrasound.

I'm nowhere near the freeway, and there's an easy two football fields between the entrance of the prison and the grass I'm planning to water, but somehow, the headlights of a van highlight both the whiteness of my thighs *and* the government-issued tags of a dark sedan hiding in the back corner of the lot.

Shit, this isn't good.

The woes of my bladder are returned to the stovetop for a second boil when I tug up my jeans and race back to my car. I assume Roxanne's whitening cheeks are from spotting the federally funded vehicle hiding in the shadows but am proven wrong when she mumbles, "That's Dimitri."

The movements of her chest match mine when I take in Dimitri's tired eyes and neck tattoos. He's sitting behind the steering wheel of a van similar to the one I spotted out the front of the ranch many times during Roxanne's first four weeks there.

Although I've seen Dimitri before, the spotlights above Wallens Ridge leave no uncertainty to his appeal. He's so handsome, a girl would be tempted to check for drool when in the same room as him. He has the same dangerous aura as Clover, but the hardness in his eyes seems self-inflicted. Like he blames himself for things out of his control.

How do I know this if we've never officially met? Roxanne has the same unfavorable trait. She was nowhere near her nanna's crash site when she died, yet she still blames herself for her nanna dying alone.

"Wait." I seize Roxanne's wrist in a firm hold before she can give Dimitri a piece of her mind as she has craved the past six weeks. "We're not the only one witnessing his arrival."

Her pulse goes from a trot to a cantor when I nudge my head to the dark sedan hiding in the shadows, then it gallops when a short man with stout thighs races out the double glass doors of Wallens Ridge. I know who he is even before the spotlights above our heads reveals his face. He's the warden who has hinted on more than one occasion how Roxanne or I could improve Claudia's stay in his 'house' without spending a dime.

It's men like Warden Mattue who force women into nunneries. We'd rather go without sexual contact than please a hideous beast like him.

As Roxanne scrutinizes the exchange between Warden Mattue, Dimitri, Rocco, and the man I learned earlier is named Smith, I keep my eyes secured on the vehicle across from us. I can't see how many occupants are inside, the tint is too dark, but I'm confident at least one person's eyes are on me.

You can't mistake the burn of a scorned woman no matter how hard you try.

A couple of seconds later, when the parking lot suddenly plunges into darkness, I startle so much I almost pee myself. "Jesus Christ. They should warn a girl before doing that."

I stop ribbing Roxanne for her quiet snickers about my cowardly jump when the occupant in the car across from us exits the driver's seat. Although it is dark out, perfect vision isn't needed to know the blonde standing across from me is beautiful. Her glossy locks fall to the middle of her back when she shakes out their natural wave, and her face is so faultless, it looks like she airbrushes out every imperfection before she leaves her home.

She's beautiful, but it's a pity her insides are blacker than Satan. She is so aware of her beauty she doesn't relish my envious gawk. She glares at me like I'm the scum on the bottom of the ocean, and I'm not the only one noticing her mocking scorn. Roxanne wants to beat her ass just for looking down at me, so you can imagine how badly she fights to free herself from my hold when the blonde's exchange with Dimitri appears more personal than two strangers having a word. They've been intimate. I know it. Dimitri knows it. And so does Roxanne.

The grinding of Roxanne's teeth almost overrides Dimitri's deep timbre when he backs up my claims a couple of minutes later. "I forgot the only time you exert any kind of normalcy is when you're flat on your back being served a healthy dose of dick. Is that why you keep showing up? Does the big gaping hole between your legs still need filling?"

"We all have pasts we're not proud of, Roxie. Even me," I remind her when their exchange sees her spunk fading before my very eyes.

Thankfully, it only takes the blonde attempting to slap Dimitri to bring back the fighting spirit her eyes are rarely without.

Dimitri soon takes charge of the situation. He gives the blonde marching orders in a way only a mafia man can without a drop of blood being shed. I can't pledge the same level of control. It takes everything I have to hold Roxanne back when the woman hisses at us like we're gutter rats before she slides behind the steering wheel of her car and floors the gas.

Even aware she's about to dig our graves won't stop me from letting Roxanne go when the blonde's sedan disappears into the abyss. My arms can't withstand the mauling of her nails for a second longer. That's how worked up she is. She's clawing at me like the blonde wants to drag her manicured nails down Dimitri's back.

Although frightened about what Dimitri's response will be to Roxanne's sudden arrival, I can't peel my eyes away from their upcoming confrontation. It's like creeping past a traffic accident. You know you shouldn't look, but you can't help yourself.

I'm reasonably sure Kai's punishment for letting us escape will be death when Dimitri threatens Warden Mattue with disembodiment when he spots the dozen red dots highlighting Roxanne's chest. He tells him he will gut him where he stands if he discovers a single finger curled around any triggers of the guns pointed her way. His response makes Warden Mattue shuffle on the spot like he too is busting to use the bathroom.

"Go..." When Warden Mattue remains frozen with his hands held in the air in a non-confrontational manner, Dimitri screams for the second time. "Go!"

Warden Mattue's scuttle leaves Roxanne standing across from three mafia men, defenseless and alone.

I'm about to back up her campaign, but the softening of the murderous glint in Dimitri's eyes when he lowers them to Roxanne stops me. He doesn't want to hurt her. He wants to wrap her up in cotton wool to ensure she can't be hurt.

The look is familiar to me because I swear I saw it in Clover's eyes when he massacred Winston and his 'little ones.'

"What are you doing here, Roxanne?"

My lips crimp when Roxanne adds an extra swing to her hips to hide the shudder rolling down her spine in response to Dimitri's deep timbre. She knows she has it, so she's flaunting it. "This isn't Smith's fault. Infrareds have their faults." She presses a kiss on Smith's cheek before she hugs Rocco like Dimitri won't kill him. "Is this new?" My brow cocks when she tiptoes her fingers across Rocco's pecs. "I don't recall seeing it on you before. It's cute and body-hugging. I like it."

Her last three words are practically purrs, and they make Dimitri see red. "Get your ass in the van, Roxanne. Smith will take you home."

She spins to reject him so fast, the hair we colored yesterday afternoon with old hair dye frames her face with perfect symmetry. "No."

"I beg your pardon?" Dimitri roars. "I wasn't asking."

"It wouldn't make a difference if you were. You can't boss me around anymore, Dimitri. You lost the chance when you abandoned me."

Dimitri looks more shocked now than he did when the blonde tried to slap him. "Abandoned you? I didn't abandon you. I set you free."

Roxanne folds her arms under her chest, which puts her cleavage front and center. "In the house my uncle, aunt, and quite possibly my grandfather were murdered in, with three snipers outside the door, and shitty-ass cell reception inside it! You may as well cut off my wings."

Her semantics is a little off, but since most of her comment is true, I let it slide.

When she pulls away from Dimitri with the strut of a catwalk model, he snaps out, "Where the fuck are you going? I'm not done with you yet."

She shrugs out of his hold before saying, "We came here to visit my friend. Since you seem to have pull with the warden, I guess we don't have to wait for visiting hours anymore." She nudges her head to me during the first half of her comment, summoning me to her side.

I take up the campaign with only the slightest knock to my knees. Don't judge. The last time I saw a man with as much anger on their face as Dimitri's is holding now, he went on a murderous rampage.

"Holy hell. What was that?" I ask Roxanne when we enter the reception area of Wallens Ridge with our lives intact. The jittering of my voice exposes my contrasting emotions. I'm torn between patting Roxanne on the back and strangling her. Her exchange with Dimitri was lusty, angst-filled, and emotionally scarring. "I need a cigarette, and I don't even smoke." Roxanne laughs before it morphs into a whimper. "Nuh-uh. None of that. You kicked butt out there. It was as hot as Hades."

"But he let me walk away... *again!*"

Before I can assure her I don't see it being a long intermission, Warden Mattue coughs, announcing his arrival. "We're not open, so you'll need to wait outside until visiting hours commence."

Anger rises in Roxanne's face. It dries the tears in her eyes and notches her determination to an all-time high. "From what I heard out there, we don't need to wait. Bring Claudia Sanchez to the visitor's room."

Warden Mattue leans over the counter to ensure his words are only for Roxanne and me. "What you heard out there was a discussion between two men. It was no business of yours. Women have no place here."

"Is that why you took Claudia's son away? Because women have no place here," I retaliate before I can stop myself. "I just witnessed you conducting multiple felonies. If you don't want those misdemeanors shared with reporters who'd promise me their firstborn to run a story about corruption at one of the most well-known prisons in the country, I suggest you bring Claudia to the visiting room as requested." I fold my arms in front of my chest. "Now."

Like a man not in fear of prosecution, he taps a plastic sign that states the visiting hours before reiterating what it says, "Visiting hours commence at nine."

He licks his lips while dragging his eyes down my body. Once his depraved gawk has my skin crawling, he shifts his focus to Roxanne. While silently suggesting ways he could be lenient on the rules, drool pools in the corner of his mouth.

His unvoiced proposal makes me sick to my stomach, but for once, a man comes to our aid instead of railroading us. "Clearly, you didn't learn your lesson out there." Rocco nudges his head to the parking lot before stopping at Roxanne's side. "She wasn't asking to see her friend. She's *telling* you that's what she's doing."

As his hand creeps for the gun jutting out the back of his trousers, my throat works through a hard swallow. I'm not freaked he's hoping Warden Mattue will step out of line so he can blow his brains out, I'm gasping about the dark SUV pulling into a parking bay at the side of reception. It's the same make and model as the car that collected me from Winston's mansion six weeks ago. The one I stole with the hope it would force Clover away from his recently purchased submissive.

As tuffs of dark hair peek above the SUV's roof, Rocco and Warden Mattue continue exchanging words. I miss a majority of what they say. My pulse is thumping in my ears too loudly to hear anything. I don't even register the stomping of a pair of black boots as they make their way up the stairs of Wallens Ridge. I'm frozen in fear, mindful I should run but too hopeful the boots belong to Clover to do that.

Disappointment smacks into me hard and fast when Dimitri almost pulls the front door of Wallens Ridge off its hinges as he yanks it open. His dark aura isn't the only thing he and Clover have in common. Their hair coloring is almost identical.

While Dimitri reminds the warden who is running the show around here, I float toward a row of chairs lining one wall to pull myself together. I can't believe I'm so fucked in the head, I am disappointed the goosebumps covering my arms aren't from Clover hunting me down like he threatened the last time I ran from him.

I should be glad I'm free of him, not upset.

I'm so out of sorts when Warden Mattue announces Roxanne

and I can head to the visiting room, I tell Roxanne I'll wait for her in the foyer. Claudia has enough lunacy in her life. I can't add more to her plate.

"Are you sure?" Roxanne double checks, conscious my bond with Claudia isn't as tight as hers but not wanting to exclude me.

When I nod, she runs her hand down my arm before she paces down a corridor we usually walk together.

With her exit shadowed by Rocco and Warden Mattue disappearing into a dark room a couple of seconds later, the reception area soon plunges into eerie quietness.

Who knew a prison housing over three thousand of the country's hardened criminals and a handful of wrongly convicted men and women could be so quiet? It's early, but still, this can't be kosher.

If the quiet isn't already confronting, imagine how perverse it comes when my walk to the restrooms across the foyer has me noticing a second pair of black boots. They're not peeking out the bottom of an SUV. They are propped under a freestanding bulletin board—a bulletin board I have to pass if I want to use the facilities.

"Smith?" Dimitri disappeared not long before Roxanne, Rocco is with Roxanne, so Smith is the only other logical choice. "Is that you?"

When the boots' owner fails to respond to my question, I decide I'd rather pee behind a bush than face whatever is waiting for me behind that bulletin board.

My ears prick when my pivot occurs simultaneously with the clumping of boots. Their stomps aren't spaced out like the men at the ranch last night. They're in close succession, assuring me I don't need to look over my shoulder to know I'm being chased.

Against my better judgment, I stop running and spin around. "Leave me alone!"

I don't know whether to be relieved or concerned when I recognize the face of the dark-haired man scaring the living shit out of me.

I'm not given the chance to assess Galib's status in my life when a heavily accented voice behind me asks, "What did I tell you to do the last time I saw you, angel?"

As pheromones overtake the fear-inducing hormones slicking my skin with sweat, I slowly spin around to face Clover. My heart smashes against my ribs when I take in his cut jaw, murderous eyes, and thinned lips. He's mad, but for some reason, the knowledge turns me on more than it scares me.

"You told me to wait, but you didn't say it had to occur at the ranch." The reminder of who he left with after our last exchange adds a snarky pitch to my words when I say, "You also said it before riding into the sunrise with your newly acquired submissive, so I kind of figured it didn't count."

I only see half his smirk before a white cloth is clamped over my mouth and nose, and my head goes woozy.

25

ESTELLE

I wake up with my jeans huddled at my knees, my sweater twisted around my midsection, and my naked backside planted on a toilet seat.

What the fuck?

When I attempt to scream for help, I realize my mouth is taped shut with the same industrial tape circling my wrists and ankles.

"I couldn't trust you not to run so I had to restrain you before pulling over." The accent coming from the other side of the closed door is Arabic, but it doesn't belong to Clover. If I'm reading the sorrow in it correctly, I'll put my money on my guard being Galib. "Once we're back in the car, I'll untie you and remove the tape from your mouth."

I want to argue, but how can I? I'm bound and gagged in a public restroom. All I can do is answer the silent screams of my bladder and pray like hell Galib keeps his promise. Escape isn't an option when your jeans are doubling the restraints around your legs, not to mention knowing the man holding you hostage carries a gun.

I don't remember much about Galib placing me into the back of the SUV idling at the front of Wallens Ridge, but I do recall his gun digging into my hip and portions of Clover's heated exchange with Smith.

Smith didn't want Clover to take me, but Clover didn't give him any other option. I was leaving with him no matter how loudly Smith protested, so why am I under Galib's watch now?

Galib partially opens the stall door when the prolonged trickle of my bladder ceases. "Are you done?"

I wipe the best I can with minimal wrist movements before grunting in confirmation. Embarrassment unlike anything I've ever experienced bombards me when he fully opens the door so he can help me to my feet. I wonder how many women he's held hostage before when he tugs up my jeans and thong without flinching or peering at anything below my waist.

Once my sweater is back in its rightful place, he bends his knees, throws an arm around my thighs, then tosses me over his shoulder. Even with my hair swishing in my face, I discover why the public restroom was quiet for a weekend. A brute of a man with thick biceps and an angry sneer is standing in the doorway of the female restroom. Although his gun isn't visible, everyone knows he's packing. That's why they don't approach even after locking their sorrow-filled eyes with me.

They watch Galib place me into the back of an SUV and slide in after me before they go back to their lives like nothing ever happened. It makes me ashamed of society until I realize I'd probably do the same. They don't know me, so why should they put their lives at risk for me?

Once we're racing down the freeway at a speed fast enough to ensure I won't attempt an escape, Galib cuts the tape on my wrists and ankles before raising his hand to my mouth. "Three... two... one." He rips the tape off before one fully leaves his mouth.

As tears burn my eyes, a voiceless scream rushes out my nose. "That hurts more than it should."

"Blame Clover for that. He only buys the good stuff."

With Galib bringing him up, I use the opportunity to discuss him. "Talking about Clover..." I don't get all my sentence out before Galib sinks into his seat and strays his eyes to the scenery whizzing by. "He told Smith he wouldn't let anything happened to me. That I'd be safe with him." When that doesn't spark a reaction out of him, I hit him with a personal jab. "But then he leaves me with you."

My endeavor to spark a reaction out of him works as it always does with domineering men. "What does that mean? I've taken care of you."

"You drugged me *before* removing my jeans and panties without permission."

A vein in his neck works overtime as he snaps out, "I chloroformed you at *Clover's* request because he knew you wouldn't come without protest before taking you to the restroom so you wouldn't pee your pants like a child."

Although appreciative he saved me a heap of embarrassment, I'm not going to let him know that. "How could you possibly know I needed to use the facilities? Do you have x-ray vision? Could you see my overflowing bladder through layers of clothes, skin, and muscles?"

"You were grunting in your sleep!"

His face reddens when I snap out, "So?"

"And... and... and..."

I arch a brow, encouraging him to continue digging the hole I'll happily push him in if he doesn't tell me what I want to know.

"And you didn't get anything out when you squatted behind the bush earlier."

My mouth falls open. "So you not only saw my vagina once, you saw it twice."

He *pffts*, sputters, and spits while snapping out, "I never saw your vagina. Not once."

"That isn't what I'm going to tell Clover when he asks why we stopped."

He stares at me, silent and blinking.

"Don't act like he didn't study our itinerary before he left me in your custody. He will know we stopped, and he'll want to know why. It's just up to you what I tell him."

It takes him a good twenty or so seconds to respond, but his delay doesn't soften the annoyance in his voice. "How is anything you say my choice, Ms. Armstead?"

"If you tell me where Clover is, I'll tell him we stopped because I needed to use the restroom. If you don't tell me where he is—"

"You'll lie and say I saw your *vagina*." He overemphasizes his last word like he's a kindergarten student.

I nod. "Precisely. So, which door would you like to walk through, Galib? The one with a steaming mad mass murderer standing behind it, or my little ol' door that merely wants to know what he's doing right now?"

His delay this time around is even longer than his first. He stews over his minimal suggestions before he requests for live infrared footage of Roxanne's grandparents' ranch to be patched through to his tablet. The voice that responds doesn't belong to Smith. It's British and grunted. It doesn't have the smooth crispness of Smith's unique twang.

It dawns on me that the heat sensors watching us are far more sophisticated than Roxanne and I realized when Galib flips over the leather screen protector on his twelve-inch tablet. It's an above-head shot that shows the heated outlines of five subjects in the open barn at the side of the ranch. The four red masses standing side by side appear shorter than the gigantic mass in front of them.

"Change the view to real-time."

When the screen switches from infrared mode to standard imagery, Galib zooms in. I'm certain his footage is being bounced off a satellite when it takes several long seconds to return to the original image. He doesn't stop when he reaches the roof of the barn, though. He continues through a crack in the worn roof, zooming in until the image of Clover standing in front of four men unblurs so well, I feel like I'm in the barn with him.

My bones jump out of their skin when Clover raises his gun to the head of the first man in a line. He doesn't give his pleas a chance to be voiced. He takes him out with a kill shot to the head before directing the barrel of his gun to man number two.

"Okay! Okay!" I shout when he executes the second man even quicker than he did the first. "I don't need to see anymore."

Galib acts as if I didn't speak. He holds his tablet under my nose, ensuring I can't miss the identity of the fourth man in the line. It's Kai.

"Why is he doing that? Why is he killing those men?" Kai will *never* be my friend, but that doesn't mean I wish for him to be killed. It's bad enough Rich lost his life, I don't want more carnage.

I still my breathing when Roxanne's voice unexpectedly comes out of the speaker of Galib's tablet. "You have no right to be angry at me, Dimi. You dumped me in a house with groceries older than dirt and men who were more worried about us *playing* them than us starving to death!"

The growl of a man on the verge of snapping sounds down the line a second before Dimitri's thick Italian timbre. "Send Clover extermination orders for Roxanne's ranch." My eyes snap to Galib's when he adds, "Warn him if he so much as rustles a hair on Ms. Armstead's head, the next rodent I exterminate will be him."

"Is that why Clover left me with you? Because he was ordered not to touch me?"

Once again, I'm torn between being angry and relieved when Galib nods. Clover is bad news, but shouldn't it be up to me how much of his crap I'm willing to take?

Knowing I'll never get an answer from the man next to me, I sink into my seat, then turn my eyes to the window. I want to say I use the time to mourn the men in the process of losing their lives, but that would be a lie.

To start with, I contemplate what story Smith told Roxanne about my disappearance for her to be so calm, then I wonder how high Clover's tally now sits. His kill count was already four before he massacred over a dozen men at Winston's mansion, so I'd hate to think how high it will be once he finishes executing Dimitri's order.

Several miles later, Galib steals my focus from the stream of cars whizzing past us. "Can I speak frankly?" He waits for me to face him and nod before saying, "Do you believe people hide more of themselves than they show?"

I take a moment to contemplate his question before nodding. "A simple smile can hide a thousand issues. Take my ex's dimple-blemished grin, for example. It hid a soul darker than Clover's."

"Precisely," Galib replies, smiling to emphasize his point. "So what crutch do children repeatedly punished for their happiness have?"

It takes me a little longer to find an answer to his question this time around, but when it finally arrives, it pains my heart to say out loud. "Mayhem, darkness, and anarchy."

I stop wondering if Clover's scars are from punishments he

faced in his childhood when Galib murmurs, "All the things Clover craved until he found something far more enticing."

What is he saying? Is he saying I'm Clover's crutch and that I am able to pull him out of the chaos he hides himself with?

I realize that is the point he's making when he says, "Even devils have guardian angels. Not all of them watch from above, though. Some walk the earth to ensure the person they're guiding only straddles the line between good and evil instead of stepping over it. I believe you could be that balance for Clover, Estelle."

Although excitement is my strongest emotion, I don't let it get away on me. "If that's true, why haven't I seen him the past six weeks? And why did he leave with her?" I hate the cracking of my voice during my last question, but it can't be helped. The image of Clover riding off into the sunrise with Andria still haunts my dreams to this day.

I'm left speechless when Galib replies, "Because the evolution of a devil is slow when his main enemy is himself. Clover was tortured as a child. He was abused both mentally and physically until he saw nothing but darkness everywhere he looked." My heart patters in my chest when he adds, "Then he found you, an angel so pure, you forced him out of the shadows he's hid behind the past twenty years."

My voice cracks for an entirely different reason when I ask, "How do you know all of this?"

Guilt pelts into me for my horrible performance earlier when he replies, "Because the shadows our father cloaked him with is the reason I serve him." I swipe at an unexpected tear rolling down my cheek when he undoes the top three buttons of his dress shirt before he fans it open. Although the circular burn below his left nipple pains my heart to see, I'm also grateful there's only one of them. His body isn't marked from years of abuse like Clover's. "Sometimes, it's necessary to sacrifice yourself for the sake of others. Clover did it for me and many others as a child. I do it for him now—"

"And I'll do it for him in the future,'" I interrupt before my head has the chance to overrule my heart. "Because without sacrifice, there will never be a chance for love."

26

CLOVER

Seven executions and endless pleas for mercy shouldn't have my blood this thick with vengeance. I shouldn't be itching for a bloodbath so soon after chasing three cowards through dense woodland and rounding up the final four as they arrived for a shift change. But there's no denying it. I'm pissed as fuck, and the sole cause of my fury is the multiple outdated packets of food in the pantry of Roxanne's grandparents' estate.

The one bag of rice that is in date has only a handful of grains in the bottom of it. There isn't enough flour to fill a cup, and the two eggs in the refrigerator are in a carton that said their expiration date was over two weeks ago.

If the money I handed Kai each Friday afternoon wasn't put toward Estelle's upkeep, where the fuck did it go? Dimitri paid him out the eye for his crew to keep Roxanne and Estelle safe, and I covered any additional expenses men who weren't starved as children don't consider. Even life inmates are served three meals a day, for fuck's sake, and the remembrance sees me storming out of the ranch via a door in the laundry/mudroom.

I dart into the dusty barn along the side of the aging wood construction like the four men lying flopped on each other aren't dead before I lay my boot into the man on top of the stack. I kick the living shit out of Kai's ribs, hopeful the thump it causes his chest will bring him back to life so I can kill him all over again— slower and more painfully this time around.

I have receipts in the thousands and images of him darting down the slot between the open barn and the ranch with his hands overloaded with groceries, yet there isn't enough food in the kitchen to feed one person for a day, let alone two for weeks on end. He fucking played me—*me*, the man who can't be fooled by anyone since I was molded by the master of manipulation. He played me like a fucking fiddle, and now it's time to return the favor.

"Come, little one."

Andria rises with so much agility, her flexibility could never be argued. She follows me to my bike and climbs onto the back when instructed before she curls her arms around my waist to hold me tight.

The healthy rumble of my bike's engine barely drowns out Idris's swallow when I request an update on Estelle and Galib's location via the hands-free device rigged in my helmet. "They're still a hundred miles out."

I understand four wheels can't move as fast as two, much less a mode of transport that doesn't have wheels, but they're further behind schedule than they should be.

When I ask Idris what caused their delay, he blubbers out a halfhearted excuse that Estelle needed to use the restroom before instructing me to take Exit 43. "There's an accident just before Exit 44. If you take 43, then Mercer after that, it will shave ten minutes off your commute time."

Although I am aware of what he is doing, he's deflecting my

agitation from one subject by reminding me about the one I'm racing toward, but I am not hyped up enough about a future kill to fully shift my focus. "Forward me the log from the Range Rover's LoJack. I want every stop longer than three seconds highlighted by the time I'm done here."

Stealing his chance to reply, I disconnect our call by hitting a button on the hands-free device.

Eight minutes later, I skid my bike to a stop at the front of an apartment building that's seen better days. I begin to wonder if Dimitri pays his goons with drugs instead of money when the removal of my helmet is quickly chased by a homeless-looking woman with track marks on her arms and matted hair begging for money.

Normally I don't have time for people who lack self-worth so much, they'd rather fill their bodies with harmful chemicals instead of food, but today, I change things up. To me, killing the fuckers who did me wrong is as natural as breathing, but there's no time for a second hunt today. Estelle is hungry, and I know first-hand how beneficial it is to feed her.

With my cock pressed against the zipper of my trousers, I dismount my bike like the heat of the blonde bombshell's cunt on my back the past ten minutes is responsible for my hard-on, then I hand the homeless woman my business card. "If my bike is still here when I get out, he will supply you with anything your heart desires for the rest of the month." I point to the petty dealer on the corner shitting bricks that one of the big guys in town has come to visit. "If it isn't..." I twist her around to show her the number of men eyeing my custom piece like they're at a strip joint. "You'll spend the rest of the month sweeping their insides into the gutter." I tap on my business card. "Show them that. It should keep them at bay."

I assumed a banquet of drugs would be the only promise I'd

have to give to have her protect my bike as if it is her kin, but the flare that darted through her eyes during the last half of my tender proved otherwise. Perhaps she isn't shooting up because she chooses drugs over food. Maybe it's the only way she can forget the horrors of her past. We all have our own ways of coping. Mine just happens to be killing.

After whispering a pledge in the homeless lady's ear that offers her both an escape and revenge, I snatch Andria's wrist in a determined hold and drag her up the cracked footpath. We climb four levels in silence, not even the increase in Andria's heart rate can be heard. It's the eerier silence of death, and I fucking love it.

"Wait here, little one," I instruct Andria when we reach apartment 47B.

I wait for her ass to hit the balls of her feet and her chin to touch her chest before I screw a silencer onto my gun, then ram my boot into the flimsy lock separating me from anyone in Kai's inner circle.

Pop. Pop.

A man I'd guess to be mid to late twenties doesn't know what hits him when one of my bullets shreds through his chest before the second one severs a vital artery in his neck. He was too busy playing a shoot-'em-up game on a console that cost in excess of a thousand dollars while his Bose wireless headphones blared out the action on an eighty-inch LCD television.

His gaming equipment is so new, I don't need to see the receipt to know it was purchased with the money I handed Kai. Bottom-dwelling gangsters don't earn the capital needed to fit out an apartment with high-end electronics and furniture. Most work for free with the hope one day they'll claw their way to good-standing.

I murdered my way there, one slaying at a time.

After checking the serial number on the first bill in a large stack next to a baggy of white powder, I move from the living area to the hallway. I raise my gun high and prick my ears when the gurgling noises of a pothead going to town on a bong sounds out of the first room on my left. I could lighten the stomps of my feet to surprise him like I did the gamer in the living room, but where's the fun in that? The thrill of the chase isn't just in reference to bedding a woman who tosses out rejections as often as she begs you to go harder, you just need to provoke someone into running, and the premise is there.

I shatter the pot lover's glass bong, forcing his eyes to mine before popping a second bullet between his blond brows. His body doesn't get the chance to register the bong piece scalding his dick when it melts through his satin boxer shorts. He's dead before half his brain explodes out the back of his head.

After checking the bathroom attached to his room and a junk room across the hall, I continue down the corridor. Excluding the scent of death lingering in the air, my next target is none the wiser to my visit. Music thumps out of a recently patched-up door and a smell worse than skin being welded off a man's arm when he's still alive sneaks through the cracks of the numerous boxes creating a fire hazard.

"Babe, is that you?" When I fail to answer the nasally screech of the blonde sitting in the middle of a bed painting her toenails with red varnish, she leans over to switch off the boombox giving me a headache. "Babe..."

After slipping off the bed, she tightens the sash of her designer nightwear around her slim waist. "He couldn't be sending you on another errand already, surely. How much does he think they eat?" I realize it isn't just me they're jibbing when she adds on, "Did he at least give you cash this time around? After the talking the supervisor gave her last week, I don't think the clerk will continue giving us cash refunds if you pay with a corporate account, and we can't keep using store credits to buy stock. We're running out of room. I might need to change our eBay listings from ten days to three."

Her giggle pisses me off, but it has nothing on the adrenaline that surges through my veins when she spots my watch through a stack of air fryers. Her pupils dilate to the size of saucers when she realizes the reaper has come to visit.

When she sprints for the only window in the room not barricaded by boxes, I give her a five-second head start. It's the least I can do since her strides are half the length of mine.

I catch her before the inch gap she places in the fire escape window causes a draft. With the chase not as thrilling as it should be, I lift her feet from the floor with a rueful clutch on her throat before pinning her to the window she hoped to use for her escape.

Her manicured nails digging into my hands as she fights to live is usually the equivalent of foreplay to me. Today, it doesn't give me the same level of satisfaction. She's attractive with plump lips, doll eyes, unblemished skin, and once the fear slicking her skin overtakes the wet varnish on her toes, she smells delicious enough to eat, but there's no tingle in my nuts and no thickening of my crotch.

My cock isn't responding to her terrified eyes at all, and it frustrates me so much, I don't kill her by crushing her airways. I drop her to the floor, lodge a bullet into the top of her head, then race out of the apartment like my thirst for carnage will never be fully sated.

"Come, little one."

Andria follows me down the stairwell with her head sagged and her hands balled at her sides. Her eyes don't even move from the ground when Idris arrives with a clean-up crew in tow, and I instruct him of my wishes. "Three deceased on the fourth floor. I want no trace I was here." When Idris nods, I hook my leg over my bike, then stray my eyes to the homeless lady keeping the vultures at bay by flashing them my business card. "Once it's done, find out who's messing with her before giving her free rein on anything in their apartment... *including* the bundles of cash on the coffee table." It's my money, so I can do with it as I see fit.

"Then?" Idris asks, knowing there's always more demands than the ones I voice.

He's right. "Then bring body bags to the ranch. It's time to cash in a previously untendered bid."

His dark brows pull together before the truth smacks him in the face. "Dimitri?"

I shake my head. "But I'm sure he'll be next when he learns I didn't follow the do-not-touch order he issued this morning."

Estelle Armstead stole the joy of killing from me, so it's only fair she returns it with the addition of her soul.

27

ESTELLE

You wouldn't believe I was a woman who never got nervous if you could feel the butterflies fluttering in my stomach now. My nerves aren't solely based on Galib instructing the driver to turn down the street Roxanne's grandparents' ranch is on. Most of them center around the fact Clover's bike is parked at the side of the barn. The same barn where he assassinated members of his crew like they're not on the same team.

"Are you coming in?" I ask Galib when he leans across me to pop open my door.

He sinks back to his side of our shared seat, interlocks his fingers, then rests them in his lap. "I wasn't asked to attend."

"Then consider this me asking." I hate the panic in my voice, but it can't be helped. This ranch gave off bad vibes before Roxanne disclosed her uncle was killed here. It's even worse now. "Will you please come with me?"

Galib takes in my pleading eyes for three painfully long seconds before he slices his hand through the air, gesturing for me to exit the

SUV first. Although he shadows my walk up the porch stairs, he maintains an amicable distance. I can't say I blame him. I threatened to throw him under the bus only hours ago. If I were him, and he had done me bad like that, I would have left me out to dry as well.

I'll be sure to remember that the next time my annoyance gets the best of me.

I begin to wonder if my mind played tricks on me when my eyes ignore the numerous demands of my heart not to stray to the open barn. There's no sign of a massacre. No blood splatters. Nothing. It truly seems as if the barn wasn't the sight of four executions.

"It pays to hire a professional," Galib whispers, reminding me that today's incident isn't a one-off for Clover. He kills for a living.

When I lower the handle on the front door, the tired headache that's plagued me the past four hours pounds my temples while my heart thrashes my ribs. Clover isn't seated at the chair he moves around like doll furniture, he's in the kitchen, staring at an almost empty box of rice and the peanut butter jar I scraped clean weeks ago.

The tightness of his jaw is undeniable when he senses my watch. It firms to the point of cracking when he grinds out, "Return to the compound to prepare for Estelle's arrival. She's coming home with me."

Before a single sputtered response can leave my lips, Galib pipes up, "That isn't part of the plan. If you want the right outcome, we need to continue on course as strategized."

"Return to the compound to prepare for Estelle's arrival!" Clover repeats, screaming. "She's coming home with me!"

My eyes bounce between Clover and Galib when Galib dips his chin, bowing out of the fight before more bloodshed occurs.

He's barely slid out the front door when Clover locks his eyes with mine. They're as dark as death and one hundred percent unhinged. "Come here, angel."

My feet move before my head has the chance to object. Not only is there a weapon holstered to his hip that could end my sprint in an instant, but I'm desperate to discover if I can soothe the absolute pain in his eyes as Galib hinted.

The scent of death and desecration fills my nose when Clover raises his hand to my face. My breathing shallows when he tracks the back of his index finger down my cheek before he lowers it to my collarbone. He isn't admiring my features. He's assessing the amount of weight I've lost the past six weeks. It wouldn't be much, probably around five or six pounds, but his response makes it seem as if it is so much more.

Although he looks set for another murderous rampage when the swell of my breasts doesn't fill his hands like they once did, my body responds positively to his groping touch. My nipples bud, and the undeniable scent of a woman in need overtakes the smell of danger he's rarely without.

His nostrils flare when he notices my body's reaction to his touch, but instead of devouring me as per the specifications in his lust-filled gaze, he returns his hands to his sides, then raises his eyes to my face.

I unearth the reason for his no-touch approach when he places me onto a chair next to the two-seater dinette. The boxes of expired food we kept in the pantry in case things turned dire are the same brand and size, but every expiration date is well into the future. Not a single item is out of date.

When Clover moves to the refrigerator to remove eggs, potatoes, and butter, my mouth falls open. How did he have the time to travel from Wallens Ridge to Erkinsvale, kill four men, *and* do a mammoth grocery shop? We only stopped once during our commute back, and that was only so I could pee. There's no way we could have fit in as much as he did in such a short period.

My gaped jaw drops even more when Clover mutters, "Sometimes you need to move quicker than your enemy. Have you ever been in a helicopter, angel?" When I shake my head, too shocked to speak, he promises, "If you do as you're told..." my lips arch into a grin when he mutters, "...*for once*... I'll take you up one time."

When my panic subsides enough to speak, I ask, "How much will that cost me?"

My knees knock for an entirely different reason when his lips curve into a smirk. I haven't seen his full smile yet, but his smirks are enough to make me weak at the knees. "I'm sure we can come to some sort of arrangement." He drinks in my squirm before adding, "*After* I've fed you."

Over the next twenty minutes, he whips up a breakfast fit for a king. It isn't a standard American breakfast with grilled bacon and fluffy pancakes. Our eggs are poached in a tomato sauce consisting of freshly diced tomatoes, onions, chili sauce, and spiced with cumin. Our toast is flatbread he grilled with a drizzle of olive oil, and we topped both courses with cheese, olives, and slices of a thick Turkish sausage.

I learn during mouthfuls of beautifully aromatic and tasteful food that although he stepped away from Islamic tradition when he left the United Arab Emirates three years ago, he doesn't eat pork in any form, hence a lack of bacon on our plates.

Although I am a sucker for the salty strips of goodness, the breakfast he prepared is both delicious and filling. I'm so full, I forget I'm in the company of a man who expects payment for every single thing he does—even the ones I wish he hadn't.

"Why did you kill Rich?"

The twitching in Clover's jaw exposes he knows who I'm talking about, but he acts ignorant. "Who?"

I place my hands under the table, praying it will hide their brutal shake before replying, "Rich. The man I invited to eat the food he bought for us with us."

"Oh. Him. The man who looked at you like *you* were the feast on offer." He works his jaw side to side before tilting his head. "Is that the man you're referencing?"

His glare warns of imminent danger, but I can't hold back. "He *helped* us, Clover. He wasn't a bad person."

His plate cracks when he slams his fist down. "He looked at you like a piece of meat!"

"Bullshit! Rich was one of the rare good guys."

He moves so quickly that before I know what's happening, I'm plucked from my seat and pinned to the cabinets in the kitchen by my throat. "So fucking good, he watched you through the drapes of your room every fucking night. So fucking good, when he couldn't jerk off at a distance, he stole the dirty panties you left on the bathroom floor when you were sleeping. He was so fucking good, the night I killed him, he had a sedative in his pocket that was so potent it could have killed you," he sneers into my ear, his voice loudening during the last two words of his statement. "That's how fucking good he was."

There's no dishonesty in his murderous gaze.

No mistrust.

He's telling the truth.

Furthermore, why would he lie?

He's never hidden who he is, so why would he start now?

Clover's grip on my throat loosens when I murmur, "I'm sorry. I didn't know. I wasn't around him enough to get the creeper vibe from him."

The longer his deadly black eyes bounce between mine, the more odd instances my first two weeks at the ranch present. I was always searching for missing panties. I assumed the dainty lace material couldn't withstand the twists and turns of the dated dryer. I had no clue Rich was taking them. I also felt like I was being watched. I was just so hopeful it was Clover, I didn't pay it much attention.

"I thought he was a good guy."

I hear the increase in Clover's heart rate in his deep timbre when he murmurs, "He wanted to hurt you."

"He didn't," I reply, my voice as low as his. "You stopped him. You saved me."

"I didn't save you, angel. I saved you for myself." I suck in a deep breath when he moves his thumb from my throat to my mouth. He drags the gunpowder-scented digit across my fleshy lips, growling when the tension crackling between us becomes too much to ignore. "Because I'd rather kill you than ever see you with another man."

Testing a theory, I murmur, "You can't kill me."

My pussy throbs when he dips his thumb into my mouth before he hooks his lethal gaze with mine. "I can't?" I shake my head, which is virtually impossible to do with how firm he's clutching my throat. "Why can't I?"

Sparks of the confident woman I was before I was thrust into the murky undertones of the Italian Cartel shine brightly when I murmur, "Because you'd much rather fuck me. You can't do that if I'm dead."

His wicked smirk does crazy things to my insides—as does his tongue. He spears it between my lips before dragging it along the roof of my mouth.

I swallow down his moan when I weave my fingers through his hair to pull him closer before I return his kiss with as much possessiveness. I should be pushing him away, but his lips are too intoxicating to maintain a rational thought process.

As he kisses me like I've never been kissed, his erection digs into my front while the cabinet fixtures dig into my back. It's a wild embrace full of lust and unquenchable desires that grows more amorous when he moves our exchange from the kitchen cabinets to the table we ate breakfast on.

He clears our plates and cutlery with a sweep of his hand before my backside takes their place. As I drag my sweater over my head, suddenly too hot to need clothes, Clover lowers the fastener on my jeans before he yanks them down my thighs.

My pussy clenches when the rigid material gets stuck on my shoes. He seems disappointed he needs to remove my heels to strip me bare, the thought of them piercing his glorious ass while he pumps in and out of me clearly as appealing to him as it is me.

"Next time," he murmurs before he yanks off my stilettos and tosses them to the side.

"Let me," I beg when he yanks at the zipper in his pants.

Not waiting for permission, I lift my hands to the top button of his dress shirt. A tinge of insecurity plagues me when he curls his hand around my hands. He doesn't snatch them away. However, he does grip them hard enough to announce his hesitation. It's mid-morning, and the sun is well risen. There are no shadows and poor lighting. It's just him and me. The beast I'm slowly learning isn't so beastly and the woman who can't say no to him.

"Please," I shamelessly beg, unashamed that his weeks of silence hasn't dampened my desire to be dominated by him. Every girl has needs, my body just refuses to believe they can be fulfilled by anyone but him.

My chest rises and falls in rhythm with Clover's when he slowly releases my hands from his grip. Not a word escapes his lips, but his eyes tell me everything I need to know. This is as huge for him as it is for me. I'm seducing a murderer instead of running from him.

I can't control the movements of my eyes when I fan out his

shirt after undoing the final button. As my hooded gaze roams stacked abs and smooth pecs, my fingertips float over scars no number of tattoos could hide. Most are long and jagged like knife wounds, but the circular burns are the width of my thumb.

"Who did this do you?" I ask while floating my finger over a wound that's clearly years old but undeniably inflicted to be cruel.

Nothing but spite is heard in Clover's tone when he replies, "A man who no longer matters."

When he attempts to snatch my hands away, I yank them out of his grasp before returning them to his torso. "A dead man?"

I've never had the wish to kill someone until Clover shakes his head.

"Why not? If he did this to you, why isn't he dead?"

I glide my eyes up to his face when he mutters, "Because, under mafia law, I'm not allowed to touch him." Dark pools of blackness drift between mine when he discloses, "It's the same with anyone I'm contractually obliged to." A rush of excitement rains down on me when he confesses, "If your name is next to mine on a contract, your life will never be claimed by me."

Is that why he was so adamant about me signing his contract? Because he knew it was my best form of protection from both him and his enemies? If so, what tsunami did I instigate when I scribbled my signature next to another man's name. Is it behind his lack of contact the past six weeks? And will our romp cause more issues for him?

My eyes snap to Clover's face when he growls out, "He may own you, angel, but your soul belongs to me." His thumb stroking the vein throbbing in my neck is softer than a feather caressing my skin but potent enough for every muscle in my body to contract. "And I'll kill any man who says differently. Do you understand, angel? You are *mine*."

The possessiveness in his eyes makes the turmoil twisting in my stomach insignificant. I nod before my head has the chance to object, then, even quicker than that, I seal our verbal contract with more than a handshake. I kiss him like his ownership works both ways. That he is now mine as much as I am his.

We kiss for several long minutes, only resurfacing for air when Clover tugs his pants down his thighs and frees his magnificent cock from his trunks. After pushing me back so my shoulders brace the table, he drags my ass to the very edge, lines up, then drives home.

I bite down on my lip to stifle a groan when he pushes in deep. The pain of taking him without preparation is intense, but when mixed with his delicious 'V' muscle grinding my clit, I don't see it taking long to switch to pleasure.

"Fuck!" he roars on a moan. "I forgot how tight you are."

After stilling the thrusts of his hips, he brings his hand to the apex of my vagina so he can toy with my aching clit. He circles the nervy bud until desire shoots down my spine instead of painful spasms, and the line between pleasure and pain is blurred.

"Open your mouth for me, angel," Clover commands when the shuddering of my thighs exposes how close to climax I am.

When I do as asked, he rubs his damp thumb across my lips before pushing it between them. The tangy flavor of my impending orgasm is weak, but the knowledge he wants me to taste myself causes my pussy to convulse around his cock.

"That's better," he murmurs when the wickedness of our exchange floods my nether regions with more wetness. I'm panting and way too hot considering all he's done is thrust into me once. I'd be scared about the control he has of my body if it didn't feel so good. "Hold on, angel. Things are about to get rough."

As his hand drops from my mouth to my throat, he withdraws his cock to the very tip before he slams back in. The power of his thrust along with the pressure he places on my airways, sees my orgasm threatening to shatter at any moment. I'm on the cusp of screaming, my body is covered with a dense layer of sweat, and even with our exchange only starting moments ago, I feel the wetness coating his balls with every grunted pump he does.

He uses every muscle in his body to control me, to take me to the brink. He makes me his with pistoning hips and a fuck so glorious, I'm left with no option but to accept it with uncontrolled moans and recurring demands for him to give it to me harder.

Thrust after thrust, he drives into me on repeat. I'm rambling nonsense, certain the tsunami forming in my core couldn't get any stronger, then he releases his tight grip on my throat.

It throws my body into a new type of chaos.

While answering the wheezy demands of my screaming lungs, I come with a hoarse cry. It's a continuous and long climax that takes everything out of me.

I'm certain I have nothing left to give, not an ounce of care or a cooperative muscle in my body, but Clover proves otherwise when he clenches my ass cheeks and drags me to the very edge of the table.

The utter ownership on his face spurs something deep inside of me. It sees me arching my back off the beaten material so I can meet his thrusts grind for grind.

"Yes, angel. Fuck me. Take what you need. Accept *all* of me into your tight little cunt."

As I buck my hips as demanded, Clover drops his focus to his fat cock pushing in and out of me. The erotic view doubles the ownership in his eyes and sees his fingers digging into my ass so painfully, I'm certain he will leave a mark.

The thought has me primed and ready to detonate for the second time. Tingles race across the lower half of my stomach, his cock faces not an ounce of resistance even with it thickening the longer he watches the intimate way our bodies are joined, and my lips are parted and ready to scream. There's just one thing I'm missing.

The threat of death.

"I knew you got off on this," Clover grunts when I lead the hand groping my bouncing breast to my neck. "The pain. The carnage. The gore." He squeezes my throat tighter with every word he speaks. "You want it almost as badly as you crave my cock." My body shudders as the most intense climax I've ever experienced develops deep in my core. "Is that why you hugged him, angel? Did you know I was watching? Did you want me to kill him?"

I can't shake my head. He's gripping my throat too tightly, but that isn't the sole reason for my lack of response. I'm unsure exactly how to answer. I was devastated Rich was killed when I thought he was a good guy. Now I'm not so sure. I'm all about justice. I just had no clue I craved it in a non-legal way until I considered the many ways I could kill the man who convinced Clover that smiling is bad.

"Answer me, angel," Clover demands, squeezing firmer. "Are you glad I killed him?"

His nostrils flare like his lungs are as depleted of oxygen as mine when I bob my chin. Victory fires through his eyes before he permits me to come a nanosecond after answering the screaming demands of my lungs.

When I shatter, he doesn't stop. I scream as he pumps into me over and over and over again, the sensation too brilliant for a nonchalant response. My skin is on fire, and no matter how tightly I clench my inner muscles to coerce him into joining me on the wild ride of ecstasy, the bucks of his hips never let up.

While pinching my clit with two fingers, he fucks me like a wild beast. Within minutes, my lips are parted and ready to screech through another feverish climax, then Clover stops thrusting mid-pump.

What the fuck?

I'm about to ask him what the hell is wrong with him when the crunching of gravel under tires sounds through my ears. We have company, and the knowledge has my climax backing away with its hands held in the air and a pleading look to return sooner rather than later.

Unfortunately, Clover wholly removes that from the table by snapping out, "You're not to tell anyone about what we discussed. As far as anyone is aware, I'm here on business. Nothing more."

Acting oblivious to my shocked expression, he tucks away his still firm cock, yanks up his trousers, then returns his shirt to its rightful spot.

He dresses me just as quickly before he shifts his focus to my ecstasy-riddled face and mussed hair. I already feel dirty, so you can imagine how perverse it becomes when he scrubs at my kiss-swollen lips with his thumb like he's embarrassed by their plumpness.

"Angel…" he growls in annoyance when I yank away before he can remove all traces of our kiss from my mouth.

My heartache speaks before my common sense. "Estelle… remember? This is just business. Nothing more."

He stops me from exiting the kitchen by grabbing my elbow. A stupid part of me is hoping it's so he can issue me an apology. I'm left sorely disappointed. "At dusk, make an excuse to leave. Galib will collect you from the back entrance."

"I'm not going anywhere with you."

He draws me so close to his face, my feet leave the floor. "I wasn't asking, angel. Make an excuse to leave at dusk, or I'll find a way to force you to leave."

In case I'm not getting the message loud and clear, he strays his once again murderous eyes to the barn siding the ranch. It's a fast reminder that he will always choose the role of a killer long before he'd choose to be a man.

He waits for me to cowardly nod before he releases me from his hold.

My plan for a dramatic exit is overshadowed by the fret on our interrupter's face. Roxanne looks panicked out of her mind, and with her safety far more pressing than my inability to maintain Clover's attention for longer than an hour at a time, I forget all about our argument while racing to Roxanne's side.

"What's wrong? Did he hurt you?"

She takes a moment to relish the edgy arrogance in my voice that advises no amount of fear will stop me from hurting Dimitri if he's responsible for the pained look on her face before she opens the back passenger door of a flashy ride.

I gasp in shock when my eyes lock on a petite brunette splayed across the dark leather material. Not much of her body can be seen since she's being protected by a snarling Doberman, but what I can see of her face isn't good. She's been badly beaten.

"Clover, hurry!" I shout before assisting Roxanne in coaching the Doberman out of the back of the gold Mercedes G-Class.

Roxanne eyes me with suspicion when Clover jumps to the snapped command in my tone like we know each other more intimately than one-off bed companions, but since it is taking everything she has to stop Clover from being mauled by the viciously barking dog, she keeps her accusations to herself.

"He's helping her, Max. I promise you that," she pushes out breathlessly when Clover lifts the barely conscious woman from the back of the car.

Unwarranted jealousy smacks into me hard and fast when she burrows her bruised and battered face between Clover's sweat-misted pecs. I'm not just green with envy she's smelling his intoxicating scent that grows more amorous during non-violent physical activities, I'm jealous as hell she feels safe and protected in his arms because I stupidly feel the same when he's not trying to kill me.

"Put her in my nanna's room," Roxanne says, answering the voiceless question in Clover's eyes before he can articulate it. "Dimitri said he would organize for a doctor to come check on her."

As Clover paces through Roxanne's grandparents' ranch like he's knowledgeable with the floor plan, he asks, "Where is Dimitri?"

Roxanne waits for him to place the unknown woman onto her nanna's bed and cover her with the bedding before replying, "Before she passed out, Demi said two men assaulted her. We only found one in her bedroom, so Dimi is... *tracking* down the second assailant."

Once Clover steps into the hallway, she releases Max a mere second before he slips his collar. He races into the room, leaps onto the bed, then takes a protective stance at Demi's feet.

Confident Max has a handle on things, Clover drifts his eyes to me. I shouldn't know him well enough to read the silent question in his eyes like Roxanne did only seconds ago, but I do. And although my first thought should be to shake my head before pleading for him to stay with me, I bob my chin instead. I'm aware of his position in Dimitri's team and conscious that all the men who hurt Demi should be brought to justice.

With Roxanne's focus fixated on Demi, Clover wordlessly reminds me about his earlier request before he races for his bike like his desire to kill ranks higher than his need to come.

My stomach gurgles when I realize how accurate my assumption most likely is.

He's a hired hitman. Of course, he'd pick gore over me.

28

ESTELLE

With police swarming every inch of Roxanne's grandparents' ranch within minutes of her arriving and a mafia presence growing more notable the longer rumors circulate that two police officers conducted Demi's assault, the hours fly by like minutes.

I haven't had time to think about my interaction with Clover and why his grapple for ownership was quickly overshadowed by a request for us to act as if we don't know each other. I could seek clarification directly from the source of my confusion, but that's a little hard to do since he's avoiding me like I have the plague. Anytime I float his way to discreetly request a word, he either moves to another location or glares at me long enough I get the hint he doesn't want to be interrupted.

I'm so bewildered by his hot and cold response today I fail to remove my eyes from him before my gawk is busted by the last person I want to know about my stupidity.

"That isn't a good idea," Roxanne murmurs while joining me on the couch.

I act dim. It isn't a hard feat for me lately. "What isn't a good idea?"

If it were anyone but my best friend sitting next to me, my blasé response would have worked like magic. Regretfully, there are times when Roxanne knows me better than I know myself. "Giving gaga eyes to a paid hitman."

I roll my eyes like I do every time she brings Clover up. "*Puh-leaze.* I was warning him to stay away."

"Oh." She wiggles her finger in front of my face, pointing out my inflamed cheeks and massively dilated eyes. "If this is your threatening face, what was the one I saw when you and Brayden went to town Thanksgiving weekend?"

The mention of Brayden's name instantly sours my mood. "Don't you dare judge me. You were all *'good riddance, I can't stand him, how dare he treat me the way he did'* to *'hey there, good-looking, can I get you a cup of coffee? One lump or two?'*"

Roxanne punches me in the arm. "I was trying to be helpful."

Happy for the focus to be on her, I reply, "You were trying to take the focus off your pressing thighs." Hating that my comment drops the shoulders she's rarely held high the past six weeks, I add, "I can't blame you. He's fucking hot, they all are, but..."

"It's crazy to think *this* is any type of normal?" she fills in when words elude me.

We've had discussions like this a handful of times the past couple of weeks, but it never had the intensity it does now. Just like I can't comprehend my craziness when Clover is in the vicinity, I didn't have a grasp of Roxanne's connection with Dimitri either until I realized his focus seldomly shifts from Roxanne. Even with his cousin battered and bruised in the room next to him, he never once removed his eyes from Roxanne. It has me confident in declaring that he didn't put thirty-million dollars on the line because he knows no one is game enough to go against him. He did it because he truly believes Roxanne is worth every penny he could possibly lose.

I drift my eyes back to Roxanne when she says, "Would it make you feel any better if I said it's not close to being normal because it isn't meant to be? There are bad and good in every person. You've just got to find the one who makes your flaws less obvious."

"What are you saying, Roxie? You're the concealer for Dimitri's blemishes?"

She shakes her head. "He isn't the one with the marks, Estelle. I am."

I'm about to remind her the scars of her past are what make her so beautiful, but before I can, the man she's speaking about as if more than lust is on the line steals her devotion for the umpteenth time today.

Dimitri looked murderous when he arrived hours ago with a blood-dotted shirt and gash to his left wrist, but it had nothing on the viciousness beaming out of him now. I don't know what Smith is showing him, but his clenched fists leave no uncertainty it has something to do with Roxanne.

As he fights the urge to go on a rampage, Dimitri seeks Roxanne's eyes like they can end his homicidal thoughts before they fully transpire. It reminds me of what Galib said earlier today about even devils having guardian angels. Dimitri seems in control of everything happening, but not a single ruling he's made this afternoon was made without first silently seeking Roxanne's approval. He's considering how his judgments will affect Roxanne more than himself, and she has no clue how influential she is to him.

It's a beautifully unique connection to witness. Even more so when Roxanne denies Dimitri's roared command for Rocco to take her to her room by sidestepping his second-in-charge with the skills of a quarterback. She knows he's going to charge across the room before his legs even start pumping, although I doubt she was prepared for him to pole drive a police officer into the ground.

While shouting his name, she fights to get past the heavy mafia presence that suddenly makes sense. One wrong move and the officers watching one of their own have his face reconstructed by Dimitri's fist will face their own form of punishment.

As Dimitri hoists the unnamed officer from the ground with the rope of a tire swing Roxanne and I put in the front tree over a decade ago, I drift my eyes to Clover. Unlike every other member of Dimitri's crew, he isn't watching the officer's bulging eyes as he asphyxiates or the numerous cuts Dimitri inflicts to his body before he lowers his pocketknife to the crotch of his trousers. He's staring straight at me, his watch an odd mix of yearning and resentment.

It has me so conflicted when he grunts, "Come, little one," my feet don't immediately jump to his clipped tone as my heart yearns. I wait a beat.

The delay is for the best. If I hadn't been apprehensive, I would have made a fool out of myself because he wasn't calling me to his side, he was summoning his sub.

As Andria scurries to answer his every whim, I struggle to comprehend how I misplaced her. She wasn't here earlier. Well, I don't think she was. I'm truly unsure. The time between Roxanne's arrival with Demi and now has been a massive blur of controversy, so she could have been here all along, and I simply didn't notice her. It isn't like she makes a fuss. Excluding the massive upheaval her dash to Clover's side caused my stomach, her visit didn't disturb the energy crackling between Clover and me in the slightest. Only his silence dampened the buzz that forever surges between us.

My stomach flips when I consider Andria being the cause of Clover's absence of late. Has she been with him all along? Was she occupying his time so well, I didn't cross his mind until Dimitri ordered him to the ranch?

Just the thought makes me sick to my stomach, and it switches my devastation to anger.

Needing to leave before I hurt Andria for doing something as meager as following the commands of her master, I pivot on my heels and dash for my room. My eagerness to get away from the person causing me a world of hurt sees me crashing nose-first into the chest of a man with orange hair and black-rimmed glasses.

"Sorry," I apologize even though I'm reasonably sure he's in the wrong. The hallway I'm escaping down only leads to one room —mine—so unless he got lost, he shouldn't be standing where he is. "I wasn't watching where I was going."

I dart past him and race down the hall, my speed only slowing when I brace my back against the door I slam shut a nanosecond after racing through it. As I suck in deep breaths, I tell myself not to be so ridiculous. I just witnessed the murder of a police officer in front of three dozen of Ravenshoe PD's finest. The last thing my focus should be on is working out how much longer Andria has to repay her debt.

With a groan, I slide down the unlacquered wood. My interest piques when my slip puts me in direct line of sight of the bathroom light. Since it's minus a light fitting, I have no issue taking in the steam floating around it. It's so dense, it is as if someone recently showered.

Anger unlike anything I've ever experienced pelts into me when I recall how wet Andria's hair was. It sloshed against her back during her hurried steps to Clover, and the material of her fancy satin dress was soaking up the dregs a quick towel dry never gets.

A squeal bubbles in my chest when I scamper to my feet and race into the bathroom. A plain white nightgown is folded and sitting on the vanity. It's similar to the one Clover dressed me in his first night here, except it doesn't have the fancy lace edging mine had.

As the walls close in on me, the truth hits me like a wayward missile.

He let his submissive shower in *my* room.

He dressed her in *my* room.

And just the thought as to why she needed to shower has me seeing red.

At the speed of a bullet being discharged from a gun, I race out of my room and down the corridor. With the officer dangling lifelessly from the tree and Dimitri cleaning the blood from his hands and face with a towel at the front of the property, I steer my focus toward the back.

Blood roars into my ears when I spot Clover mounting his bike through the laundry room door a couple of seconds later. He doesn't bother hiding his scheming ways from me this time around. He extends his hand in offering to Andria to assist her on his bike without the slightest bit of remorse fettering his features. He even smirks when she scoots into him so her front is plastered to his back.

After hitting me with a wink that has me wishing I carried a weapon, he kick-starts his bike, then yanks back the throttle. Within seconds, he's nothing but a speckle of dust on the horizon.

I want to scream bloody murder that I stupidly believed his 'you're mine' claims. I want to beat something with my bare hands, but the quickest shimmer of white reminds me that sometimes opportunities present when you least expect them.

An envelope sits right of the tire mark Clover's bike left when he shot out of here like a bat out of hell. Clover's name is scribbled across the front.

My heart beats in an unnatural rhythm when I pluck it from

the ground and rip it open like it's addressed to me. Bile burns the back of my throat when an invitation for an event occurring tonight topples into my hand. The scorching of my throat isn't because I'm shocked Clover is on the guestlist of a party being hosted by someone with clearly expensive taste, it's the familiarity of the stationery used.

I swear I've seen this invitation before, which is odd considering I haven't been invited to a single event since high school.

My already high blood pressure skyrockets toward the danger zone when I recall the last time I had similar thoughts. This is an exact copy of the invitation Galib handed me weeks ago for an event I was meant to attend with Winston. I'm sure of it.

My assumption is proven accurate without fault when I race back to my room to rummage through my drawers. The invitations are identical, but Clover's copy is fresher and without crinkles like it was recently acquired—*just like the sub he plans to take with him.*

With my jealousy at a pinnacle and my mind made up, I snatch up my car keys like my baby will be returned earlier than Smith's promise of tomorrow afternoon, then make my way to Roxanne's room like I don't have to bypass a group of scheming mafia men on my way.

29

ESTELLE

I regret my decision to wear a dress with a waist-high split when my climb out of the back of a taxi almost causes me to flash my vagina at a homeless man sleeping under the awning of the building I'm about to enter. He acts oblivious to my almost slip-up as I did Roxanne's concern when I told her Smith had patched things up with our landlord so we didn't need to stay at the ranch anymore.

She didn't believe me, but when Rocco backed up my campaign with a set of eerily well-rehearsed lies, we eventually won her over.

When Rocco gave us some privacy, I begged Roxanne to come with me. It was selfish for me to do because as much as I wish it weren't true, I know she is as spellbound by Dimitri as I am Clover.

With both of us as stubborn as the other, it took twenty minutes of tough negotiations for Roxanne to give in to my request for voluntary discharge from the crazy world she is now very much a part of.

While begging for me to be careful, she shoved a handful of crumpled bills into my hand. We hugged for almost as long as we negotiated. It was a beautiful twenty minutes that fortified my belief that we will be friends until the end of time.

After promising to update her as often as possible, I accepted Rocco's offer to drive me to my old apartment building.

To my shock, he wasn't lying when he told Roxanne that Smith smoothed things over with our landlord. Our apartment was untouched and ready for me to move back in.

I would have been excited if it didn't feel like a massive step back.

The only good that came from our belongings not being thrown to the curb was access to a wardrobe I knew would pummel Clover with the same amount of jealousy he hit me with earlier.

My dress is so risqué, I can't wear any undergarments with it. I'm as bare beneath the silky-smooth material as I was when strapped into the sex swing at Winston's mansion.

Positive I'm marching straight toward my death, I hand the homeless man the remainder of the bills in my purse after I pay my fare. He is as surprised by my generosity as me when I notice several of the bills have two zeros on them. I didn't check their denominations before handing them over because I assumed most of them were dollar bills.

Lesson learned.

Nerves take flight in my stomach when I climb the stairs of a retro building in the middle of Hopeton. After shining a blue LED torch across my invitation to check its authenticity, the doorman gestures for me to enter with a wave of his hand. "Third door on the left."

As I enter the foyer, classical music floods my ears, but the

more I pace toward the third door, the louder whispered murmurings and the clinking of glasses occur.

I consider turning around and asking the homeless man to
accompany me when I notice the lines slowly filtering into a ball-
room-size room are in pairs, but lose the chance when a man in a
black mask with silver detailing stops next to me, pops out his
elbow, then asks, "Shall we?"

I nod instead of accepting his offer with words. My stomach is
fluttering too much for my nerves not to be projected in my voice
if I were to talk.

My eyes don't know where to look when we're ushered into the
room. The invitation said the party didn't start until nine. You
wouldn't know that from the state of undress many of the attendees are in. There's a woman in a sex swing on a stage at my left. A
man is being paddled with a wooden plank on my right, and the
event in the middle of the sex-scented space is a group affair. Even
with only having three orifices to fill, five men circle a lady whose
ass is perched high in the air, and her eyes are blindfolded.

"This is a sex party," I murmur a little too loudly, considering
the number of eyes on me.

"Yes," replies the man leading me deeper into the crowd.

Although his one-word reply exposes he doesn't appreciate me
drawing the focus to us, I'm still grateful for his help. Not only
does the crowd part when he approaches, but the hovering of his
hand above the small of my back lessens the number of heated
stares directed my way.

"Keep walking," the stranger suggests when the squeal of a
woman being ravaged from all sides ripples through the air. "The
professionals play at the back. Only show ponies who want attention perform near the door."

I back away when he directs me past a scene that involves
blood. "I've seen enough. This isn't for me."

I'm so determined to leave he couldn't stop me even if he used force. I race for the exit, my speed only slowing when the reason for my attendance presents before me. Clover is entering the main part of the ballroom. He's wearing black trousers and a black dress shirt with almost every button undone. The fitted flesh-colored shirt he's wearing underneath hides both his tattoos and scars, and Andria is at his side looking impeccable.

"You should stay," suggests the man I was fleeing from only moments ago. "From what I've heard, they put on quite the performance." I don't need to follow the direction of his gaze to know he's referring to Clover and Andria. They have the attention of the room. Not a single eye isn't watching their every move. "I can understand why. She's ravishing."

If the unnamed man continues talking, I don't hear anything he says. I'm too busy shadowing Clover and Andria's walk through the at-capacity room. They don't linger near the front. They move straight for the area the masked man said the professionals use.

My heart beats faster when we reach the curtained sectionals at the back of the ballroom. Clover and Andria aren't the only faces I recognize. Several men who frequent The Commission are seated throughout the intimate space, taking in multiple sex acts, and one of the girls with a rope around her throat shook her booty on a stage not much bigger than the one she's performing on now.

When Clover's eyes turn my way, I use a thick curtain to conceal my watch. My heart begs me to leave, but my head wants to give it a taste of its own medicine. It's tired of being played for a fool—and so am I.

While watching Clover introduce Andria to high-up dignitaries, I'm unexpectedly grabbed. I'm about to ram my elbow into the groin of the person who stole nine years off my life by scaring the living daylights out of me, but before I can, the familiarity of his scent smacks into me.

After dragging Brayden deeper into the curtains, I say, "What the hell are you doing here, Brayden? Shouldn't you be sipping cocktails in Belize?"

When he *pffts* me, he coats my face with spit. "Didn't you hear? I'm un-fucking-touchable." When he leans in close, I want to say alcohol is the sole cause of his bloodshot eyes, but unfortunately, I can't. There's something much more sinister in his veins than a legal substance. "Turns out Uncle Marc and my mom were half-siblings. Grammy was quite the MILF back in the day. She went through cocks like trees at a sawmill." After chuckling at his non-humorous comment, he adds, "She hit the jackpot with Marc's dad. He's some big shot everyone fears. Hence, me being untouchable."

He shuffles on his feet while rubbing his hands together. "Then there's you. The girl two million dollars couldn't help me get over. I've missed you, Elle." When I roll my eyes before trying to walk away, he steps in my path. "I did. I even tried to check up on you, but it wasn't just his goons scrutinizing your every move." He rakes his teeth over his lower lip to hide his smug grin. He shouldn't bother. He couldn't look more arrogant if he tried. "But that's all forgotten now. I'm here so we can ride off into the sunset together." He makes a face like he was hit with a shovel before he corrects, "*Sunrise.* We can ride off into the *sunrise* together."

Since hardly anything he says makes any sense, I focus on the parts of his ramblings I understand. "You killed your uncle, so why would his father protect you?"

He *pffts* me again. Thankfully, my face skips the carnage this time around. "No one knows it was me. I didn't tell anyone what happened. I blamed it on that dude. The one you were messing with."

I stabilize his unsteady sways before saying, "You told me he's dead because Clover forced you to kill him. You said he made you hold the gun to your uncle's head and pull the trigger."

His face goes deadpanned before he sheepishly bobs his head. "Yeah, that's right. I did say that, didn't I? I forgot."

"How can you forget something if it's true, Brayden?" I almost swallow my tongue when the truth reveals itself in his eyes. Clover didn't force him to kill his uncle. He did it of his own accord. "Marc didn't have any children. He treated you like a son. You bragged for two weeks straight when he made you the executor of his will." My eyes pop when more truths are unearthed. My lungs don't get enough air when I splutter out, "You killed your uncle, your own flesh and blood for a measly two million."

"For you, Estelle. Everything I did was for you."

"Don't you dare try and pin this on me." I push him away from me, disgusted. "Nothing you've *ever* done has been for me."

"Bullshit!" His roar gains him the attention of the people I'm pushing past to escape him, but he's too caught up in proving me wrong to pay them any attention. "I've done heaps for you. I fixed your car. I paid Rich to take care of you. I even offered to buy you before *he* could taste you." The growl he releases when referring to Clover as 'he' switches to a laugh. "Do you know what he said?" He doesn't wait for me to answer him. "He said, all the money in the world wouldn't be enough." His laugh is evil and vindictive. "And now look at him... at a sex club drooling over a woman not half as beautiful as you."

When I follow the direction he nudges his head, my heart falls from my chest. Clover and Andria are no longer mingling with the other guests. They're making their way onto the stage.

The anger burning me alive changes to jealousy when it dawns on me that they're about to perform a public sex act. Not only does the crowd's ever-growing interest reveal this, so does Clover uncinching the knot responsible for Andria's modesty.

With his eyes locked on mine, he guides the lithe material off her body like he did when he undressed me before he orders her to her knees.

The crowd hisses in approval when Andria follows his command without any hesitation. She kneels in front of him in nothing but a thong with the eyes of dozens of men and women on her, yet not a single bit of modesty hues her skin.

It seems as if he did truly purchase her because she follows orders—*unlike me.*

My brattiness is showcased in the worse way when I do something far more reckless than fall in love with a hired hitman. I awaken old ghosts by dishing out jealousy as ruefully as I'm being served it.

Brayden stiffens when I squash my lips to his, but it only takes two lashes of my tongue for him to return my embrace. He weaves his fingers through my hair, murmurs something about me finally coming to my senses, then tugs me in close to ensure I can feel what my kisses do to him.

Compared to the numerous sex acts occurring around us, ours is very much a PG rating, but you wouldn't know that from the attention it attracts. Not only does it stop Clover's performance before it truly begins, but it also gains us the attention of men I'd rather avoid than associate with. Most particularly, Col Petretti.

"So the rumors are true? You killed your uncle and Winston for *her...*" He spits out 'her' while glaring at me. "You played me for a fool." Brayden shakes his head, but Col acts ignorant. He's made up his mind, and no number of blubbered excuses will change it. "Your insolence will cost you more than your life."

"But you said I was protec—" A brutal backhanded slap silences both Brayden and the room.

"Another word out of your mouth will see you gutted where you stand!"

I try to disappear within the crowd when the men swarming Col encourage his violence with whispered murmurings. They seem more interested in watching a man be bludgeoned to death than watching one have his cock sucked.

Before I get in two full steps, Col snatches up my wrist. "Not so fast, young lady. When an owner dies, his tenures are revoked." His grin makes my skin crawl. "That means you once again belong to me."

"That isn't what Ezra informed me this morning," announces a stern voice from the back of the pack. My throat works through a hard swallow when the man who accompanied me earlier parts the crowd for a second time. "Any of my father's possessions at the time of his death belong to me..." he strays his eyes to mine, "... including her." When Col tries to argue, the man states very clearly, "Her paperwork reveals her sale was not a totem auction. It was final and complete, making her *mine*." He growls his last word with the same ownership Clover used earlier today.

After checking the document Winston's son presents to him, a man with dark hair and kind eyes shifts on his feet to face Col. "It is as claimed. Atticus is her rightful owner."

My eyes shoot to Clover when Atticus calls me to his side with the same nickname he used for Andria earlier. It hurts like hell when he ignores the silent pleas beaming out of me, instead choosing to use the room's distraction to usher a once-again dressed Andria off the stage.

"Now, little one!" Atticus barks out, shifting my focus back to him. "I will not ask you again."

Believing he is the lesser of two evils and aware I can't escape a room with as many guns as there are men, I slip out of Col's grip, then make my way to Atticus.

My knees knock with every step I take, and my hands slick

with sweat, but I make it across the room with only the slightest stumble.

"Head down. You will not embarrass me here," Atticus instructs when I reach his side. Although his tone is clipped, it's nowhere near as evil as Col's was when he tried to claim owner-ship of me.

Taking my cues off Andria's walk out of the room, I balance my chin onto my chest, then rest my arms at my sides. Atticus pets my hair before he leads me out of the room with his hand on the small of my back.

Once again, the crowd parts when they see him coming, meaning we reach the exit in a remarkably quick thirty seconds.

"Don't bother testing the locks. This was one of my father's cars. A tank couldn't help you escape it."

His threat isn't required. I saw the piece his driver has tucked under his jacket when he raced around to open the door for us.

After fastening my seat belt, Atticus lifts my chin until my hair falls away from my face. "Get comfortable. The trip isn't overly long, but it is boring when you're with the wrong master."

30

ESTELLE

When Atticus's driver turns down a familiar street forty minutes later, I realize he inherited more from his father than his red hair. We're at Winston's mansion. Even the goons manning the front gate are the same ones I faced six weeks ago.

"Did you not learn from your father's mistake? He will kill you for this! He will kill everyone."

Atticus chuckles under his breath before he slides out of his car. When he dips back in to offer me a hand, I consider my options. I don't want to go with him, but I don't have any other option. Weaponed-up goons are on every corner, and if he isn't my owner, Col Petretti is. That's enough incentive to have any girl toe the line until she can come up with a better plan, so instead of running, I slide my hand into Atticus's.

I feel the increase in his pulse when he uses his painless grip of my hand to walk me past the goon who jabbed a needle into my neck, through an elaborate chandeliered foyer, and into an office off the living room. He only lets it go when Andria's usually expressionless face mars with the faint lines of disappointment.

"Come, little one." Andria leaves Clover's side before all of Atticus's command leaves his mouth. Her steps are so fast, her feet barely touch the floor. She more floats across the room than stomps. After kneeling at Atticus's side, she rubs her cheek into his dress pants. He pets her hair before lifting his eyes to Clover. "Thank you."

Even with confusion by far my strongest emotion, my insides can't help but flutter when the briefest smile graces Clover's lips. It isn't a full grin, but it's more than a smirk.

"What did I miss?" I mumble under my breath when Atticus removes his mask, exchanges documents with Clover, then guides a subdued yet somewhat excited Andria out of the office, leaving me alone with Clover. "Isn't he the man who—"

"Showered and dressed Andria in your room when we found out Brayden had purchased a ticket to tonight's event," Clover interrupts, his tone an odd mix between angry and relieved. "Yes, he was."

He moves so agilely I don't realize he's crowding me toward a wall until his big imposing body doubles the cantor of my heart. After drinking in my face like he's memorizing every pore, he shoves my head to the side so he can drag his nose down the throb in my throat.

Goosebumps prickle on my nape when he growls, "You smell like him."

"As you do her," I snap out, too riled with jealousy to let it be pushed aside for lust.

I feel Clover's lips raise against my neck before he sinks his teeth into the sensitive skin. His bite is nowhere near as painful as the ones he did to my butt cheeks six weeks ago, but there's no doubt he's marking me. Claiming me. Making me his. I'm just confused as to why. Shouldn't he be doing that to his submissive?

When I say that to him, he lavishes my love bite with his tongue two times before he pulls back to admire his handiwork. Once he's satisfied with himself, he locks his eyes with mine and says, "Atticus is Andria's master. Her *true* master." He rubs at the skin opposite to the mark he just left, softening it for his teeth while adding, "But she didn't belong to him. She belonged to another man."

As the truth smacks into me, my mouth falls open. "His father?"

Clover murmurs in agreement before he lavishes the right side of my neck with his lips and teeth. He bites me, sucks me, then discloses, "But the rules we're governed by meant he had to sit and watch the woman he loves be hurt over and over again." My heart pains for both Andria and Atticus. "He had no way to break the cycle... then he stumbled onto an angel so beautiful even men who have everything can't turn her down."

"Me."

I only realize I whispered my comment out loud when Clover hums for the second time. "When Atticus was forwarded information about your sale, he knew his father wouldn't be able to resist you. You were exactly his type. Blonde, beautiful, and bratty enough he would require the help of his understudies to break you as he had Andria a year earlier." Once he has my head as piqued as my heart, he inches back. "I almost killed Atticus just for suggesting I let his father purchase you, but then I remembered how stale things were between Col and me. He wouldn't sell you to me. He would only loan you out, one transaction at a time." The desire to kill blackens his already dark gaze. "My intuition was proven accurate the night of the auction. When Winston purchased you instead of me, Col pushed aside my pre-drafted contract and had Winston sign an agreement for sale."

So that's what he was looking at the night of my auction.

The reason for the anarchy in his eyes makes sense when he murmurs, "Although Atticus was right about his father's interest in you, he missed one vital component about his obsessive-compulsive traits." As he scrubs at my lips with his thumb, his blood heated with annoyance, he murmurs, "His father's desire to immediately claim you. He had never done that before, not once in over thirty years, so not only were we left scrambling, but you were also left vulnerable."

"They didn't touch me. You arrived before they could."

My confession softens the murderous glint in his eyes, but it doesn't wholly remove it. "That doesn't matter. The fact he wanted to touch you warranted a bloodbath." His jaw tightens. "Then I had to let you leave with *him* because the only way Atticus could frame Brayden for his father's murder was by Ezra seeing you together only minutes after the massacre." I don't need to announce my confusion because he immediately works on unmuddling it. "Atticus wanted Brayden to take the fall because you weren't the first girlfriend he sold. Andria wasn't auctioned like you. Brayden handed her over to Col like agreeing to date him gave him the right to sell her." My back molars smack together so fast, I almost crack a tooth. "But not only did the rules state Atticus couldn't kill his father no matter how cruel he was, my gun was also muzzled by the same bureaucratic tape." He leans in close to ensure his words are only for my ears. "Have you heard of Jalaal Latif?"

I haven't frequented the social scene much after high school, but even a part-time socialite would have heard that name. He's one of the richest men in the world. He tied for third spot in *Forbes Rich List* only last year. "He's an oil tycoon, right?"

Clover notches up his chin. "And according to mafia law... my father." My heart beats erratically when he discloses, "He purchased me off my biological father when I was ten. I thought it was to exploit my exemplary archery and marksmanship skills." His nostrils flare as his fists ball. "I was wrong." He doesn't need to say the burns and cuts on his body are from Jalaal. The hate in his eyes tells me everything I need to know. "I left when I was eighteen only to be lured back two years later."

"Cyra," I whisper. Clover's eyes snap to mine, confused as to how I know his story before he's shared it. While running my index finger across his right hip, I confess, "Your tattoo artist did a good job hiding her name, but when you look really close, you can see the outline behind the warrior's head."

My pulse thrums for an entirely different reason when he snickers out, "For a woman forced to do things against her will, you certainly like to look, angel."

I don't deny his claim. He's standing too close to me for my hazy head to think up a good lie, and I honestly believe he'd see straight through it. He has a knack for reading me like no one ever has.

"What happened to Cyra?"

At first, I was jealous he once cared enough about a woman to tattoo her name on his body, but then I realized he wouldn't have covered it for no reason.

My throat becomes scratchy when Clover mutters, "She learned the consequences of lying to a madman."

I suck in a sharp breath when he squeezes my throat between his index finger and thumb. It isn't a painful hold, but it is firm enough to show he could have killed me within seconds the morning he arrived at my apartment. He didn't because he didn't want to.

As a smirk tugs at his lips, pleased I don't fight him even when my lungs start to panic, he murmurs, "Many men think they can do what I do. That they can kill without remorse and live without guilt." He loosens his grip enough tiny parcels of air pacifies the cries of my lungs. "Not many can. Eddie couldn't when Brayden promised him twenty thousand to kill his girlfriend so he could pocket the remaining eighty thousand off the tender he accepted without any intention for bloodshed. When Eddie fucked up, and evidence started pointing in another direction, Brayden had no choice but to hire a professional."

"He hired you to kill Roxanne." I'm not asking a question. I am stating a fact. I'm also so fuming mad, my voice is unrecognizable. I invited Brayden into our home. I introduced Roxanne to him as my only lifeline, yet the entire time we were dating, he wanted her dead.

I still when a disturbing notion enters my head. Brayden didn't start sniffing around until nine months after Roxanne's accident. If he hired Clover to finish the job, what caused such a long delay? From what I witnessed my first twenty-four hours in Clover's presence, he doesn't let time get away from him. Once a contract is signed, his target is all but dead.

"How come you didn't go through with it?"

Clover looks torn between wanting to strangle me and kiss me when he murmurs, "To start with, she was rarely alone. Then..."

When he works his jaw side to side, I blurt out, "You saw me."

My emotions only swing one way when he reluctantly notches up his chin.

I want to kiss him—badly.

The only reason I don't is because I can't stomach the thought that I put Roxanne's life in danger. "Is your contract with Brayden still valid?"

A sigh rattles in my chest when Clover shakes his head. As the wish to murder darkens his murky gaze, he discloses, "Brayden withdrew his tender when he fell in love with the target's roommate."

"And the terms of your contracts mean you couldn't kill him for disclosing that."

"Don't remind me," he growls out, quickening my pulse with his surly tone. "I was this close to pretending that term didn't exist..." he holds his index finger and thumb apart an inch, "... then he convinced Col I had killed his uncle, which saw him being offered protection under Mafia Law."

"Is that why you vanished for weeks on end? Because you were hiding?"

I'm more excited by his growl than scared by it. "I don't hide, angel. I was waiting."

"For?" I ask, truly confused.

"For Brayden's obsession with you to rear its ugly head," he spits out through a tight jaw.

I scoff. "Then that's where you went wrong. Brayden isn't obsessed with anyone but himself."

I'm forced to swallow my words when Brayden's voice commences playing out of the pocket of Clover's trousers before he's even pulled his cell phone out of his pocket. Although Brayden is in the midst of a mental psychosis, it's obvious who his breakdown centers around. He mentions me several times before he ends his agitation by popping a bullet between his uncle's brows.

The second video shows him handing Rich rolled-up bundles of cash. I assume he's buying drugs—it was obvious tonight alcohol wasn't the only thing boosting his ego—but my opinion changes when Rich hands him a delicate lace material.

He isn't buying ice.

He's purchasing my underwear.

My eyes lift to Clover when he discloses, "With the Governor of Mafia Law watching him as closely as Atticus and me, Brayden was once again forced to bring in outside help."

"Rich," I fill in, confident I'm on the money.

Clover nods. "He spilled many secrets during the hour I spent with him." I shouldn't be turned on by his murderous gleam, but I am. "It pissed me off so much, I didn't care about Brayden's thin cloak of protection, he was to be the next name on my docket."

"What stopped you?"

Jealousy pummels into me from all angles when he murmurs, "Andria." He grins about my reddening cheeks before muttering, "It isn't as you're imagining, angel. She reminded me that more than Atticus's life would be on the line if Brayden didn't take the fall for Winston's murder. Yours would be as well."

It takes me a couple of seconds to understand what he's saying, but when the lightbulb in my head finally switches on, gratitude smacks into me hard and fast. "If Atticus was stripped of his mafia standing, Col would consider himself my owner."

"Yes." You wouldn't know Clover's reply is a one-word response for how long it takes him to deliver it. It was more a roar than a word. "But now not only do you know you are mine, so does Col."

I'm confused. It doesn't linger for long. The document Clover and Atticus swapped at the start of our exchange is very basic, but the prose is undeniable. For the safe and untouched return of Andria, Atticus promised me to Clover.

He didn't pocket a dime for killing Winston and his 'little ones.'

All he got was me.

For the first time ever, I witness the greatness of Clover's full smile when I ask, "What *exactly* does the untouched clause entail?"

He leans into me deeper, towering over me with his big brooding frame. "It means any chastisement for bad behavior or praise for matters above subservience obedience were only to be handled by the submissive's true master."

"So you didn't... she didn't... there was no..."

"If you're asking if we fucked, angel, no, we did not." When I attempt to shift my focus to sexual activities slightly below sex, Clover squashes his finger to my lips. "Nor did she suck my cock, undress me, bathe with me, or any other thing responsible for the groove between your brows." He rubs at the line he's mentioning. "She stayed with me to fortify my ruse I didn't free you from Winston's madness because I was fascinated with you, and she obeyed me because she was instructed to do so by her master."

Even with honesty prominent in his tone, I can't help but ask, "Then why did you tell her to kneel after ordering me out of the room?"

The seriousness of our conversation shouldn't allow for snippets of lust, but there's no denying its presence when he smirks about my snapped tone. "Because I needed your obsession of me to force you to make a mistake. Both then and tonight."

I roll my eyes. "My obsession? *Puh-leaze.* I am *not* obsessed with you."

Air whistles through my teeth when he grips my throat with enough force both my lust-filled heart and rational-thinking head take notice. "Lie to me again, angel, and see what happens."

"I didn't lie." While fighting through the exquisite tingles the firming of his grip shoots down my spine, I murmur, "I'm not obsessed. I am delusional for believing we could be so much more."

31

ESTELLE

I wake up disoriented and confused, but with every muscle in my body thrumming in the aftermath of the best sex I've ever had. Last night was crazy. It was passionate, dangerous, and deadly. A lethal combination for someone who once thought the murky water of the underworld was too gloomy to swim in.

As my teeth graze my kiss-swollen lips, I roll onto my hip, anticipating to find Clover at my side. My eyes pop open when my hunt comes up empty-handed. The thump of my achy clit matches the beats of my heart when I rise to a half-seated position to scan Clover's room.

After having an asset transfer approved by Ezra James, the Governor of Mafia Law, Clover brought me to his residence. Although that was his plan all along, I felt more like a guest than a captive. The air shifted when Ezra questioned me about Brayden's participation in the massacre at Winston's manor. He was still suspicious, and although I could have thrown Clover under the bus along with Brayden, I didn't.

The documentation to transfer Andria's ownership from Clover to Atticus proved Brayden deserved to be punished. He sold her to Col when she was seventeen, and he received a percentage of the profit every time she was auctioned. To me, that makes him a monster right alongside Col and Winston. So instead of telling Ezra what I saw, I told him I saw nothing. As far as he is concerned, I was bound, gagged, *and* blindfolded.

Since that wasn't out of the norm for Winston, Ezra believed me. I should feel guilty that I deceived him. It should make me panicked I'll go to hell instead of heaven when I die, but I don't.

You can't feel guilt when you're handing out justice.

I'm not exactly sure what Brayden's punishment will be, and in all honesty, I don't care. He came into my life because he wanted to kill my best friend. Death will let him off lightly.

My heart beats for an entirely different reason when Clover enters the room. He's as naked as he was when he fucked me into oblivion, fed me, then did it all over again, but he has instruments strapped to his body—dangerous weapons that shouldn't make my pussy throb, but they do. Very much so.

After taking in the knife taped to his thigh, the gun strapped to his ankle, and another two semi-automatic weapons holstered around his torso with leather shoulder straps, I raise my eyes to his face. My thighs press when I realize he's assessing me as readily as I am him. It's clear he likes what he sees. His twitching cock is a sure-fire sign, not to mention the grogginess of his voice when he murmurs, "You should be sleeping."

"As should you... with me."

His smirk is more dangerous than the weapons strapped to his body. "I wish I could, angel, but I can't. Business calls." After entering a massive walk-in closet, he covers up with black trunks, dark trousers, and a buttoned-up white shirt. "Galib has been instructed to wake you at eight to eat. If you want to go back to sleep after that, you can, but only once your stomach is as full as your cunt was last night." The mattress dips when he sits on the edge to put his shoes on. "Roxanne's appointment is at ten, depending on the outcome, I'll either be back a little after that or in a couple of days."

I choke on my spit. How can his timeline be so differing? And what appointment is he talking about? Is Roxanne sick?

When I express my worries out loud, Clover finishes tying the laces on his military boots before twisting his torso to face me. Even with unease hardening his features, he has the dark and sexy aura down pat.

I sit quietly as he explains the plan Roxanne and Dimitri compiled last night. Although worried as hell Roxanne has bitten off more than she can chew, I also understand her objective. Dimitri's crimes should have never been forced onto his daughter. She's an innocent who doesn't deserve the hand she was dealt, so she needs as many people in her corner as possible.

"Angel..." Clover growls when I slip out of bed to scoop up the clothes I let drop where they fell last night.

After stuffing my feet into my jeans sans panties, slipping the under-shirt Clover wore last night over my head, and pulling my sex-mussed hair out of the collar, I spin around to face him. His expression exposes with no uncertainty that he's opposed to my unvoiced suggestion, but I act ignorant. "I won't leave your side. I'll do as asked the instant you ask, and if it stretches to a three-day affair, you'll see me eat every day instead of assuming I am." I'm a bitch for using his neurosis that I almost starved to death against him, but if it gets him on board with my plans, I'll use it, then make it up to him later. "It isn't like you'll let anyone get close to me. You'll gut a man just for looking at me."

"And I'll make you watch while I do it."

When my knees pull together, Clover grins a predatory smirk.

"I knew you'd get off on this." He paces my way, his walk as arrogant as the gleam in his eyes. "The carnage. The mayhem. The *gore*." He growls his last word when his closeness leaves no doubt to my aroused state. I find his protectiveness erotically satisfying, and my body is no longer willing to hide that.

My heart erratically beats when Clover crowds me into the wall he fucked me against last night, shoves my head to the side, then drags his nose down the throb in my throat. Once he has my senses heightened beyond reproach, he presses his lips to the shell of my ear and growls, "Fan those wings, angel. It's time for you to learn that hell's playground isn't reserved solely for the devil."

EPILOGUE
ESTELLE

One year later...

"*H*arder. Move those legs. You stay still, you die. If you die, I'll bring you back just so I can say I fucking told you so before I kill you again."

Clover moves from behind the boxing bag to in front of it. It's rainy outside, and there's as much moisture pouring down my cheeks as there is the tinted windows of Clover's mega-mansion. We've been working out in his home gym for the past hour. I stuffed up earlier today, and Clover isn't going to let me forget it until I either collapse from exhaustion or withdraw from the three tenders I told Galib to accept on my behalf this morning.

No, you didn't hear me wrong. Clover is no longer the only hired hitman in Hopeton.

Well, technically, he is since I'm a woman, but you get what I mean.

I don't accept payment for the services I offer, though. I do it for the men and women who were done wrong but don't have the funds to hire a professional like Clover.

This morning's contract was for a man who raped his co-worker's fifteen-year-old daughter when she let him sleep on her couch after one too many drinks at their workplace Christmas party. The victim's mother lost her husband to prostate cancer two years earlier, and with his insurance only covering his excessive medical bills and three children to feed, she had no choice but to return to the toxic work environment that took the word of a rapist over a fifteen-year-old girl.

The plan Clover obsessed over for weeks on end was tight. I was meant to be in and out before my target woke, then I trod on a squeaky dog toy I didn't factor into the movement sheets Clover made me go over three times last night.

The ear-piercing squeak of the plastic chicken not only woke my mark, but it also saw him leaping out of bed so fast, the knife wound I hit his chest with before he wrapped me up in a bear hug barely slowed him down.

When he realized I was a woman, he whispered words in my ear that left no doubt he was guilty of his crimes. The only good that came from his derogative comments was confirmation I don't get off on danger like Clover once believed. His darkness is the only chaos I'll ever seek.

I tried to fight the man off. I activated months of training, and almost had the advantage, then he slid his hand between my legs to cup my pussy.

That's when Clover moved in.

I'm guessing by now you realize how that went down. The cleanup crew didn't just have a missing johnson to contend with. Clover took his time with my mark, and by the end of their session, I learned that the comment Clover made about tweezers at the Blue Dragon over a year ago was accurate. They come in handy for all types of situations.

I stop smiling about the memory when Clover bands his arms around my chest and squeezes the living shit out of me. My lungs and heart immediately feel the impact of his grip, and my legs still to reserve power.

"Get out of my hold, angel. Now!" Clover growls into my ear, annoyed by my lack of fight.

After silently promising my lungs they'll breathe again soon, I attempt the many maneuvers Clover taught me the past twelve months, both defensive and aggressive.

Nothing works.

He's too big for me to budge and far too strong.

"Now, angel!"

"I can't," I murmur on a wheezy breath. "You're too strong."

My reply should weaken his grip on my body, but since it's Clover, a man who's always known I was stronger than I portrayed, he hugs me tighter.

When I whimper, he growls. "You're done. If you can't fight past the pain to ensure you win, you can't put yourself in danger." I understand he's more worried about me than angry when he murmurs, "What would have happened if I weren't there? What would he had done to you?" He doesn't wait for me to answer him. "He would have raped you like he did that little girl. He would have torn you apart."

The pain in his voice mimics the absolute despair in the mother's tone when she rang 911 to report her daughter's assault. She was as gutted as I was when I learned about the many horrid things Clover faced in his childhood. He was tortured and abused so badly I'm shocked his voice can replicate worry.

Remembering what he went through fills me with so much anger, I refuse to walk away. I'll push through the pain so I can prove to Clover I have what it takes to protect him as well as he does me.

I didn't become a vigilante solely because I want to help the men and women of Hopeton. I did it for Clover as well.

Mafia Law states he can't kill Jalaal, but since I've refused his numerous demands for us to wed the past six months, I'm not collared by the same rules.

I'm not a mafia entity. I am an everyday citizen who has an undeniable hate for men who abuse children, and I plan for Jalaal to learn just how perverse my hate is at the earliest possible convenience.

"Good. Keep going," Clover instructs when I do a small jump to bring my legs to the side and lower my body.

He grunts when I thrust my arms up to loosen his grip, but he stabilizes his legs too well for me to throw him over my shoulder.

With one tactic failing, I jump into another. I strike down hard on the hands crushing my insides. When he loosens his grip, I bump him back half a step with my backside before dipping down to cup the back of his ankle.

He falls to the floor with a thud when I pull his leg out from beneath him. When he attempts to get back up, I keep him to the floor by squashing my foot to his crotch—*his rapidly thickening crotch.*

Just like his darkness inspires reckless yearning in me, my ability to protect myself is one of Clover's biggest weaknesses. He was lured back into a world that caused him years of pain because Cyra, a child Jalaal purchased a year after Clover, convinced him she couldn't protect herself.

When she 'allegedly' died at the hands of her abuser, Clover was devastated enough to ink her name on his body. You can imagine how foolish he felt when he discovered everything she told him was a lie. She wasn't scared of Jalaal. She was in love with him, and she used the demons of Clover's past to force Jalaal to respond.

She also wasn't dead—until her lies caught up with her.

Clover has never admitted he killed her, but Galib has assured me multiple times that her name doesn't need to be added to my hit list, and although I blame Cyra for some of Clover's hard exterior, I'm also grateful. The last year of my life has been extremely adventurous, both sexually and spiritly, thanks to Clover's unusual quirks.

You don't realize how choking expectations are until someone forces you out of your comfort zone. Clover's attention made me look at life differently, and even though he'll never admit it, I did the same for him.

The misty sheen in my eyes clears away for lust when Clover swipes my legs out from beneath me. I don't hit the dark blue canvas like a sack of potatoes. Clover adjusts his position to ensure I land on top of him before he steals the air from the lungs by rolling me over so he can drag the prickles on his cut jaw down my midsection.

I'm wearing a super tight crop top and yoga pants combination. I knew we were working out because I stuffed up, so I went for an outfit I knew would force Clover to slot an intermission into his grueling itinerary.

I was right—*as usual.*

When Clover burrows his head between my legs and inhales a big whiff, I raise my ass off the canvas to mash my pussy with his face. His heated breaths double the scent he's sucking in when he informs, "I could smell your cunt heating up only an hour in today." He peers at me over the swell of my breasts. "Why do you think I went easy on him?" He bites on the clover tattoo on the inside of my thigh that lines up with the one on his cheek anytime his head is between my legs before he ensures there's no misunderstanding as to where I'm going when I die. "You were so fucking hungry for my cum, I only cut off his cock. I didn't feed it to him as planned."

I'm so wet over both the yearning in his eyes and the protectiveness in his voice, my yoga pants dampen with more than sweat, and I'm not the only one noticing.

"You fuckin' love the carnage." After ripping off my yoga pants, their stretchy material no match for his strength, he parts my legs, tugs his gym shorts down his thighs, then grinds his thick cock against my aching pussy. "You just needed me to show you how badly."

His groan rolls from his throat to his cock when I nod, agreeing with him. The sensation is almost as delicious as the ecstasy that races through my core when he impales me with one ardent thrust.

After pumping into me three times to ensure his fat cock doesn't face an ounce of resistance, he curls his big brooding body over mine. Spasms of excitement shoot down my spine when he shoves my head to the side so he can growl into my ear. "And I will continue showing you even when you are my wife." With a hand curled around my throat and his cock thrusting in and out of me, he forces my eyes to his. "No more stalling, angel. You are *mine,* so you will take *all* of me... including my last name. I won't accept any less." I'm about to breathe out 'soon,' but his next command exposes it would have been a waste of breath. "When we visit my home country next month, we will wed. Do you understand, angel?"

I nod without pause for thought. Organizing an assassination *and* a wedding isn't kosher, but neither is our relationship. It's dark and chaotic, but since love always moves faster than evil, I have nothing to worry about.

The next book in the Italian Cartel Series is Smith, you can download it here: Smith

Facebook: facebook.com/authorshandi

Instagram: instagram.com/authorshandi

Email: authorshandi@gmail.com

Reader's Group: bit.ly/ShandiBookBabes

Website: authorshandi.com

Newsletter: https://www.subscribepage.com/AuthorShandi

If you enjoyed this book, please leave a review.

ALSO BY SHANDI BOYES

Denotes Standalone Books

Perception Series

Saving Noah *

Fighting Jacob *

Taming Nick *

Redeeming Slater *

Saving Emily

Wrapped Up with Rise Up

Protecting Nicole *

Enigma

Enigma

Unraveling an Enigma

Enigma The Mystery Unmasked

Enigma: The Final Chapter

Beneath The Secrets

Beneath The Sheets

Spy Thy Neighbor *

The Opposite Effect *

I Married a Mob Boss *

Second Shot *

The Way We Are

The Way We Were

Sugar and Spice *

Lady In Waiting

Man in Queue

Couple on Hold

Enigma: The Wedding

Silent Vigilante

Hushed Guardian

Quiet Protector

Enigma: An Isaac Retelling

Twisted Lies *

Bound Series

Chains

Links

Bound

Restrain

The Misfits *

Nanny Dispute *

Russian Mob Chronicles

Nikolai: A Mafia Prince Romance

Nikolai: Taking Back What's Mine

Nikolai: What's Left of Me

Nikolai: Mine to Protect

Asher: My Russian Revenge *

<u>Nikolai: Through the Devil's Eyes</u>

<u>Trey</u> *

<u>The Italian Cartel</u>

Dimitri

Roxanne

Reign

Mafia Ties (Novella)

Maddox

Demi

Ox

Rocco *

Clover *

Smith *

<u>RomCom Standalones</u>

Just Playin' *

<u>Ain't Happenin'</u> *

<u>The Drop Zone</u> *

Very Unlikely *

False Start *

<u>Short Stories - Newsletter Downloads</u>

Christmas Trio *

Falling For A Stranger *

<u>**One Night Only Series**</u>

Hotshot Boss *

Hotshot Neighbor *

<u>**The Bobrov Bratva Series**</u>

Wicked Intentions *

Sinful Intentions *

Devious Intentions *

Deadly Intentions *

www.ingramcontent.com/pod-product-compliance
Lightning Source LLC
Chambersburg PA
CBHW070544190726
48291CB00017B/2212